The Blood-Red Sunset

Philip Matyszak

Monashee Mountain Publishing

Philip Matyszak has a doctorate in Roman history from St John's College, Oxford University and is the author of many books on Ancient History including the bestselling *Ancient Rome of Five Denarii a Day* and *Legionary: The Roman Soldier's (Unofficial) Manual.* He teaches e-learning courses in ancient History for the Institute of Continuing Education at Cambridge University. *The Blood-Red Sunset* is the sequel to *The Gold of Tolosa* and *The Servant of Aphrodite,* and this is his third novel in this series. For more information about the author visit: www.matyszakbooks.com

First published in 2020 by Monashee Mountain Publishing, Rossland (Canada)

www.monasheemountainpublishing.com

ISBN 978-0-9881066-7-3

Cover design by: **Ravastra Design Studio**

The Blood-Red Sunset

Foreword

Notes by the editor and translator

Welcome to purgatory;

As Tundale approached, he saw butchers standing amid the flames. Some held sharp knives and savage cleavers, others saws, forks for skewering meat over a fire, broad axes and instruments designed to drill holes into bone. Some held very long knives and others, sharp hooks. Tundale saw with horror how these fiends butchered the souls. Some decapitated their victims, others cut off their legs at the thighs or at the knees, and some hacked the souls into pieces. Yet once they had perished - in agony - the victims were restored as they had been before, only to be seized again by the butchers!

The author of this amiable text was a Benedictine monk known only as Marcus. His *Vision of Tundale* was written in the twelfth century AD to describe the harrowing tortures of Purgatory that await as punishment for what today we might consider relatively minor offences. (One of Marcus' colleagues recommended a pit of boiling oil from which one could only escape by climbing a red hot ladder. This was considered suitable chastisement for married people who had sex on a Sunday.)

Many copies of the 'Vision' survive – Marcus was a best-seller in the Middle Ages. The particularly fine first edition from which the above text was taken comes from the Scots Monastery at Regensburg in Germany. While studying the passage quoted, post-doctoral research student Sian Hughes of Cardiff University noted faint markings on the page. This caused her to suspect that the vellum had been scrubbed clean of the original text and replaced with Marcus' pious visions of torture.

This is in itself unsurprising, because parchment is expensive even today, and in the twelfth century a book was as prized for its pages as for what was written upon them. Therefore, when a monk had a powerful urge to record a vision such as Tundale's it was not uncommon for the monastery to let him do so on a text that was deemed surplus to requirements. In the later Middle Ages books due for recycling were cleaned with powdered pumice, and their contents were lost forever. We are fortunate that this volume was given the milder treatment of having the ink washed away with a mixture of milk and oat bran.

The monastery generously gave permission for the text to be loaned to Johns Hopkins University where the pages were non-destructively examined with the multi-spectral techniques by which a number of other ancient texts have been similarly retrieved, such as the famous Archimedes Codex.

The researchers had been hoping to discover a work of lost literature such as the missing books of Tacitus, or Trajan's *History of the Dacian War*, for early samples of the text had suggested that these were both possibilities. In the event it became apparent that the researchers had on their hands a folio by Lucius Turpillius Panderius, soldier and spy of the late Second Century BC - one of those texts which the press has taken to calling the 'Panderius Papers'.

As soon as the first computerized pages appeared on my computer screen, it became clear that translating this work would be challenging even in comparison to previous texts by this writer. While capable of the elegant prose (and extreme vulgarity) of an educated Roman, Panderius has perversely chosen to use the camp Latin of a soldier, replete with obscure jargon, abbreviations and brutal cruelty to Latin ablative cases. He also has a typically Roman weakness for obscure puns and in-jokes that were probably incomprehensible to contemporary civilians, let alone Latinists of later millennia.

As nearly-incomprehensible Latin is my speciality, it has again fallen to me to render Panderius' work into English. As a literal translation would be meaningless, I have rendered the text into the colloquial English which is the best equivalent of Panderius' colloquial Latin, while removing those expressions which would bring a blush to the cheeks of a hardened pornographer.

It is now clear that this work deals with the last struggle of the Legions against those same over-whelming hordes of Germanic warriors who slew tens of thousands of Romans at Arausio. Defeat at Arausio and other battles had brought the Romans to their knees, and one last Germanic victory would have seen Italy over-run and the Roman Republic wiped out.

It is now evident that Panderius' story of those desperate days has been extensively used as source material by later Roman writers such as Plutarch, Sallust and Velleius Paterculus. Plutarch is particularly guilty, because whole paragraphs that biographer's Lives of the Roman commanders Sulla and Marius seem to have been copied almost verbatim from the Panderius manuscript.

Such blatant plagiarism is to be condemned, not least because it means that we already know much of what Panderius has written. Therefore the main value in Panderius' account lies in how his narrative ties together those parts of the story which we have already and adds to these facts Panderius' own behind-the-scenes perspective. These scenes reveal Lucius to be courageous and tough but also surprisingly perfidious and regrettably callous, amoral, ruthless and vindictive – in short, a typical Roman of the late Republic.

P. Matyszak, B.A. Lon. (Hons.) M.A. D.Phil, Lit.hum. St John's Oxon.

Rossland 2020

Glossary

Auxilia Allied troops armed and trained in Roman fashion who fought alongside the legions

Ballista Medium or heavy artillery firing boulders

Canaba The civilian village which generally grew up around army camps

Capsarius Medical officer of a Roman military unit

Chiton Greek-style woman's dress

Cohort Army unit of six centuries (about 500 men) recently created as part of the Marian army reforms

Lictor Official who carries the fasces (rods and axe), the insignia of a Roman magistrate

Maniple Tactical unit of 60-120 men, still used in the army of 100 BC but later obsolete

Optio Centurion's sidekick and replacement if the centurion fell in combat

Pilus Prior The centurion in charge of the first cohort of a legion (This unit was twice the size of a regular cohort)

Praetorium The administrative building/tent of a Roman army commander

Primus Pilus The chief centurion of a legion

Proconsul A former consul whose command has been extended due to the military situation

Scorpion Light artillery firing bolts

Sestertius Roman coin worth a quarter of a denarius (A Roman solider earned around a denarius a day)

Signifer Standard bearer

Tribune Army officer equivalent of a legion commander (not to be confused with Tribunes of the Plebs)

Liber I

'What are you doing here?'

'Huh? Oh, the Proconsul sent me. The scroll with the cavalry patrol schedules is meant to be somewhere in this bucket, but the accursed thing seems to have gone missing.'

Minatius regarded his tent-mate with bemused affection. 'Haven't you figured out the filing system yet, you dolt? You are looking the records section, cavalry patrols are in current operations. Hold on.'

The young Italian aristocrat briefly regarded the rack that took up the rear of the army command tent. It was a substantial affair, loaded with scrolls stacked somewhat carelessly into leather buckets. 'Here.' Minatius stepped over to a bucket at around waist height, pulled out a papyrus scroll and briefly examined it. 'The completed patrol reports are in that bigger bucket over there. This is the summary. So ... ah! Here we are. Patrol schedules for the next tenday. What do you need them for?'

'I don't need them. The Old Man wants them. Why is none of my business. When the Proconsul says he wants a document I don't cross-examine him as to motive, I just do my humble duty and scuttle off to obey.'

Minatius frowned. 'That's odd. When did he send you for them? For the last two hours he's been in a meeting with the *Primus Pilus*, and before that the two of them were discussing lines of march and possible encampments for the army. You would have known that if you had been with the other junior tribunes at the meeting instead of skulking off on your own again.'

'Yes, yes. Sometimes I wonder if I'm cut out for the military life at all. Anyway, Catulus told me yesterday that he needs this information for the ninth hour today, and I completely forgot about it until just now. Thanks for finding it for me. I had better be getting it over to him.'

'No problem.' replied Minatius. 'Hand it over and I will give it to him. He sent me to get the fodder requisitions for the pack animals, so I can give him the cavalry report at the same time. That way you also avoid getting one of his lectures for being absent this afternoon. When he does catch up with you, just say you have been abed with a headache or something.'

Returning to the scrolls, Minatius quickly ran his glance across a row of buckets and deftly removed the document he needed. A thought struck him, and without turning, he asked. 'Hey, how come the guards at the entrance didn't tell me you were in here? They usually … uouf!'

For a moment Minatius thought that his companion had punched him hard in the ribs. Confused, he turned, saying 'Why did you …?' when a wave of pain overwhelmed him. He dropped the scroll from his hand and groped across his tunic. It took several moments before he recognized the dagger buried to the hilt in his side.

When he did, his eyes opened wide and Minatius opened his mouth to say something. Instead he coughed violently, spraying a film of blood across the bookcase in front of him. Then the hot, choking blood filled his mouth and poured out over his chin on to his tunic. Appalled, he looked at the spreading stain across his chest and clapped a hand across his mouth so that the blood dribbled between his fingers. Still clasping the dagger hilt with one hand, he tried to raise his other arm against the killer who stood watching him with a mix of horror and fascination. The tent had become strangely dark, and the last thing Minatius saw on this earth was the canvas of the tent floor as it rushed up to meet him.

There was silence for almost a minute before the killer knelt beside Minatius and inexpertly felt at his throat for a pulse. Finding none, he looked at the corpse for a few seconds, and then tried to extract his dagger by pulling at the hilt with two fingers. This proved harder than he expected, and in the end the killer had to wrap his entire hand over the hilt and pull. This succeeded in extracting the dagger, but as he had feared, it came out with a gush of blood that covered his hand.

The killer carefully wiped dagger and hand on a clean part of Minatius' tunic, noting with hysterical detachment that he would have to stop his hands from shaking so violently once he was out again in the army encampment where everyone could see him. He stepped behind the rack of scrolls and peered carefully through the slit he had made to enter the tent on his clandestine mission. No-one was looking his way. Good.

He was about to step out into the alley behind the tents when a thought struck him. Quickly he ducked back into the commander's quarters and retrieved the cavalry schedules from beside the dead Minatius, tsk'ing as he did so at the blood that had splattered across the scroll's exterior.

Meanwhile, on the other side of the Alps, I had troubles of my own. Trouble can appear in many forms, some more grim than others. In terms of immediate terror, the young woman sitting beside me was on the low end of the scale. She was wearing a Greek-style chiton, and had short, mousy-blonde hair tied in an untidy bun. When she saw me looking at her she gave me a wave and a cheerful grin, though in truth I was looking more at the three feet of empty air above which her petite posterior was floating. The sight had me very, very worried.

The shaman had crossed to the other side of the fire and seated himself in a more conventional manner, his knees neatly crossed before him as he took another swig of the ceremonial drink I had been offered as I stepped inside the lodge. He paid no attention to the girl who had so unexpectedly appeared, which I took as another sign that she was not really there.

Nevertheless, it seemed only polite to do the introductions, so mustering my imperfect Greek I said light-headedly, 'Shaman, meet Momina. Momina is a spooky priestess whom I last saw trying to get me killed while we were robbing a temple in Gaul. I can tell you a lot more about her later – although of course, that is assuming that I have a 'later'. I have to say that is looking decidedly iffy right now. Momina, meet the village shaman. He's the bastard who has almost certainly adulterated this drink – and has he done it with drugs or poison, I wonder?'

Momina, or at least my imaginary phantasm of her, gave the shaman a polite nod of acknowledgement, and then pouted thoughtfully as she addressed my question. 'Well, the potion is both really. The drug is a powerful hallucinogen – and a large dose is certainly fatal, so if I were you I wouldn't take any more of it. You probably have troubles enough. You've already taken an overdose of that drug, and when that has incapacitated you sufficiently, these people are going to kill you. They would have done it already, but they're farmers who don't fancy taking on a trained swordsman. Someone might get hurt.'

Momina indicated the Gauls crowded around me. They were following events with deep interest.

Well, yes. Even with my thoughts getting increasingly incoherent, that the crowd wished me ill was obvious from the knives now held openly by some of its members. The scene of my probable murder was a crude alpine hall with low rafters partly hidden by a fug of wood-smoke. Spears were propped randomly against the walls, with the occasional agricultural implement leaning between them. I was standing right in front of a large fire, and my audience was crowded around the shaman and myself, listening with great amusement to my side of the current conversation. Even though this was meant to be a friendly village, I had been wearing a sword and now I shifted my balance unobtrusively to check that the friendly weight was still at my hip.

'That sword won't do you a lot of good here,' observed Momina. 'You're well outnumbered. And, um, don't expect any help from your escort outside. They've already stripped the armour and weapons from the bodies and are currently dragging them to the midden to be buried. Somehow it didn't occur to them that those over-friendly young lasses might be carrying daggers. Sorry about that.'

I looked blearily at the grinning murderers who crowded around me and frowned. 'If I'm just imagining you are here, and no-one else can see you because you are just a hally, a holluc, a figama-thingy of my imagination, why is there a clear space around you?'

'Oh. I'm here', said Momina brightly. 'Well, 'here' so long as we don't get too literal about the meaning of the word. These boys can sense that, even if they can't see me. You can actually see me and speak to me, but that's because of your large draught of that extremely nasty brew.'

'How about him, then?' I pointed an accusing finger the shaman sitting across the fire from me, and then hurriedly pulled back my arm as the sleeve of my jerkin began to smoulder.

This evoked ribald chuckles from the spectators, which Momina ignored as she answered, 'No, he can't see me. What I'm doing is actually rather complicated, because I'm also quite a long way away. You're lucky that you have a reputation as being quite a dangerous fellow, or they wouldn't have wanted to drug you before they stabbed you. But we need to do something before your entertainment value expires, um, along with the rest of you.'

'It was meant to be a simple trade agreement', I moaned. 'Some surplus cattle and cheeses for good Roman gold. I've done the same deal with half a dozen other villages in this bit of the Alps without even a hint of trouble.' I waved a hand at the moustachioed faces around me. 'What do these idiots have against me?'

The 'idiots' swayed back as my hand passed within inches of their noses and no-one seemed to notice that when my hand dropped back, it landed on the hilt of my sword.

'You can get to that later', remarked Momina without a hint of impatience. 'Right now, let's focus on getting you out of here. Well, you're getting out anyway, of course, but getting out alive would be good. Let's try for alive. Now, see your friend opposite? As village shaman, he's accustomed to the effects of this stuff. That's why he happily put you off your guard by taking the first swig from that goblet. It's actually rather a clever mix of herbs and a particular little mushroom - I'll give you the recipe later, if you're interested.'

'Now the thing is, I'm using the effect of the drug to let you be able to talk to me, so it's keeping other things out of your mind. You're a lot more clear-headed than you should be.'

'In a few moments I'm going to let go of you and focus on the shaman. I'm sorry to say that the things that come into his mind are going to be ... very unpleasant. He should put on quite a show once the nasties get to him. While he's going off, you might want to push over the fellow behind you and dive out of the door. It's just three steps back, no matter what the drugs might tell you. No, don't stab him. You haven't the time, and he's just got married. Won't even know that he was going to be a father, poor boy. Now get ready, okay?'

I hadn't even realized that Momina was in my mind until she left it. Suddenly the room felt and looked as though it was deep underwater. I rocked back on my heels and tried to focus my wandering thoughts on the shaman. Something was coming for him through the crudely-plastered walls. I screwed my eyes tight and then opened them suddenly, but even that could not bring the thing into focus. It was clear though, that there was something disturbingly wrong about it. It was very large too. Many times larger than a spider should be, and though this was not a spider, there was something about it that put me in mind of one.

Evidently the shaman could see the creature more clearly than I, for his eyes suddenly bulged with terror and he desperately scrambled backwards. This brought him into contact with one of the tribesmen who had transformed into … something. Whatever the tribesman had become was terrifying enough to cause the shaman to roll right through the fire and grab one of the spears from the wall.

Being right next to a flaming human wildly slashing about with a sharp-tipped spear takes one's whole attention. I was as riveted as everyone else until Momina said clearly in my ear, 'Go. Now.'

I let myself fall backwards, and the man behind me

caught me in a reflex reaction. His kindly conduct was repaid by a vigorous punch to the testicles that promptly reduced his chances of future offspring. The man's collapse was unnoticed in the general chaos, and I wriggled past several sets of legs and dived out of the door. Thanks to the accursed potion, I had forgotten that the hall entrance was by way of a flight of wooden steps and I half-rolled and half-bounced down these before hitting the ground with a jarring thud that brought me partly back to sanity.

The village hall dominated a shabby courtyard with a cluster of ramshackle slate-roofed cottages beyond. Drawing my sword I looked around wildly in the gathering twilight. After a moment or two I located the hitching post where our horses were tied and headed for them at a lurching run. Behind me an indignant shout signalled that my absence from the party had been noticed. My horse was the dun in the middle of the group at the hitching rail, and some swine had stolen the saddle. The horses of my former escort were likewise unsaddled, so with a curse I leapt gracefully onto the bare back of my steed. Or at least that was the intention. Instead I planted my face firmly in the beast's tail and rolled aside just in time to miss the irritable kick it aimed at my stomach.

Men were spilling out from the hall, and my befuddled mind grasped that this was no good thing. A wild slash with my sword came close to decapitating one of the escort horses, but severed the harnesses of both. My own horse was tied with a slip-knot and I pulled this loose while trying desperately to swing a leg over the horse's back. It later occurred to me, when I tried to collect my jumbled memories of the entire episode, that the escort must have been killed nearby and the smell of blood was still heavy in the air. This would have greatly unsettled the horses, and at my wild scream they took off in a blind panic.

It was not the most dignified of departures for I had dropped my sword and was clinging to the horse's side like a limpet, my arms firmly clasped around its neck and one knee hooked over the back. It was however, a very speedy departure. I was vaguely aware of the horses bowling over a cluster of men before we were out on the string of potholes that passed for the village's main (and only) street. Then the horses were hammering for the forest with me literally holding on for dear life.

'Well done, Lucius!' This from Momina. Since my view presently consisted of nothing but the velvety skin of the horse's neck, I could not see my least favourite priestess but I imagined her lounging on the air beside me as though on a couch in an invisible carriage. My struggles to get properly sat on the horse only succeeded in dislodging me further, and it became depressingly clear that I could not hang on for much longer.

'Don't worry. You're clear of the village now and headed into the trees. They've only got four horses back there, and two are plough horses. By the time they've got themselves saddled up and after you these horses with you will be long gone. You won't be of course. Let go now.'

'Sorry. That mud patch was the deepest around here so I couldn't arrange a softer landing. You've got few bumps and bruises, and those cracked ribs will be better in no time. Now I need you to walk up the slope here, yes, okay, crawling works too … there's a bear's den over here where you can shelter for the night and work off the effect of that drug. No, the bear's not there. Silly thing made its home too close to the village and the hunters got him. But you'll be comfortable, well, that is, as comfortable as you can be while the drugs are wearing off. You are in for a wild night.'

Cornelius Sulla is a considerate man, which is why he had placed a bucket beside me so that I could be sick into it without interrupting my debrief. It is Sulla's boast that no man is a better friend than he, or a worse enemy. Sulla affords me the dubious honour of considering me a friend, which is why early this morning he had personally led the cavalry troop that set out to investigate why I had not reported back to camp the previous night.

He had found me at the side of the road leading to the village, very much the worse for wear. After hearing only my quick précis of events, he abandoned me and rode on to demonstrate the 'worst enemy' part of his boast to the unfortunate villagers. His cavalrymen were reluctant participants in the slaughter until they discovered the bodies of their comrades buried, as advertised, in the midden. Thereafter they went about their business with grim enthusiasm, and by the time I had staggered down to the village it was mostly burning buildings interspersed with pale, stripped corpses.

'You were my envoy, and that means an attack on you is an attack on me', Sulla informed me when I mentioned something about – quite literal – overkill. 'I take attacks on me very seriously. I have a reputation to uphold hereabouts.'

Indeed. Sulla's enemies in the Roman Senate had managed to deny him the glory of participating in the coming round of conflict with the horde of Cimbric invaders poised to sweep across Italy. Instead he had been given the demeaning but essential job of arranging local provisions for the armies that would be doing the actual fighting.

So we were now located in a camp deep in the Alps on the Cisalpine side of the mountains (i.e. the Italian side), and from there Sulla sent a steady stream of supplies to the legions. Being Sulla, whatever he did, he did well. As a result of his efforts both armies had been surprised and delighted by the quality of their rations, though I noted that the better quality supplies went east, where Lutatius Catulus and his men were trying to confine the invaders to the eastern Po valley, rather than west, where Caius Marius had done a rather better job keeping the enemy from breaking through via the Piedmontese Alps – so good a job in fact that the western threat was now nullified by Roman victory and attention had shifted to the much larger threat in the east.

Helping Catulus more than Marius had been fair enough in my opinion, because as Consul of Rome,

Marius had made sure that he had mostly veteran troops fighting with him. Catulus had been left with raw levies and the rag, tag and bobtail whom desperate recruiters had qualified as fit for military service, usually on the basis that they were male and breathing. So we had balanced things a bit by feeding Catulus' troops better, though it also helped that Sulla rather liked Catulus and loathed Marius with a passion.

Now we were at the staff meeting, though I would infinitely preferred several hours of misery on my camp bed. A post-mortem on last night's events was well under way. I had left out all mention of being coached through my misadventures by a priestess several hundred miles distant, not least because I was pretty sure that I had imagined her presence in any case. Mind-altering drugs can do that.

'What did you do to upset the villagers?' Sulla was asking. 'I thought they were friendly enough. We can raze a village or two as an example, but in the long term we need them to provide supplies and that's one less village to do the job. Did Cimbric spies get to them?'

I shook my head wearily, and contemplated leaning over the bucket to try another set of dry heaves. My stomach was looking forward to it, but my gut muscles ached already. Getting drugged had been bad enough, but the aftermath was truly horrible. 'Not the Cimbri. They have sent spies of course, looking to turn the Gauls hereabouts against us. However the people know that they would be exchanging bad masters for worse. Anyway, assuming we fight off the Cimbri, we'll go home and leave the people hereabouts to their own devices and they know it. Cimbric agitators are not the problem.'

'Well what? People don't just happen to get as murderous as that village became. There has to be a reason. The risks of attacking a Roman envoy are too high to just do so on a whim.'

This was not a conversation I wanted to have, especially in front of witnesses, and several of Sulla's staffers were present. Blearily I raised my head and informed Sulla. 'It's a complete mystery to me. Doubtless it will always remain so. However, the problem will stop in a few days and we won't have any more restless villagers to worry about. Not for that reason anyway.'

That was all that the meeting needed to hear, so I shut up and glared at Sulla, defying him to ask more. Instead, my commander regarded me thoughtfully with those pale blue eyes of his. After a second or two he remarked, 'That kind of mystery, is it? Very well, I'll leave you to sort it out.'

'Thank you, sir. Now on a completely different topic, there are some troop reassignments we need to go over.'

Two days later, and at another Alpine village, Aulus Maphronius pulled his horse to a halt. Before him stood the village's assembled population. Behind him, a squad of twenty auxiliary soldiers were moving from line of march into attack formation. They did this with a notable lack of enthusiasm, which the ebullient Maphronius appeared not to notice. Cheerfully he addressed the sullen villagers.

'Right, you stinking peasants, you know the deal. I'm here calling for volunteers to join the Roman army, and you are going to supply them. Or we can do the goddess Hygiena a service and burn this flea-infested dungheap to the ground.'

Maphronius turned his attention to the village headman. 'You. You know what you have to supply.' In reply the man simply glared at him.

Nothing daunted, Maphronius reeled off the list. 'Five boys, blond, aged between ten and fourteen. That's our volunteer lads over there, is it? Don't look so worried, boys – what could be worse than living right here? I mean, look at this place. Next, four men, twenty to thirty years of age, with no physical defects. Good. Ready for a life of military derring do, eh? I'm sooo pleased to see it. And those further volunteers who have preferred to make cash payments rather than serve. I trust you got a good price for your mangy livestock at the last market? You can thank me for giving you time to raise the coin. Most recruiters are nowhere near so considerate, but me, I have a good heart.'

Maphronius licked his lips as he came to his final demand. 'And of course, two women, thirteen to nineteen years of age, to accompany the volunteers as cooks and helpmeets. And if you have not found me an attractive pair, headman, I'll crucify you myself.'

The recruiter watched carefully as two sobbing girls were pushed through the crowd, and he nudged his horse forward for a closer look. 'These two rats?

Seriously, is this the best your village can do? Maybe we should do a search through the huts to see what else you are hiding, eh? You girl, look at me! Hmm, properly washed down and de-loused, you might look almost human. Okay, they'll do. Gaius!'

At Maphronius' shout a scowling auxiliary elbowed through the ranks, a papyrus scroll in hand.

'Gaius, set up over there, and take payments from those volunteers offering cash in lieu of service. And note, gentlemen, that short payment gets you a whipping as well as twenty percent interest on the amount outstanding. We all understand that? Good, let's get started. I'm a busy man and can't waste all day on you peasants. And who in Hades are you?'

This final remark was addressed to me as I stepped out from between the huts into the midday sunlight. Unlike the trousered and cloaked Gauls assembled to my left, I was wearing a simple tunic. Beautifully white, and of expensive lambswool, but simple in any case. I spread my hands to show that I was also unarmed.

'Maphronius of Padova! My name is Turpillius Panderius. In absolute truth, I have to say that I am delighted to meet you.'

Maphronius scowled, and his hand drifted downwards to the sword at his hip. Unlike my civilian self he was wearing a vest of light scale armour. The measuring look that he gave his auxiliary escort spoke volumes. As Maphronius nudged his horse towards me, I held up a hand. There was a gentle jingle of chainmail from behind me and I knew that five Syrian bowmen in full battle array now stood at my shoulder, arrows nocked on their vicious composite bows, though the arrow tips were pointing at the grass – for now.

'I wouldn't, Maphronius. They'll turn you into a pincushion if you ride another step towards me. And also don't think of riding away. Please. At this range your pretty armour won't stop one of their arrows, but your horse might get hurt. And unlike yourself, that horse has some value.'

The recruiter kept scowling, but he pulled his horse up so sharply that the animal tossed its head angrily at the bit. 'What do you want?'

'In a word, Maphronius – you. I want you, because your recruiting scam has been alienating Gauls up and down this corner of the Alps – Gauls whose support we need for operations against the Cimbri. And of course, on a more personal note, there are the thanks I owe you for setting those villagers up to kill me. It was only a matter of time before you found out I was investigating your recruiting scam, but murder? That's a bit extreme. Why didn't you take your profits and run?'

'Those villagers didn't have a lot of choice did they? Kill one Roman envoy or lose every young person in the village to your recruiting efforts. Now they are all dead, and that's on you. I had one really bad night and that you also need to pay for. So now the bill … ', I gave Maphronius a cheerful smile, 'awaits payment.'

My little speech had given the Maphronius a chance to compose himself. His answering smile was close to a sneer. 'You can't touch me, you little creep. This whole thing goes way above your pay grade. There are people of considerable power and influence waiting for these boys, and they have already paid for them. If they don't take delivery they'll want your head instead. My connections go all the way back to the Senate in Rome.'

Actually, my own connections in the Roman Senate were better, more direct and stronger, but I had no intention of getting into a dick-measuring contest with this idiot. It was regrettably true that a number of powerful people were going to be severely annoyed once Maphronius' operation was closed down. Attractive young catamites are an expensive commodity, especially if naïve and blond. They were also strongly disapproved of in the very puritanical north of Italy, so both money and reputations were at stake. Which is why Sulla expected me to handle things discreetly without making waves.

'You can't touch me.' Maphronius said triumphantly, and this time his smile was genuine. 'My authority to act as a recruiter comes from the provincial Praetor, not your Cornelius Sulla. So if you don't like the way I am performing my duties, the only thing you can do is put in a complaint. Please go ahead. Doubtless a formal complaint will result in a comprehensive and independent investigation of the charges, and doubtless that investigation will exonerate me completely. It might ruin your career, however.'

Confident now, Maphronius laughed. 'Good try, Panderius. Now get lost. I have work to do – work that is no concern of yours. Gaius – stop standing around like a gawping fool and get on with things. We haven't got all day.'

I did my best to look crestfallen. 'Yes, indeed. You are absolutely correct. Neither I nor Sulla have any authority over you nor any right to interfere with your recruiting, filthy and corrupt though your methods may be. However … . Gaius, would you step over here for a moment?'

As the soldier approached, I dipped a hand into my tunic and came out with a small folded paper. This I gave to the auxiliary while explaining to Maphronius. 'Your escort is a different matter. They are Sulla's troops, loaned to you for the course of your operations. I checked. As this requisition document explains, these men are being transferred to my command with immediate effect. We need them, you see, to contain this inexplicable wave of unrest we are encountering in the local villages. Gaius, please form up your men and prepare to march out with me.'

'Oh, and Maphronius …', I was walking forward as I spoke. 'That's also a requisition for your horse. We lost three horses in the process of you trying to get me murdered in that village, so I'm taking yours – now.'

With that I reached up and grabbed Maphronius where his tunic fluttered loose between his armour and his armpit. One pull, and he came tumbling down to land with a crash on the ground at my feet. The auxiliaries of his former escort responded to the man's plight with unrestrained laughter.

As the recruiter lay gasping I informed him, 'It's always a good idea to cut your men in for a share of your profits. You were just too greedy, too reliant on your connections back in Padova. Goodbye,

Maphronius. Squad! Prepare to move out!'

'Wait!' The panic in Maphronius' voice was sudden and very apparent. 'You can't leave me here like this. I won't last ten minutes - they'll kill me, you know they will. It's the Praetor's orders. You have to supply me with an escort. If I go missing there will be an investigation. Eventually one of the auxiliaries will testify that you left me here unprotected. So you can't do that - you can't just leave me here.'

I nodded agreeably. 'But you shall have your escort, Maphronius, just as those orders stipulate. It is not that far to the camp – a morning's ride perhaps? And to protect you,why, you have those Gauls from right here whom you have just recruited into the Roman army. Unless anyone else wants to also accompany Maphronius and see that he comes to harm? No harm. I meant to say 'see that he comes to no harm'.

There was an excited babble from the tribesmen as they were brought up to speed by the Gauls in the auxiliary guard. I gave the horrified Maphronius a big grin. 'Oh look. Suddenly everyone wants to be in the army. See, the mothers of those children you were, um, recruiting, even they are rushing to join your new escort, and they are not even eligible. Still, we should not discourage such enthusiasm, should we? Your safety is guaranteed.'

'So it is my official belief that I'm leaving you in safe hands. Gaius, would you note for the record that when we left Maphronius was in good health and with an escort of, hmm, at least ten men, all volunteer recruits for the Roman army whom Maphronius had recruited personally. We need not mention the half-dozen women, some of whom appear to have gone back to their huts for meat cleavers.'

The enormity of his peril hit home, and the eyes of Maphronius went wide. 'Money', he gasped as he struggled to sit up. 'Lots of money. It's all yours, if you just get me out of here. You'll be rich.'

'Sorry. We found your strongbox in your tent. The one in the false bottom of the chest where you keep your ceremonial armour. You can't bribe anyone, because you actually don't have a sestertius in the world.'

'But wait - I can name names. Who paid me to acquire what kinds of human product. I kept it all, letters, receipts, times, meetings, places. Padova is a very moralistic place. If news what those people did gets out, they would be ruined. I've got the proof and I can give it to you.'

'We've got it. You kept the documentation in the strongbox with your money, remember? Now stop snivelling and take what's coming like a man. Or like a woman, as the case may be. I see that the mother of one of those girls you intended to rape has found herself a gelding knife.'

There was nothing else to say. The auxilia were formed up in line of march, so I took my newly acquired horse by the reins and signalled the troop to move. Maphronius curled himself into a ball and gave a despairing wail that I did my best to ignore. Making sure that the horse was between me and the soldiery, I muttered to the village headman, 'No remains can ever be found. Got it?'

Without looking at me the headman replied. 'There will be no remains.'

I was going to ask what he meant by that, but then decided I didn't want to know.

'There is one further item of business', I mentioned diffidently at the end of the staff meeting that week, 'Although it does not concern us directly.'

Sulla raised a pale eyebrow at me and indicated that I should continue.

'It appears that the local army recruiter has gone missing.'

'What?' This from a burly centurion sitting further down the table. 'Has another accursed village gone rogue and killed him?'

I shook my head. 'Definitely not. All the signs point to the man abandoning his post and deserting.'

'Ugh. Yet another who has lost faith in Rome's ability to beat the barbarians. The man is probably halfway to Greece by now. Bit of a problem getting an army together if the very person doing the recruiting believes that we are going to lose. Curse him for a coward, then.'

'Cowardice is certainly a motive', I said smoothly, 'but probably not the only motive. The man was running a recruitment scam.'

'Eh? A recruitment scam? How does that work? Surely you either deliver the recruits or you do not? It is hard to fake a sturdy peasant ready and willing to serve.

Or ... you mean they were not that willing and he pressed them into service anyway?'

I nodded. 'He did that certainly. Also he ordered men to serve who were too old, or too sick, or who had large families to support. Such men were allowed to secure release from the army for a payment of 350 sestertii.'

Sulla gave a gentle whistle. 'That's almost a year's earnings for these people. No wonder we have been able to pick up so much livestock on the cheap. They've been selling off their assets.'

Trust Sulla to put things together so quickly. Giving my boss a respectful dip of the head I went on.

'Furthermore, it seems this beauty was in the business of extorting the villagers to give up young, attractive boys, pre-purchased to order by wealthy pederasts across North Italy. Oh, and he was getting through two teenage girls per week. When he was done, he sold them as whores to brothels in Mediolanum.'

'And all this happened under your nose?', someone asked pointedly.

'I couldn't stop it even if I knew. We're in the business of logistics, and recruiting is done by the Praetor. We have no jurisdiction.'

At the mention of a high Roman official, several heads around the table came up sharply and I pressed on quickly. 'I'm not saying that the Praetor had any idea of what was going on. Obviously this man – his name was Maphronius by the way – was upsetting the locals with his activities. And 'upsetting' is putting it very mildly, so this interfered with the willingness of the people to sell supplies to us, and this would have ultimately affected our operations. But even so, all we could have done was make the Praetor aware of the situation and wait for him to put a stop to it.'

'However, it seems that Maphronius knew that he couldn't keep up his extortion for long. He was operating for just over a month. Then he got spooked and decided to take his profits and run.'

'What spooked him?'

'I did, actually, although quite inadvertently. We needed his auxiliary escort to contain unrest, so I substituted his men with a less-qualified bodyguard. For some reason Maphronius must have decided that this meant we were becoming aware of his activities and he decided to pack his bags. By my estimate he got away with some 5,000 sestertii.'

There was a general exhalation around the table. That sum of money would buy one a mansion in Rome or a prosperous farm in Campania. 'I didn't know there was that much money in these mountains', someone remarked.

'There isn't. The bulk of the money came from those pre-ordered bum-boys. Maphronius had better run fast and far, because we found where he was stockpiling the kids and they have been released back to their families. Some very important men paid a lot of money for those boys, and are going to get nothing in return. They are going to get highly indignant and all the more so because they won't be able to say what they are indignant about. Expect something of a political shitstorm.'

Sulla shrugged. 'A storm that will hit the Praetor's office. As Panderius has pointed out, it's nothing to do with us. We just happened to be doing logistics in the same bit of the mountains and we didn't even notice the problem until it was too late. All they can hold against us was that the man was operating from our camp.'

'Nevertheless, since Panderius precipitated the storm by changing the escorts, it might be better if he lies low for a while. I'll arrange a temporary posting somewhere safely far away. With the rest of you, if anyone comes inquiring about anything to do with this sordid affair, tell them that you know nothing and refer the questioners to me. Okay? Well, that's about it. Thank you for attending everyone, and Panderius, please do me the kindness of remaining for a moment after the meeting. We have a few things to discuss.'

'Wait a moment, though.' Something had occurred to one of the junior tribunes. 'When you say that you changed Maphronius' auxilia for lower quality escorts, were those escorts, um, I mean … actually … they...'. The young man visibly wilted under his commander's basilisk-like glare. Yet Sulla didn't take on tribunes who were slow on the uptake and the lad recovered fast. 'Do you know?' he said brightly, 'I've completely forgotten my question. Apologies.' The tribune ducked out of the room, elbowing past several more senior officers in his haste to be gone.

Once the room had cleared, I dropped on to a couch while Sulla filled two beakers with red wine. I took an appreciative sniff. 'Massarian. A local vintage, but aged in a good oak cask to take the sharpness from the after-taste.' After swirling the drink around in my cheeks I swallowed and inhaled through an open mouth to let the final flavours caress my palate. 'This is the best specimen of the type I've ever tasted. Over ten years old then?'

'Twelve. A gift from a local nobleman. It's always good to share wine with someone who appreciates what he is getting. So what did you do with the body?'

I took a cautious sip of the wine. 'Obviously I have no idea of what you are talking about. But it does occur to me that if properly sliced and diced, a man could easily disappear. There were at least three pigsties in that village I was at last week. Talking of which, it might be an idea to get your hams elsewhere.'

'Oh.' Sulla went on, ' And the treasurer reports that a tribal chieftain has just made very generous donation of 2,500 sestertii to the legion welfare fund. Our treasurer is even more impressed that the chieftain insisted that his donation be anonymous. A man called Balenaeus. I believe that you and he have become rather good friends and drinking buddies?'

Sulla looked at me over the rim of his wine beaker. 'Yet somehow I get the feeling that Balenaeus was only half as generous as he might have been.'

There was an unstated question in that observation, which I chose to answer with an observation of my own.

'We got the boys back undamaged, and that's a good thing. But the girls – ten of them – they've been effectively ruined as far as life in the mountains goes.

No man will touch them after what they have been through, so they'll never marry. The only hope for those girls is if someone buys them out of their brothels very soon and sets them up elsewhere in the Alps with dowries so substantial that suitors will be very careful not to ask any embarrassing questions about their past.'

I shrugged. 'It would be the charitable thing to do, but it would take around 2,500 sestertii, and where would that amount of money come from?'

Sulla burst into laughter. 'Lucius, Lucius. That soft heart of yours will be the death of you. Seriously, all that money for peasant girls you have never met, and who can never do a thing for you. What were you thinking of? What next? Are you going to start adopting stray puppies?'

'I am sure that I do not know what you are talking about, Sir. I was just making general conversation. Anything specific I would put down on a small scroll with a red leather case. I believe you came into possession of something similar recently?'

'If I did', replied Sulla serenely, 'I certainly would not tell you about it. For the next few months the scroll in that leather case is going to be the single most-sought after item in north Italy. Would you believe that some buyers were so stupid as to put their names and seals on the bill of sale? Lust can totally blind some people. But who am I to criticize? I cannot speak ill of those who help to push me another step up the electoral ladder, and it looks as though the vote from much of north Italy is locked up come the next elections. I don't like being indebted to that degree Lucius, so you had better think of a big favour I can do for you. And think of it soon.'

'Well, you can start by telling me why you're sending me to the army in Picenum. And why not as intelligence officer? The man not doing the job there at the moment is as incompetent as they come, and no-one is going to say a word if he is replaced. It was an intelligence failure that allowed the Cimbri to get into Italy through the passes in the eastern Alps. Yet you have me training Catulus' bunch of brats? Are you going to tell me why, or am I supposed to figure it out for myself?'

'Well, for a start, it's a demotion for letting Maphronius get away and that will appease some of those after your blood. Secondly, Catulus needs someone to discreetly investigate the death of a young Italian aristocrat who was in his charge. He died of a lung haemorrhage.'

'I'm not a doctor … .'

'The haemorrhage was caused by eight inches of sharpened steel being thrust with considerable force through the young man's ribs. The dagger went through his left side and stopped just short of his heart. Finding out who was on the other end of that lethal dagger falls well within your highly specialized skill set. Catulus asked for you personally, and this recruiting scandal gives me the perfect reason to send you there. We're pretty sure that the killer is another of the young men sharing the command tent, so that's why you are in charge of their training.'

'One of the others, eh?' I mused. 'So if the investigation succeeds, I've to accuse the scion of a top Italian or Roman family of committing a murder? And if it fails, I'm in Catulus' black books. This seems to me very much a lose-lose situation. Um, about that favour you mentioned a moment ago. Actually something has come to mind. Instead of Picenum, I'd like to be posted to Southern Italy. There are wines I need to research, and the cooking! Do you know … .'

'Stop drivelling. This is important. There's more than just the death of some Italian sprig at stake here. The Cimbri did not get through the Alps by just happening to find those unguarded passes – someone told them where to go. Catulus has a spy in his camp and it has to be someone close to the top. We think that this Minatius kid was killed because he found out who it is.'

Sulla stopped and looked at me seriously. 'You have to stop the leak, Lucius, or there won't be any point in sending you south, or anywhere else in Italy. Stopping the Cimbri is going to be hard enough as it is. If they know our every move before we make it, then Catulus does not stand a chance. Italy as we know it will not exist. More wine?'

The *canaba* is the generic name for the village that inevitably grows up around every Roman army camp. Some soldiers actually bring their wives and children with them on campaign, which is less foolish than it sounds when you consider the risks sometimes facing a defenceless woman on her own. Those without womenfolk can rent them in the huts and tents that also supply cheap wine, gambling, and greasy inferior food. Despite the fact that many of the facilities provided by the *canaba* are available cheaper and better within barracks, most soldiers hit the village at every chance they get.

Tonight the place was relatively quiet, and I made my way between the makeshift hovels and tents unmolested, apart from the occasional hopeful invitation from prostitutes who stepped from the shadows at my approach. Turning to talk to them gave me a chance to glance behind and ensure that no-one followed me as I carefully picked my way through the nameless piles of stinking debris that littered the pathway.

I was brooding on my parting conversation with Sulla. If emissaries from various disgruntled aristocrats came looking to find what had become of the boys they had purchased, then it might be an idea to move the soldiers of the recruiter's former bodyguard out of range of any enquiries. When I mentioned as much to my boss, he replied in a neutral voice, 'Don't worry. I have plans for those men.'

'Sir!' My voice was sharp with alarm. 'You can't blame them for what happened. They were seconded to that duty and they hated every second of it. Yet they were told by their centurion that if they complained or told anyone what was happening, he would personally make their life a living hell.'

'Which centurion?' Sulla asked in a mild, almost

bored, voice.

I shuddered as if someone had tossed a bucket of cold water over me. It's not a nice thing to inadvertently sentence a man to death. 'Look, he probably did not know what was going on himself. He was just asked to do a favour for a well-connected friend. It happens all the time.'

Sulla's expression remained neutral, but I recognized that dangerous whiteness around his eyes. 'That man knew that something suspicious was going on. With my men, in my camp. Something that could harm my men and give ammunition to my enemies. Yet he chose not to come to me with that information, as if I and my reputation did not matter. That is disrespect, and I will not be disrespected. His name, Lucius – uh!'

Sulla held up a warning finger. 'If the next words that come from your lips are not the centurion's name, then we are done. Our friendship is over. And be very clear to yourself what that means. So?'

Like a coward, I had blurted out the name and then got out of the tent as soon as I decently could, even though Sulla afterwards was all smiles and crude jokes. He was my friend and mentor, and I liked and admired him. But nevertheless, there were times when I wondered if Cornelius Sulla was completely sane.

By now I was reaching the edge of the *canaba*, and the wafting smell of manure told me that I was approaching the tents of Bassianus, the Syrian horse trader. He greeted me with a smile as I ducked under the tent-flap and gestured toward a richly embroidered couch.

' I got your message. Have a seat and I – !'

His words were cut short by the dagger I pressed hard against his neck, just above the Adam's apple where his curly beard ended. The man swallowed hard and the action caused my knifepoint to dig a small bead of blood from his skin.

'Is this any way to treat a friend?', asked Bassianus hoarsely, almost cross-eyed in his efforts to look downward at the peril facing him.

'We have never been friends. Now, in the next few seconds I can drive this blade up, through your jaw, through your palate, and right into your brain. You will never even know that you're dead. Now tell me honestly – did you arrange for that Italian boy in Catulus' camp to be killed? I will know if you are lying.'

Bassianus chuckled, and then winced as the action dug my knife tip deeper into his throat. This close to the man, he smelled of sweat, incense and horses as well as a musky odour I could not define. 'No, we did not arrange for the killing', he rasped, 'now take that blade away, please.'

Reluctantly I did so, and the horse trader reached into his robes then dabbed at his throat with a silk handkerchief. His dark eyes glittered in the lamplight as he looked at me. 'Mind you, we did not kill that boy only because I did not think of it. Nor was it necessary. You said you would find your own means of getting transferred to Catulus' command. I take it that has been accomplished?'

I nodded curtly. 'I'm being sent to investigate the murder. That very convenient murder. Also that very unnecessary murder, because I would have been transferred there anyway. I'm putting you on notice, Bassianus, I will investigate that murder and I will find out who is behind it. And if it was you, I'm out. Our whole deal is off.'

Bassianus inspected the bloodstain on his handkerchief with a sour expression. There was little love in the swarthy face that turned back to me.

'I shall let your behaviour pass on this occasion. Your recent meeting with Sulla was probably somewhat stressful – in fact I would imagine that working for Sulla is rather like dancing on the edge of an active volcano. Catulus' camp is merely a scorpion-pit of rivalries, treason, and as we have now discovered - murder. Compared to your last week here, being there should be like a holiday.'

'And as to that Italian boy – Minatius, wasn't he? I don't see what you are so worked up about. He's dead. Well, soon enough so also will be the other little brats that you are meant to educate in warcraft. It's all a waste of time and everyone knows it. That Minatius, he just got to the head of the line for Hades. The others will follow.'

Bassianus gave me a gap-toothed grin of pure, distilled malice. 'Haven't you heard? The Cimbri are coming, and everyone is going to die.'

PHILIP MATYSZAK

Liber II

It's not far from the Alps to the Cispadane plain, but I took my time getting there. A bodyguard of three men accompanied me, along with all my campaign kit slung across the back of an uncomplaining donkey.

My horse was called Maphronius in memory of its former owner. He was a gelded sorrel with the placid temperament that I look for in my steeds. I've nothing against a spirited stallion that charges gallantly into battle with his rider – in fact I'm happy to watch and admire their technique. My own preference is for a horse which stoically takes the tumult of combat in his stride and never gets excited enough to either charge into enemy ranks before his rider can stop him, nor get so worked up by combat that he fails to retreat along with everyone else. I've seen horses do both and neither incident ended well for the person on top.

Besides, Maphronius (the horse) had a beautiful reddish-brown hide which contrasted nicely with his flaxen mane and tail. Not only was the sorrel handsome enough for me to cut a fine figure in the saddle, but steer him into the trees and once in the shadows between the trunks his colouring made him practically invisible. Such was the case at the moment, as he waited peacefully hidden in a stand of larch at the roadside where one of the last alpine foothills led down to the plain.

I was dismounted, and on the rock before me I had spread a large handkerchief upon which was placed a pewter beaker containing a somewhat rough

Piedmontese wine. Maphronius was deeply interested in the loaf of fresh bread I had broken open and I periodically tossed him chunks that he snuffled down with enthusiasm. Between bites of fresh-baked bread I was attempting to chew one of the remarkably tough smoked pork sausages that are inexplicably considered a local delicacy. Before me the plain spread out south-eastwards, the further horizon lost in a bluish haze.

The farmlands seemed to slumber peacefully under the summer sun, but my eye picked out occasional distant feathers of smoke. It was too early for farmers to be burning off stubble after the harvest, and too late for fields to be cleared for spring planting. Somewhere beneath those plumes of smoke, horror was happening. Farmhouses were being plundered, children butchered, and their mothers raped while their menfolk were tortured, killed or enslaved according to the whim of their attackers. The Cimbri were loose on the plain, and were slowly and methodically plundering it from end to end. It was a fate that awaited all Italy if Rome's outnumbered armies were to fail within the next few months.

Behind me and further back in the trees, my escort were sprawled in the shade. They were Marsi, tough, seasoned fighters from a warrior tribe. They had very clear ideas about fraternizing with superior ranks – such as that it was never going to happen. It also did not help that I was Roman and they were Italian. The Romans might be the top group in Italy right now, but Italy had many other peoples, and some of them – including the Marsi – reckoned that the Romans were getting more than somewhat arrogant and pushy with the other peoples of the peninsula. Consequently, my orders were obeyed with brisk efficiency, while attempts at more general conversation were met with blank, unfriendly stares.

On the other hand, the newcomer might offer more value in terms of conversation. I had been watching him for the better part of an hour now following the road as it wound tortuously uphill. In fact, it was to observe him better that I had pulled off the track for an early lunch. A Roman soldier, evidently and an officer too, unless Catulus allowed his troopers un-precedented freedom in their style of dress. Which he didn't because the men accompanying him were clearly Campanian cavalry, with their standard armour, colourful shields and crappy little javelins. The fact that everyone was geared up for instant combat reminded me that it was probably time to unpack my own kit from my saddlebags, and get my escorts to do the same. The young officer's behaviour was decidedly odd. He was keeping off the road and using every scrap of cover as he inched his way uphill, yet his breastplate was polished so brightly that the lad could have done extra duty as a signal beacon. Every now and then he would plant himself firmly against the skyline while he examined the hill ahead of him and then resume skulking through the bushes. The cavalry behind seemed accustomed to such antics and merely plodded stolidly in his wake.

A quick assessment suggested that the approaching party would follow the road past the stand of trees in which I was hidden, and their dauntless leader would probably cut into these trees, all the better to hide his shining armour. Accordingly I gulped down the last of my wine, and stowed the beaker. Then I wiped my mouth with the napkin and, giving the rubbery sausage a reproachful look, wrapped it in my napkin and stashed it and the bread in my pack.

Then I stepped behind a bushy young spruce tree giving Maphronius a warning glare as I did so. Maphronius is a genial sort with a regrettable habit of snorting a friendly greeting to any other horses passing by. However, the sorrel was considerably less stupid than some legionaries I have known and it was dawning on him that a snort got him a whack across the nose with the little leather sap I carry behind my belt while silence at the right time was rewarded with treats. Right now Maphronius had that bread loaf in mind, and was trying to assure me of his good intent by nuzzling me hard in the back – silently – as the young officer approached.

Said officer's attempts at remaining out of sight were rather cancelled by the fact that a blind man could have tracked his approach. I had honestly been unaware there were so many bushes in the clearing until this rider conscientiously located each one and noisily rode his horse through it. Finally, I could take it no more and stepped out to tap the young man on the thigh as he passed.

'Might I enquire what in Hades you are playing at?'

'Yaaaah!' At the rider's startled yell his horse reared and the young man toppled off its back over the tail.

Since I'm not stupid enough to try to catch a man in full armour, I simply put out an arm to break his fall as he crashed to the woodland floor. A grinning Marsic escort stepped up briskly to grab the horse's bridle before it could bolt. A quick glance told me that the horse was a spirited young stallion. I might have guessed.

Beneath a helmet knocked askew the rider looked at me with eyes wide with shock and pain. I ran through a mental inventory. This was not Gnaeus Domitius Ahenobarbus, because my informants had told me that Ahenobarbus was not only younger than this fellow, but already sporting the beginnings of the russet beard which was his family's distinguishing feature. (Ahenobarbus means 'bronze beard'. If they were horses, the entire clan would be sorrels.) It wasn't Lucius Antonius, because that young man was more heavy-set and clean-shaven. Anyway, I knew Antonius because he came around to my brothel in Rome whenever he could afford it.

Gaius Claudius Marcellus Porcellinus was from a junior twig of that aristocratic family tree, and small, mousy and slight, with dark hair. This lad had blonde curls peeping from the sides of his helmet, and his eyes were the blue of the summer sky above. That ruled out Titus Lafranius the only surviving Italian among Catulus' young tent-mates, so I was looking at …

'Publius Cornelius Dextrianus. I assume Catulus sent you to find out what was keeping me?'

'Hey!' One of the Campanians had stepped into the trees to find out what had happened to his officer.

Seeing his man down and a stranger in civilian dress standing over the body was hardly a reassuring sight. 'What's going on here?'

'Shut up, get your men dismounted and set up a defensive perimeter. I want a lookout on that ridge – there - within the next two minutes and no-one gets too comfortable. We may be moving out in a hurry. Get to it!'

At my barked commands, the cavalryman hesitated and looked Dextrianus, who responded with a feeble wave. 'The lookout's already moving into position', the cavalryman informed me grudgingly. 'I'll get that perimeter formed.' A thoughtful pause. '…Sir.'

We exchanged nods and as the cavalryman left I turned my attention back to my youthful charge.

'What's that business about lookouts?' Dextrianus wanted to know.

'Well, Prince Morningstar, your escort commander and I are curious to know whose attention you attracted while you were twinkling your way uphill. That armour is conspicuous from very far away. Probably the only reason you haven't been ambushed yet is because you look so much like the bait for a trap. How in Jupiter's name did you get that breastplate so shiny? And why in Jupiter's name would you want to do such a stupid thing?'

Dextrianus struggled to sit up, brushing strands of dried grass from his forehead as he did so. 'I am a warrior. Warriors do not hide from the enemy.'

I was less than a decade older than the lad in front of me, yet right now it felt closer to a century. Patiently

I told him, 'Look, you are not a warrior so get that idea out of your head. The other lot are warriors.' My gesture took in the plain below us. 'You are a soldier and that is a very different thing.'

'How so?' Dextrianus was genuinely curious.

'A warrior thinks mostly of himself and does that thinking mainly with his testicles. His objective in fighting is to win honour and glory even if he gets killed in the process. We are soldiers. That means that primarily we are components in a unit, and any individual soldier is only as good as his unit as a whole. A soldier's objective in fighting is to win, preferably while killing as many warriors as he can. The world needs fewer warriors.'

Dextrianus slowly levered himself to his feet, wincing at unexpected twinges from his muscles. 'Being a warrior sounds like more fun though, you have to admit that.'

'Freely. Soldiers are not in it for fun. It's a job. Warriors are enthusiastic amateurs.'

'Sir?' Another Campanian cavalryman was trotting towards us, poorly concealed urgency in his manner. 'Horsemen coming our way – fifty to a hundred. Lookout could not see clearly, but he reckons they're hostiles. They are tracking. About thirty minutes out at their current pace.'

'Tracking' meant that every few minutes one of the lead riders would dismount, examine the ground before him and then the horsemen would move on. There's a lot you can tell from tracks even when you know pretty much where your target might be. If you are following horsemen, how professional are the riders? Do they keep well spaced? How often do they pause to check their back-trail? How fresh are the horses, and what quality might they be? A quick poke through the droppings can establish whether these are grain or grass-fed horses. Grain-fed have more stamina and might be harder to catch, but they and probably their riders also, are correspondingly more valuable.

Dextrianus looked abashed. 'This is on me, isn't it? My escort commander was really grouchy about that breastplate too, so I was trying to keep it out of sight. Also', he grinned at me shyly. 'We knew you were somewhere on this road so I was trying to sneak up on you. Guess that did not work out too well either.'

Ignoring this, I turned to the cavalryman who was pretending that he was temporarily deaf. 'Who is the best rider in your unit? And is he on the best horse?'

'Fufidius. And yes.'

'Fetch him and get two men who know this country.' Turning back to Dextrianus I gestured at the armour.

'Take it off.'

'What? Why?'

'Because this Fufidius is going to be wearing your armour while he sprints uphill for the pass. Hopefully those cavalry will dash after him, and if they stop tracking they might not notice that we have snuck off in a different direction. Not for a while anyways. Behind the ridge-line there was a trail forking off. I want to know where it goes. Now, see that donkey? Right-hand saddlebags, there's a set of chain-mail and a Phrygian helmet. When I get back I want you dressed in that, and Fufidius taking his turn at being the sun god.'

'Where are you going?'

'To the ridge-line to see for myself. If we are really, really lucky, that's a unit of friendly Gallic cavalry coming to see if we need any assistance. Somehow I'm not feeling very lucky.'

This was not completely true. It was very probable that, as the pickings in the plain started to run low, it had occurred to some of the Cimbri that there might be booty to be stripped from travellers coming over the Alps from Raetia. They were probably planning to set up their own lethal version of a customs post and had Dextrianus not blundered into me, I and my Marsi might have been among their first customers as we made our way downhill. So while 'lucky' did not quite cover it, I was feeling less unlucky than I might have been.

It was a few hours before I was happy that we had shaken the unknown cavalry unit off our trail. As expected they had hurried off after the highly decorative Fufidius in his new armour, while we had quietly slipped down the cart track behind the ridgeline. As soon as he had topped the pass the speedy Fufidius should have ditched his armour and be now heading up the road to warn the guards at the next town that the route was compromised. Thereafter Fufidius would make his own way back to the army of Catulus – doubtless stopping at a few taverns as he did so.

'I wonder what those Germans will think when they find they have missed us?' Dextrianus mused. He was slightly too big for my chain-mail and kept wiggling his shoulders in an attempt to get comfortable as he rode beside me. He seemed philosophical about the loss of his armour, especially once I had explained its complete unsuitability for small unit operations. But then, he was of the aristocratic Cornelii and so stinking wealthy that he could afford to order up new armour on a whim.

'The Germans – if that's what they were? They're probably not too upset. Honour demands they fight us if we insist, but if I read that lot right, they were after booty. Twenty-five well-armed cavalry can hurt them a lot, even though they'd probably win in the end. So when they discovered that we'd slipped off their path I suspect they were quietly relieved. As for us, well, I'm already late so another day's detour won't harm.'

'Where are we headed? Until now I was more interested in what we were going from rather than what we were coming to.'

'As I understand it from those lads of yours who have patrolled this area before, if we keep going down this track we'll get to an offshoot of the road to Feltria. From there we turn south and follow the river Adige to a small fort alongside the river where we can bunk down for the night. It is manned by a cohort of Picentine regulars, I believe. They're heavy infantry and the fort has stone walls, and that means that once the gates close behind us we can laugh at a thousand cavalrymen. We should be there just after sunset if we keep up this pace, or even sooner if we can walk-trot-canter once we reach the better road. Then we rejoin the main army tomorrow morning.'

Sarni, the place was called and for me it was love at first sight. While most Roman forts are wooden and built on a standard plan, this one was adapted from a castle built by the Maurici tribe who had once dominated the area. It was situated on a rocky spur that pushed into the Adige, forcing the river to turn briefly east before swirling around the sides of the castle to resume its southward course. Because two sides of the fort were flanked by the river - and much of the western side as well - the fort had just two gates. The main gate was a very solid affair flanked by rectangular stone towers, and the other a small, well-protected postern that allowed access to the river for one or two people at a time.

Torches were already flaring in their sconces outside the main gate as we rode up, with the great black pile of the fort outlined against the delicate blues and gold of a summer sunset. The sentry's challenge came loud and reassuringly prompt, though after our arrival there was a long delay before the gate was actually opened.

'We don't know where the Cimbri are right now.' the fort's commander explained as he entertained us to a late supper in his rooms. 'They moved camp a few days ago, and with swarms of their cavalry in the area, it's been too dangerous for our scouts to keep track. Just in case they turn up here, our gate is barricaded six ways to breakfast, which is why it took so long to let you in.

We were hoping that you were the first outriders of the Marian army.'

Dextrianus nodded, his face still stuffed with a mouthful of braised lamb that the commander had served with spiced cabbage. I had made a note to pop down to the kitchens and discuss the recipe with the cook – for a country fort the commander's cuisine was remarkably good. We waited politely for the young aristo to gulp down his food before he remarked eagerly, 'Once we have the Marian forces, the combined armies of Rome should crush the Cimbri.'

The commander was a veteran soldier with an arm withered from an old wound. He and I exchanged looks. 'Depends', I remarked in a neutral voice, 'I was at Arausio when two consular armies took on the Cimbri. Not our finest hour.'

Which was one way to describe one of the most comprehensive defeats in Roman military history. Of an army of 80,000 men, five people had survived the massacre – six, including myself. I was getting used to the sideways looks and mutterings that followed me around any army encampment. I was the man who had survived, and no-one was quite sure whether that meant I was protected by the gods or somehow infected with the ill-fortune of calamity.

'But our defeat was avenged at the Six Waters,' argued Dextrianus enthusiastically. 'Half the threat has gone already.'

The commander helped himself to some more wine and offered the jug to me. I refused politely because whatever the skills of the cook, the vintner's abilities were sadly lacking. My own suspicion was that the brewer had fed a barrel of grape juice to his donkey and placed a bucket beneath to catch the product once it had marinated in the animal's bladder. Sad really, because the nearby Athesis Valley produces some good Rhaetian-style wine, and I'd rather been looking forward to getting re-acquainted with those sweet, smoky flavours.

Worse, we were now discussing one of my least favourite topics – the victories of that jumped up little sow's tit, our multiple-times consul Caius Marius.

'It was good generalship', I allowed grudgingly. 'Marius positioned his army perfectly, so that the Tuetones would have to cross a river and then charge uphill. They were probably exhausted even before they reached the Roman lines.'

'Tens of thousands of the Germans killed and thousands more taken prisoner,' agreed the commander. 'Now that the Teutones have been disposed of, the western passes are free of any threat and Marius is on his way here. Let's hope the Cimbri have learned nothing from the experiences of the Teutones.'

After the battle that had defeated the western arm of the Germanic invasion, Marius had again acted astutely. The man had the morals of a rabid weasel but there was nothing wrong with his political instincts. He had declined to celebrate a triumph for his victory and instead had turned his army around and hurried to reinforce Catulus.

Marius carefully did not say – but made it very clear that he was not saying – that while he had utterly crushed one half of the barbarian threat, Catulus had not even been able to keep the Cimbri out of North Italy, where they were now ravaging the plain around us. Of course, the Cimbri were better fighters and had a larger army than the now-defeated Teutons, and Marius' men were more numerous and higher quality than the legions of Catulus but Marius was certainly not saying that either.

The commander took a long swig of his wine, winced, and set his beaker down again. 'Reckon you are going in the same direction as the Cimbri. They will be heading south, looking to push Catulus off the position he's taken downstream from us near Tridentum.' I vaguely recalled that Tridentum was a small market town. The commander continued, 'If Catulus can't hold them at the Adige, the Cimbri will swarm right across the rest of the plain past Mediolanum. It could split the armies – Marius coming up from the south and Catulus stranded in the north.'

'How many Cimbri?' I asked casually. It would be good to get a local opinion, even though I was pretty sure of the numbers from the intelligence reports I had requested from Rome (I hadn't spent my time taking in the sights on my way to join Catulus – I had also requested and received reports about the young men I was supposed to be training, and I had perused with interest a highly detailed report on the murder scene in Catulus' tent, the latter sent in answer to my equally detailed set of questions.)

'How many Cimbri?' The commander shrugged. 'Hard to say. It's difficult to get past their cavalry screen to count the main body but one of the spies says he watched them for six days going through the Alpine passes. Given the width of the road, he reckons around one hundred thousand men – give or take thirty thousand or so.'

There was a choking sound from Dextrianus who knew, as did we, that the 'thirty thousand' margin of error was in itself several thousand men more than the total forces under Catulus' command.

'Do you think he can hold the bridge at Tridentum?' the commander asked me. His voice was casual but his eyes were fearful. If the main army was defeated or pushed back from the Adige, this little fort would be a lonely island in a barbarian sea.

I shrugged, reached for the wine, thought better of it and instead opted for an extra helping of cabbage. 'We have to hope so, for all our sakes. If Catulus gets beaten at the Adige, Dextrianus and I go down along with him. Personally, I've not seen his camp yet so I can't judge.'

Dextrianus jumped in. 'We've a strong position. There's a legion camped on the east side and Catulus has set up on some low hills west of the river. It's an excellent position for a stand. If the Cimbri take the bait and attack it will be the Six Waters all over again. If things go badly, which they won't, Catulus can use the bridge over the Adige to move his army to the safer bank. He's made it hard for us to lose and easy for us to win. You'll see. We'll defeat the Cimbri just as Marius defeated the rest of the Germans. We won't even need Marius to reinforce us, you'll see.'

There was little to add to that optimistic statement, so we finished the meal in silence.

The next day just before dawn we set out to rejoin the main army. Just before breakfast time we were all back at the fort at Sarni.

'Couldn't resist my kitchen, eh?' said the commander cheerfully.

'Indeed not. That dinner was so good I got to wondering what your cook might manage for breakfast. In the end my appetite overwhelmed me. I stand here a hostage to my stomach.'

My stomach did not, in reality, feel at all like having breakfast dumped on it. In fact my stomach felt rather as if someone had poured a keg of cement into it instead. From the commander's grim expression it seemed very likely that he was feeling the same way.

We stood in one of the stone towers overlooking the gate. Every now and then someone on the road below noticed the commander in his officer's breast-plate and hurled a spear at him. These missiles fell well short, occasionally landing with a clatter on the ramparts. Such spears were gratefully picked up and stored by the garrison who threw nothing back in reply. We were going to need all our munitions and simply throwing them back would have been a waste of time.

The road outside was packed with a flowing stream of humanity, and beyond it a wider pool of men pushed across the meadow, so that from the walls we could see nothing but a tight-packed mass of warriors extending from the fort to the trees over a third of a mile away. Pale figures flickered between the trunks of the trees suggesting that the woods also were packed with barbarian warriors.

The entire mass was heading south, and in that direction the first wave of the Cimbric army had already reached a slight rise in the road and vanished over it. From there the enemy stretched in a jam-packed murmurous mass all the way to the fort and then back past it out of sight behind a bend in the road. They came in their hundreds and hundreds, never stopping, never thinning out, with more coming around the corner at one end to replace the hordes swallowed up by the rise at the other. A heavy, musky smell of under-washed bodies rose from the throng below us, giving it an almost herd-like quality. Seldom in my life had I seen so many people all at once.

We were heading back to join the army of Catulus when we had met the first Cimbric outriders a few miles from the fort, and just a glimpse of the main army following behind had completely ruined my day. Once we had dashed back to safety, the first thing we had told the commander was that whatever he was using to block the fort's gates, he needed more of it. Much more.

Now the Sarni garrison were standing to at the walls, cloaked and silent as they watched the Cimbric army stream by. Like most garrisons, the cohort at Sarni was under-strength. Two hundred and seventy men we had, including three sick and the Campanian cavalry we had brought with us. 'We're a fart against an earthquake', one of the men had muttered to the commander as we climbed to the watch-towers and that comment barely did justice to the odds against us. So we stood and watched in grim silence until Dextrianus arrived.

'Why haven't they stormed the fort?', the young man wanted to know.

I turned to ask where he had been, and then noticed that Dextrianus had managed to get himself re-equipped in a decent set of infantry armour, doubtless scrounged from the fort's stores. I made a note to ask what he had done with my own kit, since I was going to need it rather soon. Dextrianus leaned on the tower's balustrade and contemplated the vast crowd below.

'Jupiter, Juno and Minerva', he breathed. 'How in Hades are we supposed to kill so many?'

'Hey, pretty boy!' Someone in the crowd of Germans spoke basic Latin. A bearded warrior in a chequered cloak, it turned out. He made an obscene gesture at Dextrianus. 'Why not come down and give me your bum? It will be so much worse if I have to come up there and take it.'

Dextrianus gave a cheerful wave in reply. 'Sorry, friend. I'm married.'

'Describe your wife to me then, so that I can give her your regards while I'm enjoying her. We're going to have all your wives and their mothers and daughters too!' This last was greeted with a localized cheer from the barbarian mass and followed by a quick shower of missiles that were gratefully collected by the garrison.

It turned out that there was also a rare bowman in the crowd passing by - and one with none too bad an aim at that. An arrow zipped past my ear and hit one of the wooden roof supports with a meaty thunk. I studied the quivering shaft for a few thoughtful moments then announced, 'Time for me to get armoured up, I think. Dextrianus, where did you leave my chain-mail?'

As I made my way down the reassuringly solid limestone slabs of the tower steps I also pondered the matter of breakfast. The question was not so much if I wanted to eat (I didn't), but whether I should. There was a near-certainty that we would be fighting by the end of the day and I needed the energy. On the other hand, stomach wounds get infected that much more easily if half-digested food gets spilled everywhere.

Also with infection in mind, before I pulled on my newly-reclaimed armour I rummaged through my pack for my cleanest dirty tunic. When threads from dirty linen get driven into a wound along with a slash or stab, it's my experience that infection is more likely to follow. And that's not just my opinion – many of the barbarians on the other side of the wall preferred to fight bare-chested (or simply bare) for the same reason.

I wondered if Dextrianus had worked out the answer to his earlier question about why the Cimbri had not attacked us. The Cimbri were ignoring the fort - for now – because in fact they couldn't attack it. In all the horde of men that had passed by there was not a single ladder or item of siege equipment. So our attackers would have to go into the woods and cut down trees make assault ladders. Then they would have to try storming the walls of the fort, and for all their overwhelming numbers there was only so much fort for the attackers to assault. Those with no room to attack the ramparts would have to wait in line for space to become available.

Since two-thirds of the fort was protected by the river and we had the other ramparts manned, an attack on the fort would take hours if not days. And all the while that the space in front of the fort was taken up by the attack the rest of the Cimbric army would have to sit and wait patiently for the road to become clear again. So for the moment, Cimbric army and Roman garrison were each pretending that the other side did not exist – aside from the occasional romantic invitation of the sort extended to Dextrianus.

So I had breakfast. Then I had a hunk of bread and cheese for lunch. Then, getting tired of watching the endless stream of Cimbri on the other side of the wall, I passed the time in a dice game with a bunch of soldiers in the forecourt, losing thirteen sestertii while my Marsic escort watched on with aloof disgust.

The afternoon had already faded into the long twilight of evening when the last bloc of Cimbri approached. They sent us a herald who waved the traditional staff over his head as he nervously approached the walls. That staff was a standard length of ashwood, about which two willow wands had been plaited. The ash was meant to represent the staff placed between armies, and the entwined willow wands depicted snakes representing the warring forces - though on this occasion a more realistic staff would have an earthworm on one side and on the other an overgrown python.

The herald had the plaid trousers of a Picentine Gaul, which made him one of the many Italian Gauls who had thrown in their lot with the invaders. This was none too surprising, since apart from a natural inclination to be on the winning side, the Picentine Gauls had the further incentive of thoroughly disliking the Romans. And for that no-one could blame them. Much of the Roman settlement of the eastern Padus valley had been done by arriving with well-armed retainers who simply pushed the Gauls off land they had held for generations.

Since only Roman citizens could appear before the courts in Rome, the summarily evicted Italian Picentines had to seek a Roman champion who would be prepared to take up their cause. Not unexpectedly, there were few takers because Roman politicians and judges were more interested in the votes of Roman citizens than in appeals from landless barbarians. So when the Cimbri had arrived, many Gauls saw the opportunity for payback – and doubtless some of the burning farms I had seen as I descended into the valley yesterday had been Roman settlements suffering as part of that retribution.

Yet it was not the herald who interested me so much as the young chieftain who accompanied him. In contrast to the definitely rotund herald, the German was a skinny lad, not much more than twenty, with spiky straw-blond hair cut short in a manner clearly motivated by convenience rather than style. When he tilted his head back to survey the ramparts I saw a bony face with small prissy lips and deep, shadowed eyes. His escort were some twenty paces back and from their restless manner, they had evidently been ordered to stay there.

The herald boomed out, 'Men of Picenum, we are here to offer you a choice. Surrender or die. Our quarrel is not with you but with your Roman masters. Give up your weapons and the Romans in the fort and your lives will be spared. Otherwise … '. The herald looked uneasily at the young man, who gave him no attention. The herald gulped and continued, indicating with his staff a knot of Cimbri working in the meadow between the woods and the road. 'Otherwise, you may see the sharpened stakes we are preparing. By morning, if you have not laid down your arms there will be hundreds of stakes in that field, and every one will have on it the impaled body of a man from your garrison. You cannot win – but you can surrender with honour if the odds against you are overwhelming. Give up your weapons and open the gate.'

The commander and I exchanged glances and I shrugged. 'It's up to you.'

One of the men on the walls called out something, his tone both questioning and appeasing, yet too soft for those of us on the gate tower to make out what he was saying. Certainly it did not sound like defiance. I looked at the commander again. 'Or maybe not up to you, after all.'

The commander said nothing, his face grim.

The men on the walls looked anxiously at the gate tower, and gestured for the herald to approach so that we could not overhear whatever they had to say. The herald called back something encouraging and trotted closer until he was almost right below the ramparts, his upturned face a pale oval in the twilight. Talking urgently, the herald gestured back towards his leader doubtless stressing the man's clemency and generosity.

There was a sudden burst of activity from a knot of men on the rampart and something fell untidily downwards. This was, I later discovered, the contents of one of the fuller, riper slop buckets from the latrines. It hit the herald square on his upturned face and reduced the man to a spluttering incoherent mess. At the same time our men on the walls burst into derisive shouts and howls of defiance which were answered by similar jeers from the chieftain's bodyguard. The young man himself observed his herald dispassionately. Then he threw back his head and let loose a peal of uninhibited laughter before spinning on his heel and sauntering back to rejoin his men

Beside me the commander observed. 'It looks as though we will be fighting after all.'

Liber III

Those who have never tried it might be surprised to know that waiting for combat is a great deal worse than the actual fighting. When you are in the thick of it you're too busy to think and powered by that frenetic energy that only comes along with the likelihood of imminent death. Actual combat is breath-taking, frantic and so exciting that some people become addicted to it. Waiting for the fight to begin is boring and horrible, especially if you have been in action before and your mind is busily serving up gruesome images of what several pounds of razor-sharp steel can do to human flesh.

People deal with pre-battle stress in different ways. Probably the worst solution is to kill that looming sense of dread with judicious shots of wine. That works, but fighting drunk means that you will probably get killed along with your sense of dread. There are soldiers who sit alone, obsessively sharpening swords that could already split a hair lengthways. Others gather in groups, and talk bold as they pretend their bowels are not gradually loosening. I know of one fellow who would mutter long passages from Homer's *Iliad* as though reciting a prayer - anything to take the mind off the horrors to come.

Personally, I tend to prowl around whatever space is available and as the waiting goes on and on I get wound up tighter than a catapult rope. When the time to fight actually arrives, I'm usually so tense and irritable that inflicting serious injury or death on someone feels like a really good idea.

The moon that night would be almost full, but we had about an hour between the last glow of twilight and moonrise. As the evening gloom thickened, we could hear the Cimbri preparing. There was the thud of hatchet on wood as siege ladders were made ready, and the clash of steel as warriors practised with warm-up bouts. Since the Cimbri had nothing against mixing wine and warfare, there were also sounds of raucous revelry around the campfires, and the smell of wood smoke and roasting meat drifted over the ramparts.

Gradually, the blue-gray smoke from the campfires blended into the dark of evening and the flames themselves became ever more visible. Then the Cimbri came at us in a sudden, silent assault. It was cleverly done. By my estimate there were around twelve hundred men in the besieging force, and of these around eight hundred continued drinking, carousing and making a general racket. The others rushed the ramparts in nearly complete silence under cover of the growing darkness.

However it's impossible for a crowd of men to sprint across unfamiliar terrain while carrying bulky ladders without the occasional collision, and there's always the one dickhead who won't obey orders and gees himself up with a wild battle cry. So we had warning of all of a hundred heartbeats that the first attack had begun.

I was pacing the ramparts anyway and was among the first to react to the sentry's warning yell. We had sheaves of javelins stacked at intervals against the rampart wall, along with large lumps of debris from what used to be the stable and latrines. There was nothing but darkness with hints of moving shadows beneath the walls, so I flung javelins almost at random. Given the narrow frontage of the fort I reckoned I could hardly miss hitting someone in the crowd below.

Then someone thinking more clearly than I tossed down a flaming torch to reveal a few dozen shadowy shapes disappearing into the darkness. The empty ground in front of the fort was littered with javelins that we had thrown in vain. I felt at my depleted stock of ammunition and bitterly regretted the missiles I had wasted on the enemy's feint.

The commander yelled, 'Don't throw anything unless you can see a target!'

Excellent advice, if not exactly timely. Still it was effective enough, for moments later what looked like a solid wall of warriors charged into the torchlight. This time my javelins were used to greater effect. I aimed at the front runners of those with ladders, working on the principle that dropping a man in front would greatly increase the problems of those carrying behind. It's harder to throw downwards than it seems and mostly I missed, but given the mass of warriors below the javelins had to hit something – though mostly that seemed to be shields.

In a matter of moments, ladders were thunking against the walls. I abandoned my javelins and stooped to pick up a masonry lump of former toilet block. As I stood, a spear hit me on the shoulder, but its force was largely spent and the missile bounced from my armour back into the darkness. It almost caused me serious injury though, for sheer surprise caused me to drop my lump of stone and I almost crushed my foot.

It's amazing how light even a large lump of masonry about the size of my head can feel at moments like this. Stooping, I retrieved the stone and in one movement dropped it down the ladder in front of me. The first warrior must have climbed like a monkey, for he was only a few feet from the top when the stone hit him, taking him down and dislodging the warrior below him also, and the man after that. Thereafter, with a shoulder-twisting wrench, I pulled the ladder sideways and toppled it from the wall. Further along the ramparts, other soldiers had rigged long poles with Y shaped ends which they fitted to the top rung of the siege ladders and pushed them off the wall. This worked especially well with ladders placed at a steep angle and it was reassuring to watch them topple backwards replete with their human cargo.

There was a furious hammering from further along, and as my bit of wall was temporarily ladder-free, I grabbed a handful of javelins and rushed over to help ruin the evening of the axemen trying to stave in the gate. This was not really necessary, as the defenders over the gate were already engaged.

They had a fire going on the ramparts, and little clay bottles filled with olive oil were buried deep in the coals. First someone would drop a boulder over the ramparts, and then someone else would use tongs to fish out a red-hot clay bottle and drop it into the chaos caused by the falling rock. Judging by the shouts and screams as each bottle exploded this unusual weaponry was having its effect. I guess that's what happens when people are stuck in a fort with nothing to do but think of novel ways to be nasty to attackers should they ever arrive. They come up with interesting ideas.

There was a downside to the fire, because the flames illuminated the men on the ramparts, and the few archers among the Cimbri were firing a stream of arrows at them. Three men were down already – two with what looked like flesh wounds. These two were being tended by medics, and while I watched the third, with an arrow angled upwards through his throat, had his corpse unceremoniously rolled off the ramparts into the courtyard below.

Then as suddenly as it had started, the attack was over. The Cimbri retreated, pulling their dead and wounded back into the shadows as they withdrew. The wall was suddenly silent apart from the sound of men sobbing for breath and the curses of those with wounds both serious and minor.

I'll freely confess I am no Achilles who delights in battle. There are those types who claim that they never feel more alive than when arrows are hissing past and the swords sing in combat. Me, I'm all too well aware that in those circumstances 'feeling alive' might only be temporary, and I can't claim to enjoy something that will be waking me up in a cold sweat some night a few months hence. That said, I have no moral objections to taking human life (with the firm stipulation that the life in question should not be my own) and as far as I was concerned any barbarian who put a ladder up against our ramparts deserved whatever he got.

I'll also concede that if one has to fight, defending the walls during a siege is probably the best way to do it. There's no other form of warfare where one can pop down to the kitchens for a mug of milk and a slice of beef on bread during a break in the action. Secondly while besieged the odds are massively in the defenders' favour, because they have solid stone walls and years to prepare for the event. It also helps if the enemy are new to siege warfare and have to work things out as they go along.

Take the exact science of siege ladders, for example. As the night went on the Cimbric ladders showed a steady improvement on the early, often fatal prototypes. There's not much room for error with a siege ladder. For example, there's the embarrassing moment when one rushes forward to lean a ladder against the walls only to discover that it stops four feet short of the ramparts.

At least then one can slink away to cut a longer ladder, with only damage to your pride as the besieged howl in derision. Worse are the ladders that can reach the ramparts only if stood almost vertical. Those, the defenders leave until they are loaded from end to end with warriors before slowly and sadistically pushing them backwards. After some thought about this our attackers came up with long, long ladders that sloped gently up to the ramparts.

There are two types of long, long ladder. The first lets around a dozen warriors ascend it before it breaks disastrously in the middle and drops everyone hard on the ground. Dropping twenty feet while carrying sharp swords and spears is a dangerous business, even without armour that exaggerates rather than mitigates the force of a fall. The second type of longer ladder is made up of near-complete tree trunks. It cannot break, but requires almost forty men to haul it into place, and while they struggle with their load they are almost defenceless against a shower of well-aimed javelins from the walls.

Yet the Cimbri learned as the night wore on, finding the sweet spot between length and strength, and when they got their first ladder exactly right they did not swarm up it, but carefully dragged it back and retreated to make two dozen more just like it. Defending against attacks became harder, especially as the Cimbri attacked in waves, one after the other. After a while our commander worked out that the Cimbri were actually attacking in shifts. Only a third of them could attack the narrow frontage of the fort at any one time, so while that third were attacking one third were resting and the other third preparing their next assault.

This meant that we on the ramparts had to throw back attack after attack without respite. Eventually the commander was forced to respond in kind, resting a third of his men while the others fought on the walls. The reduction in our manpower, combined increasing exhaustion and slowly mounting casualties meant that on several occasions towards the end of the night the Cimbri successfully scaled the walls.

When this happened, there would be a shout of 'Breech! Breech!' Those of us who were closest would snatch up broad legionary shields and rush the Germans as they tried to move along the walls to make room for their friends still coming up the ladder. The trick was not to fight, but to push the attackers backwards with the shields until our sheer body weight pressing from both sides created a packed mass of bodies.

Not only could those on the ladders not then join their playmates crushed against the walls, but also in that tight-packed mass of humanity the Cimbri had no room to swing those huge broadswords which were their favourite weapon. We used spears and the Roman short stabbing swords to deadly effect on these occasions. After several soldiers almost came to grief on the puddles of blood left on the flagstones after such engagements, someone came up with the idea of using the well-defended postern gate to bring buckets of sand from the riverbank. Thereafter I fought with a good grip under my feet, but with bloody sand stuck between my toes – which was annoying and painful.

As with everyone else, the strain of defending had taken its toll on me. By this time I had a solid assortment of bumps and bruises, and a cut over one eye that would not stop bleeding. I stank of sweat and my arms hurt relentlessly from the strain of wielding a sword for hours on end. I was so weakened that I no longer dared to pick up masonry lumps to hurl over the walls and my stomach ached after I had vomited several times from sheer stress and exhaustion.

The final push came just as the dawn slowly paled the sky behind us. The Cimbri came on in a howling horde apparently undaunted by a night of setbacks. Their archers had run out of arrows some time ago, and we were low on javelins, so barely a missile was exchanged until the ladders hit the walls. Grimly I picked a ladder and slashed at the first blond head that poked up. By now the Cimbri had mastered the art of climbing with a shield hooked in one hand, so I had to yank the shield aside and nearly overbalanced while stabbing downwards at the snarling face below.

In the nick of time it registered that the person next to me was not Italian, and I converted my stab into a backhand slash that sent the warrior leaping backward to be impaled on a spear wielded by one of the defenders. By the time I turned back my man was off his ladder and on to the walls, with the cry of 'Breech!' coming from perhaps half a dozen points along the ramparts.

The advantage of being completely surrounded by the enemy is that you can slash about frantically without worrying what or whom your sword might hit, while your opponents have to be careful not to stab each other. The disadvantage is that you can't keep it up for long, especially if already debilitated after a night of constant action. I became vaguely aware that the warriors to my right were being distracted by another attacker, and so turned my attention to the man on my left.

This was a young warrior who died with my sword stabbing under his armpit as he lifted his broadsword for a downward swing. As the man behind him pushed the corpse aside to get at me, I glimpsed the warrior to my right going down. Then an armoured figure was at my side, fighting like a berserker. Back-to-back we fought across the walls and then half-slid half-stumbled down the steps to join a ferocious melee in the courtyard.

My rescuer was Dextrianus, who seemed to have lost not a whit of energy through the long night. He fought Thracian style, with a longer sword in his right hand and a shorter sword in his left. Both weapons he used with lethal skill against nonplussed opponents unaccustomed to this form of combat. Fighting two swords at once is hard enough, but Dextrianus made it all the harder by concentrating totally on offense, perhaps on the assumption that his opponents would be too focused on not dying to harm him.

I gratefully dropped into the role of sidekick, meticulously stabbing anyone who tried to edge around that whirling storm of blades, and once dropping to my knees to hamstring an individual with my dagger when my now-blunted sword simply bounced off his expensive-looking armour.

There was a triumphant shout from the ramparts. Sobbing for breath, I looked up to see a flying wedge of Italian infantry clearing the walls, their bodies dark outlines against the pale blue sky. Some twenty Cimbri were trapped in the courtyard, and we drove them slowly into the corner where the barrack block joined the walls. There, too exhausted to fight any more, both sides lowered their weapons and we stood glaring at each other. Above on the ramparts, the clash of weapons died away. This Cimbric attack had failed, but

I was seriously uncertain whether the next one would also.

'Commander!'

The shout from above brought the commander hurrying over, and Dextrianus and I tagged along, sheer curiosity temporarily overcoming our exhaustion. On the walls we saw the young Cimbric leader from yesterday, though now without his herald. A herald which he did not need in any case, it transpired. Ignoring the risk from a well-aimed missile, the young man sauntered to the walls as though headed for a picnic in the woods. Seeing the commander staring grimly down at him, he smiled and gave a cheerful greeting. The lad's Latin was harshly accented, and his cruelty to the vocative case was grating, but neither of these linguistic failings hampered clear communication.

'Hello, to you being Italian in charge. Throw down a rope that I might climb to talk to you.'

'What do you want?'

Blondy shrugged. 'Your fort of course. But I perhaps offer you in exchange for it.'

'What?'

'The rope. Then we talk properly.'

While a rope was being fetched, I reflected that there had been no official cease-fire, or even talk of a truce. By the rules of war, as soon as the young man was hauled on to the walls, we were well within our rights to gut him like a fish. On the other hand, the rules of common sense dictate that when the enemy vastly outnumber you, it's a good idea to be nice to their leader. Besides he seemed to take it for granted that we'd throw down the rope and talk, and after a hard night such as we had just gone through, frankly it was easiest just to go with the flow.

Once on the walls the young man looked keenly around. His quick, intelligent eyes noted our numbers and defences and he was quite shameless about it. He even walked to the edge of the rampart and examined the courtyard, all the better to see how the gate had been blocked.

'Now to see your, um … the name for the place where food is kept?'

The commander exploded. 'Why in Hades should I show you that?'

'Because if you have a little food, we will do a siege. If you have a much food, we need to talk.'

The commander shrugged. 'Yes, we have a much food. Would you care to join us for breakfast?'

'I see the food, please.'

On his way to the stores the young man crossed the courtyard and had a word with the twenty Cimbric warriors still trapped against the barrack block. The state of these warriors was, as with everything else at the moment, a bit uncertain. They were certainly not prisoners, because they had neither surrendered nor given up their weapons. On the other hand they were not free either, for if they tried to leave the corner in which they were hemmed fighting would break out again in earnest.

So there was a sort of wary cessation of hostilities, during which the Italians took the chance to study their Cimbric opponents with great curiosity. It occurred to me that the garrison here had probably never seen Cimbric warriors before yesterday. So far the fighting had been in the north and east of the river, and never before had the Cimbri penetrated this far south. Someone emerged from the stores with an armful of loaves and proceeded to lob them into the crowd, throwing the bread impartially to Cimbri and Italian garrison alike. Impromptu breakfasting broke out.

In the storeroom the young leader of the Cimbri regarded the stacked sacks of foodstuff impassively. After a minute he turned on his heel and stalked back to the ramparts from where he firmly dictated a string of orders to the anxious crowd of Germans who had gathered below. In due course the fat herald came trotting up, and was hauled up the wall to join us despite his spluttering protestations.

While the herald regained his breath and his dignity he smoothed his tunic and listened intently to the rapid monologue of his boss. When the boss was through, the herald closed his eyes, took a deep breath and began.

'This is not a discussion. Metus, the son of Boiorix has spoken and this is how it will be. You have fought gallantly, and have clearly shown that you can keep fighting. This we do not want to do. We are warriors and we prefer to fight our enemies face-to-face on the field, not while they hide behind stone walls. '

'He says that you have supplies, but he has the men. If this fight continues, it may take another night, perhaps even the night afterwards, but this fort will fall. If we go down this path, then - ', the herald gestured at the clearing before the woods, '- the impalement stakes await any survivors. We will do this if we must. Alternatively - ', the herald paused, and then presented his ultimatum.

'We can't leave an armed presence behind the army, even an insignificant presence such as yourselves. The fort must be ours, so you must leave it. When the sun is above those trees there, the garrison must be formed up in the courtyard in marching order. You can keep your weapons, such personal effects as you can carry, and put your wounded on those carts behind the stables. We will even allow the cavalry to take their horses. But you must be gone by mid-morning.'

The commander was about to speak, but was silenced by the Cimbric leader holding up a hand. The herald continued. 'Killing you all is not the only way to take you out of this war. Look over the walls, and you will see the effigy of a golden bull being brought to the gates. As you leave, each of the Italians of the fort will place their hands on the head of that bull and swear by whatever gods you hold most sacred that you will never take up arms against the Cimbri again. Then you can go. You will not be harmed.'

'I repeat, this is not a negotiation. You either agree and leave, or disagree and fight to the death. While you discuss it, we shall depart - and by 'we' the son of Boiorix means also those men of his in the courtyard. Call them up here, please.'

Ten minutes later, though I really did not feel like eating, I chewed hard on a dried fig, and swallowed it with the help of a mug of cool river water. Then I glared across the table at the commander, and repeated for the tenth time, 'Take the damn deal.'

We were back in the commander's quarters, and I had spent the past few minutes refuelling with whatever rations were on hand and, between mouthfuls, battling with the commander's misplaced sense of honour. My bruises were beginning to settle, and the consequent aching stiffness did little to help my foul mood.

'You know and I know that the Cimbric kid was wrong. We probably won't last another two hours, let alone two days. A few more assaults like that last one will finish us. Practice makes perfect, and they've gotten accursed good at attacking our ramparts. The fort is done for. We have done all we could and there's no point in dying just so you can take a few Cimbri along with you. Do you really think that killing another dozen or two more of that lot outside will make even the slightest dent in that horde we saw pass by yesterday?'

'It is our duty to defend the fort', the commander insisted stubbornly.

'And you have. You and your men have defended the fort against great odds, and held it for longer than anyone would expect. You have done your duty, and no-one is going to blame you if you quit now, especially as you leave with your honour and your weapons. On the other hand, if you do not quit – do you know who is going to blame you? Your children, and the wives and families of those brave soldiers who fought so well for you last night who will now die for nothing. Be reasonable, man.'

For the first time the commander seemed to weaken.

'I have two grandchildren', he admitted. 'It would be good to see them again. I wonder where they got this golden bull from? An odd thing to be dragging around with an army. They probably looted it from a local temple and decided that if it's a religious artefact, that's good enough to swear on.' A thought struck him. 'But what about you two? The herald's terms were for the Italians of the fort. There was no mention of what happens to the Romans.'

'That's okay. You go ahead and get your men ready to move out. Dextrianus and I will make our own arrangements.'

As it became clear that the Italians were going to accept the deal and leave the fort on terms, there was a general relaxation of tension around the Cimbric camp. Some shinned over the ramparts on the siege ladders they had spare, and once in the fort gave a hand with dismantling the barricades piled up behind the gate. Others wandered up to the gate tower to enjoy the view. Several inspected the bodies neatly laid out in the courtyard, looking for dead friends to carry away for burial.

So it came to pass that two warriors, who having just urinated into the river, wandered back from the fort's postern gate towards the woods. They were having a quiet but intense argument, and to keep it private they skirted the main body of men still camped in the field. The younger warrior seemed particularly incensed.

'So you made me strip off my armour, and then sent

it flying over the hills with that Fufidius individual. It was expensive, that armour. The breastplate alone would have kept a workman in good wages for a year. I lost that, all that, and did not say a word. It was mine, it's gone and I'll get another. But that sword. It was my grandfather's. He brought it back from the Macedonian wars, and now I've lost it. No, not lost it – you made me leave it behind, and replace it with this, this … '. Dextrianus shook the iron-tipped spear he carried, apparently at a loss for words.

'And these trousers,' he went on plaintively, 'apart from the disgusting lack of personal body hygiene on the part of their previous owner, these trousers have fleas. I can feel them biting my testicles. There's also something alive in my helmet. It's crawled out of the padding. Now that tunic of mine, the one that we put on the corpse we stripped, that was finest lambswool. Admittedly, no-one is ever going to get the bloodstains out of it, but that's hardly the point.'

Personally I felt little better about the blood-stiffened leather jerkin that was uncomfortably tight around my bruised ribs. And Dextrianus was certainly right about wearing trousers. Any trousers are an unventilated abomination fit only for barbarians, let alone the second-hand leggings we had removed from their deceased owners after those owners had just completed a night of strenuous exercise. It had been hard enough finding a pair whose former wearer's bowels had not relaxed in death, and I had to keep hitching up my belt to stop the horrible garment from dropping around my ankles.

I cast around for a topic to take our minds off our mutual suffering. 'Look, it's only a few hundred paces to the woods. Once we get there and are out of sight, you can strip as naked as a faun for all I care. That sword, was it that what gave your instructor the idea for you to learn to fight Thracian-style?'

Dextrianus nodded, and put a hand up to prevent his helmet slipping over his nose. 'That and because I could fight left-handed anyway, of course.'

Of course. The fact that Dextrianus could fight left-handed was baked into his name. All Romans have three names - the *tria nomina*. It's one of the things that distinguishes a Roman from the rest of the world. For example I was Lucius – a name chosen because I had been born at first light (prima lucis) – Turpillius was my family name, and Panderius because my family came from the island of Pandateria. It's that last name, the cognomen, that tells you most about a person. Were I particularly good looking, I might be Lucius Turpillius Pulcher. If I had a ferocious temper I might get the cognomen 'Bestia', as in Lucius the Beast. The great Roman war hero Quintus Fabius Maximus might have performed his great deeds to gain his cognomen, because being called 'the great' is so much better than his previous cognomen of 'Verrucosus' (warty).

The cognomen Dextrianus is an example of Roman humour. Let's start with the suffix '-anus' which means 'formerly'. So if someone from the Scipio family adopts someone from the Aemilius clan, the adoptee becomes Scipio Aemilianus. A Roman born left-handed who chose to remain that way might end up with the cognomen 'Sinister' (lefty). However, many parents felt it better to re-train their children to adapt to a right-handed world. If a child so trained managed to become particularly adept at using his right hand (dexter) he is said to have been 'adopted' from that side, hence the cognomen 'Dextrianus'.

'You are that good with either hand that they should have called you 'Ambidextrianus'', I remarked. Inserting a hand under my belt I scratched at my buttocks, taking the opportunity to look about as I did so. The woods were now a few yards off, and no-one was paying us much attention. Once in the trees, we had to run parallel to the road for around half a mile until we were out of sight of the camp. Then it was a matter of waiting until the fort's garrison came by, hopefully complete with the Campanian cavalry and our horses.

Along with the garrison, the Campanians would have sworn not to fight any further in the war. However, turning loose two extra horses which the troop had brought along with them presumably did not count as fighting. I sincerely hoped that someone had remembered to pack clean tunics and underwear in the saddlebags, and also that the swearing ceremony was short enough for everyone to be gone before our absence was noted, but long enough for us to have time to wash in the river before something permanent rubbed off on to me from those scrofulous trousers.

Liber IV

'Now, by the hound of Hekate, that's rather odd.'

'What's odd?' I growled, urging my horse uphill and then reining in beside Dextrianus. My mood was none too good and my body had aches in places where I hadn't previously known I had places. I was severely short of sleep, having spent the previous night curled up under a bush and resting as soundly as a cat on the roof of a kennel filled with Molossian hounds.

Things were not helped by Dextrianus creeping up on me an hour or two before dawn. I nearly cut his throat before he leapt back and announced in a stage whisper that he had heard movement on the side of the thicket where he was sleeping. An extended period of extreme alertness revealed nothing more suspicious than a shadowy fox evidently interested in the lingering scent of our evening meal but thereafter I was unable to get back to sleep. This had not helped my mood at all.

That morning we had crossed the bridge of some obscure tributary of the River Adige and were making our way up the hill on the other side when Dextrianus pulled his horse to a sudden stop just short of where the rise topped out. 'There's a lot of Cimbri over the river', he informed me, 'but what in Hades are they doing?'

'Let's get off the road first.' I instructed and made sure that my trainee never came far enough uphill for his silhouette to appear against the skyline. This required several sharp nudges with my knee because

Dextrianus was too fascinated by the activities downhill to pay much attention to basic fieldcraft.

'Do they think they are Gods? They seem to be re-arranging the landscape simply for the pleasure of doing so.'

The Cimbri did indeed appear to be acting strangely. They were swarming like ants around the edge of the forest, hewing down trees and dragging them to the river's edge. Others had attacked a rock outcrop and were in the process of breaking it down into a jumble of boulders. There was an overall air of focussed industriousness but I found it rather hard to make out the point of it all.

The first clue came when another team emerged from deeper within the forest dragging a complete birch tree trunk from which they had stripped the branches. This trunk they took to where another group were busily breaking down the river bank to create a wide, crude landing. As we watched a number of logs were rolled together while the bark was skinned in long strips from the birch trunk. Bearing strips of bark and rope a crowd of men swarmed over the logs, and within moments a rough-looking platform had taken shape. Barely pausing to admire their handiwork, the mass of workers moved on to the next pile of logs and began assembling them in the same way.

'They're making rafts', breathed Dextrianus, 'But to what end? Those are green logs – so full of sap they'll wallow about in the water. And some of those tree trunks they have stacked up at the riverside are far too big for rafts unless they plan on transporting giants –

with giants on hand to bind those trees together.'

There came a shout from the outcrop, and groups of men began rolling the rocks toward the river using long poles as levers. Well, that explained the road roughly carved between outcrop and river. They were going to transport rocks on the rafts. Large rocks, some several times the size of a man. A horrible suspicion began to grow within my mind and I turned towards Dextrianus.

'How far to Catulus' camp at Tridentum?'

Dextrianus pushed out his lower lip. 'I'm not sure. Not that far – five miles? Seven? Not more than seven, probably less. Why?'

'That horse of yours - is it fast?'

'It certainly is. Probably faster than that horse I last saw a few days back vanishing up the pass along with my armour. Why - what's going on?'

He received no reply for I was already galloping down the road, no longer caring whether or not the enemy on the other bank could see me. At stake was the fate of half of Catulus' army - and that fate depended firstly on whether I could reach the camp in time, and secondly whether there was someone competent in command of the camp who would listen to me.

As it happened, the senior officer on the eastern bank of Catulus' camp was an aristocrat called Marcus Aemilius Scaurus, son of Rome's famous (or infamous, depending on your political and ethical persuasion) Aemilius Scaurus. Now it is not the case that all aristocratic officers are imbeciles – on average they are as intelligent as the next man and also much better trained for command. However, wealth and privilege allow them to sidestep the filtering process that usually prevents the grossly incompetent from rising to a position where they can do serious damage. So one finds a higher percentage of aristocratic imbeciles in high command than one would in a random sample of the population. The younger Scaurus was one such imbecile.

Fortunately, reports that the Cimbric army were gathering for an attack had caused Scaurus to call a meeting of his *comitium* (his senior advisors). They were in the praetorium – the command tent – when I burst in and informed the group that they needed to break up the meeting and evacuate the army over to the west bank immediately. As in right now, please gentlemen.

'It's Panderius', someone remarked. 'We were expecting him. Why are you dressed as a barbarian cavalryman, Lucius?'

'Because I had to ride around a large Cimbric army to get here. And this garb caused me no little difficulty with your sentries, let me tell you. Now let me explain why you have to evacuate. There's almost no time.'

'I'm in charge of this meeting', Scaurus informed me sharply, 'And advisors far senior to you have decided that we can easily hold the camp, especially as we can get reinforcements over the bridge should we need them. This is just a feint designed to panic us into doing just as you want us to do – evacuate the camp. So you don't get to just barge in here and give us orders. Sit down and be quiet.'

'Listen to me -'

'Why? Who ever listens to a junior tribune?' Scaurus chuckled and looked around the table for support.

In my frustration I chose to take the question literally. 'Well sir, those who listen to a junior tribune are those who find his information more important than his rank. On the other hand, those people who are too stupid to process information or too pigshit ignorant to even hear that information in the first place, such people would probably have to rely on the rank of the person giving it to them – sir.'

'And if that is the case', added a cool, disdainful voice, 'Perhaps the word of a Scipio of the Cornelii Scipiones might add weight.' In the few minutes since we had arrived in camp Dextrianus Scipio had somehow managed to ditch his Germanic clothes and pull on a tunic. Now he came to stand beside me, looking every inch the young aristocrat.

Fortunately the senior centurion at the table was none other than Petraeus, a veteran with whom I had previously campaigned in Africa. Ignoring the slowly enpurpling Scaurus, he asked, 'What's going on Lucius?'

'The Cimbri are going to take down the bridge.'

Scaurus began to say something, but Petraeus silenced him by holding up an imperative hand. 'How? We have that bridge better guarded than a Vestal Virgin in an army camp. Have you seen the earthworks at either end?'

'And have you looked upriver, Petraeus? Right now, floating downstream there's tree trunks weighing tons and rafts loaded with rocks that weigh only a bit less.

Not just a few, not even dozens, but over a hundred of the accursed things. How long can the bridge pilings hold out before the repeated impacts collapse them? And how long can this side of the camp hold out once the bridge is downed?'

Petraeus looked at me wide-eyed as he uttered a string of highly obscene oaths. Then he leapt to his feet yelling at the guards stationed at the tent-flap 'Sentries! Sound the alarm. You lot – ', he looked wildly around the table,' - get your men mustered in battle gear right now, formed up to march. We need to be out of here now and anyone not ready will be left behind. How long have we got, Lucius?'

'Judging by the speed of the river current, half an hour, tops. The Adige is pretty fast hereabouts. Even if we get everyone mustered immediately it's going to be very close.'

'You heard him, gentlemen. Why are you still here? Let's move!'

'Hey!' Scaurus had decided to reassert himself as he rose angrily from his chair. Petraeus rounded on him swiftly.

'And you sir? Are the cavalry prepared? How soon can you get into your armour?'

Scaurus opened his mouth to reply, but Petraeus didn't give him the chance. 'You had better get on with it then, hadn't you sir? Lucius, you're with me. And get out of that damn fancy dress before someone kills you by mistake. Come on!'

In a matter of minutes the camp was heaving like an overturned anthill. Most of the army was already stood-to in the expectation of a Cimbric attack but now men were rushing back to their tents to stuff their packs full of belongings, or loading squad gear on to confused and restive donkeys. Centurions rushed everywhere bawling out mostly disregarded orders and striking out indiscriminately with their vine rod staves of office.

Petraeus led a flying wedge of guardsmen through the chaos at high speed achieved mainly by shoving aside, and in at least one case trampling over, anyone who got in his way. I was caught in the middle of the wedge hopping and swearing as I tried to get into armour while on the move. A patient orderly trotted along beside me passing bits of armour as soon as the previous piece was strapped, buckled or belted into place. The final item was a short legionary sword and rather than slip it into a scabbard that I did not yet have, I decided to disregard the scabbard altogether and keep the sword in hand.

My *ad hoc* gymnastics prevented me from seeing where we were going until we reached one of the earthworks overlooking the river. The waters swirled under the bridge, making splashes of greyish white foam where it battered against the bridge pilings. I looked at the pilings, spaced an even eight feet apart and mentally compared the gap between the pilings with the rafts the Cimbri had been building. I recalled that each raft had been at least ten feet wide, which showed that someone had done his homework. There was no way those rafts were going to go under the bridge without hitting at least one piling - hard. The bridge itself had a plank floor wide enough to take eight men abreast, and I was pleased to see the first legionaries already crossing at a brisk jog.

Petraeus had been looking upriver and now he turned an anxious face to me. 'You had better be right about this Lucius. I've put my cock right on the chopping block on just your say-so. If nothing comes down that river we might as well jump off that bridge ourselves rather than face the hell there will be to pay.'

'Look', I replied.

Petraeus had been looking for rafts and had missed the mostly-submerged tree trunk that slid with the current like a giant shark. Together we watched as it glided toward the bridge and then under. For a moment I thought we had a clear miss, then came a muffled clonk and the bridge shook slightly as the trunk hit one of the leeward piles a glancing blow.

Looking upriver I saw another trunk, and then another, and then the first of the rafts twirling ponderously in the rushing waters, half awash from the weight of the boulders piled atop it. Then more rafts appeared, each with an escort of semi-submerged tree trunks. Petraeus groaned softly. 'Oh, crap. I really wish you had been wrong, you know. No matter what it would have cost us personally this is going to be worse. Come on.'

We forged our way back across the camp as cries of alarm rose behind us. The pilings were now constantly being hit and the bridge shuddered repeatedly under the series of hammer blows. Even with good Roman workmanship those pilings could not have been driven that deep, and in any case, the repeated shaking would eventually work loose the dowels and joints of the superstructure. If the impacts continued, the question was not if, but when the bridge would fall, especially as it was now packed end-to-end with the weight of an increasingly panicked mass of heavy infantry.

So of course this was the moment when the Cimbri attacked. Petraeus and I reached the wall on the far side of the camp just as the mass of warriors formed up, and I was still catching my breath when they came at us in a massive, screaming wall of humanity. There was a momentary impression of bare chests, colourful cloaks and bearded faces contorted into bestial snarls, and then my attention was focussed on the men directly in front of me as they dropped to all fours to climb the final section of the earth rampart.

I split the first man's skull with a vicious downward blow and had to twist the sword loose, opening the skull like a melon in an untidy spill of blood and brains. Then it was a double-handed back-swing with blood streaming off the blade as I sank my sword into another warrior who had come almost beside me. Ready to take his place, a dozen others were scrambling up between the sharpened wooden stakes with grim, implacable determination. At the last moment I whipped my head aside as a spear blurred through the air and then I was ducking back as an entire flock of them came hurtling through the air at me.

A wild glance left and right explained why I was the subject of such special attention – I was practically the last living Roman on the rampart. 'Come down, Lucius!'

bellowed Petraeus from some twenty feet behind me where he was mustering a shield wall of legionaries to face the Cimbri pouring over the wall in a human wave.

Three giant steps were all it took for me to go flying down the back wall, and I ended up falling and rolling under the feet of the legionaries, one of whom pressed a sword into my hand as I rose dazedly to my feet. My original weapon had got lost somewhere during my descent, fortunately without doing me any damage as I rolled. Once I was on my feet it was rearguard work all the way, exhausting, stabbing work against a human tide that pressed right up against the shields sometimes so tightly that even when a man was stabbed the corpse could not fall but instead remained upright, pressed by the crowd behind against the shield of the legionary who had killed him.

Something had struck me across the nose and now blood was pouring down my chest, feeling sticky under my armour. I was a step back from the front rank, now putting my shoulder against the back of legionaries where the line buckled under the weight of humanity pressed against it, and now throwing myself into vicious combat at points where our formation was beginning to break. Finally I felt other Romans behind me and realized that we had retreated across the camp to the point where we were back-to-back with the soldiers lined up to cross the bridge.

At that point the cavalry appeared. Their horses had been secured in the picket lines in the middle of the camp, and either Scaurus or a capable subordinate had pulled them to the downstream side of the walls. This manoeuvrer went largely unnoticed by the Cimbri until some three hundred horsemen crashed into the rear of their line. Fighting confused men who mostly had their backs to the horses allowed the cavalry to cut through the horde like a knife through butter, and the legionaries to their front took advantage of the tumult to do some serious killing of their own. I waited for the cavalry to pull back, rally, and strike again, but instead the block of horsemen went on, right into the Roman lines.

There were cries of shock and outrage as the cavalry bulled through the packed mass of infantry leaving behind a mass of disordered men upon whom the Cimbri fell like wolves. It soon became clear that the cavalry were pushing toward the bridge, and then on to it. Those already on the bridge were pushed aside and I saw bodies fall over the railings, arms flailing as they tumbled to their deaths in the river below. I made a mental vow that next time I saw Marcus Aemilius Scaurus I would kill the swine on the spot, and damn the consequences.

(I never got the chance to fulfil that promise, for Scaurus and his men did not stop once they had gained the safety of the west bank but instead kept running all the way to Rome. There Scaurus gave the breathless news that Catulus, his army, and probably Rome itself were lost. Yet when the senate questioned the other cavalrymen the truth quickly revealed - that Scaurus had fled before the outcome of the fight was known. Thereafter the gates of Rome were shut to him and he and his men were considered deserters. Aemilius

Scaurus senior refused to intercede for his child, and all that Scaurus junior got for his desperate pleas was a cold statement that the old senator no longer considered that he had a son. Disowned, disgraced and facing certain prosecution, the coward took the coward's way out and killed himself.)

Satisfying as this development was when I later heard the news, at the time all that we on the east bank knew was that the cavalry had abandoned us. Again, I thought bitterly, remembering the Roman catastrophe at the battle of Arausio where a Roman leader had also led his cavalry at high speed from the battlefield, leaving the infantry - and me - to our fate.

'Useless damn cavalry', muttered the legionary next to me. 'Come on, its near our turn.' He looked at me more closely and added 'Sir'.

There was a brisk little artillery duel going on across the river where Cimbric archers were shooting at legionaries so jam-packed on the bridge that every arrow was a certain hit. The archers were not getting it all their own way though, because the Romans on the west bank had been alerted to our peril and the camp's scorpion bolt throwers and ballistas were busily laying down suppressive fire. Every now and then I caught a glimpse of a boulder soaring overhead, aimed to land somewhere in the crush of the Cimbric horde.

Then my feet were on the planking of the bridge, and that planking had a decided upriver slant. The bridge now swayed rather than shuddered under the impacts against the pilings, and when I stumbled I looked down to see large gaps that had opened in the planking. Falling would have meant death, for the press of bodies was relentless. Fortunately those same bodies packed around me kept me upright as I was helplessly carried along by the crowd.

As it happened, my earlier worries that I would eventually have nightmares about the defence of the fort at Sarni proved groundless. Instead I even now occasionally wake up sweating when my dreams put me back on that accursed bridge with the sour stink of river mud and the shouts of frightened men ringing in my ears, the tilt and sway of the structure growing ever more extreme, and all around the sudden hiss and thwack of arrows burying themselves in flesh.

Then suddenly the pressure in front of me eased and I nearly fell on my face from the force of those pushing from behind. I half-ran, half-stumbled off the bridge and was abruptly pulled aside by waiting soldiers who were diverting the flow of humanity upriver, downriver and into the camp. Being among those shoved into the downriver group, I had a disjointed view of the last moments of the camp on the eastern bank. Already plumes of smoke were rising from looted tents and buildings and a mass of warriors were gathering at the riverside.

Apparently Petraeus still commanded the rearguard, though I did not see the desperate charge with which he and his men pushed the Cimbri back one more time, just long enough to allow them space for a final frantic sprint across the collapsing bridge. The Cimbri did not follow because already the bridge was breaking into sections which slowly crumbled into the swirling waters before the last men were across. Some of the rearguard managed to cling to planks or other debris and these men we fished out downstream as they struggled to safety. Others were pulled down by their armour and simply vanished underwater. Petraeus was among those who survived, and was later richly rewarded for his heroism.

And thus it was that I finally arrived in the camp of Catulus - sweating, dirty and bedraggled, wearing blood-soaked and ill-fitting armour and already the participant in two solid defeats before even I had joined the army proper. My two main ambitions in life were to get my report to Catulus and then locate a bed in which I could sleep for a month.

In fact I got to sleep for around eighteen hours solid. In their failed attempt to strand half the army of Catulus on the east bank of the Adige, the Cimbri had removed the bridge which was their only way of getting at the Romans who were now all on the west bank. In the end the Cimbri took their time looting the camp and then trudged off northwards, probably to squeeze themselves over the same little bridge by which Dextrianus and myself had crossed the river two days ago.

On awakening I was delighted to be reunited with my gear and also with Maphronius, the noble steed of whom I was growing increasingly fond. After we had brought the news of the impending Cimbric attack to the eastern camp, I had rushed off with Petraeus and had left Dextrianus at something of a loose end. He, sensible fellow, had decided that the best thing he could do was take the horses and beat the rush for the bridge by leaving early and at speed. Consequently he was comfortably ensconced on the western bank even before I had reached the ramparts to the east, and had already alerted the quartermaster that I would soon urgently need a tent and bedding. His faith that I would actually arrive at all was rather touching.

The camp on the western side of the Adige was now in a state of some confusion, having had its population doubled by a mass of military refugees most of whose equipment was now in Cimbric hands. Fortunately a mild summer night had allowed many men to simply cover themselves with their cloaks and sleep outside on their shields. In a bustle of activity new tents were now being requisitioned or fashioned from whatever materials were available, and teams of men were busily strengthening the camp's fortifications in readiness for when the Cimbri finally got themselves across the river.

I had been allocated a small tent not far from the praetorium, and now wandered back through the chaos towards that tent, wearing a clean tunic and sporting a towel around my neck. One good thing about a Roman army camp is that if it has been established in one place for over a week or so our engineers somehow manage to get a good set of baths installed. So I had spent an hour soaking my bruises in a hot tub and thereafter had bribed one of the bath attendants to give my back a good massage. It was a clear sunny morning, and even the stink and dust of the camp couldn't interfere with my good mood.

Until I got back to my tent anyway, and found that someone had urinated all over my bed. The bed was a field cot really, a straw pallet suspended by ropes across a wooden frame. The straw could be easily replaced, and my blankets were dry and folded at the end of the bed, so no major damage had been done. But still, as they say, it is the thought that counts. After studying the bed sourly for a few moments, I folded back the tent flap to let the place air and shouted for an orderly to sort out new bedding. Evidently it was time to meet my trainees, the happy bunch of cadets whom I had allegedly been sent to instruct in the art of warfare while simultaneously working out which of them had killed one of his companions.

'One of you lot pissed in my bed', I informed the little group gathered in the training area just before lunch. Titus Lafranius the Italian trainee, snickered. Antonius and Dextrianus looked at Domitius, while young Porcellinus looked at the ground in front of him. They were a motley group, these students, with little in common apart from their ingrained sense of aristo-cratic superiority. They had been sent by their parents to share the tent of Catulus, and while they were there to learn the art of command the way Romans learn best – by watching and imitating a good example. Yours truly was their instructor, but also a common plebeian, and my urine-soaked bedding was the group's way of reminding me of my place in the scheme of things.

At first glance my trainees seemed a standard bunch of smirking teenagers rather resembling those who occasionally gathered outside my brothel in Rome, elbowing each other and nervously making dirty jokes as they dared one another to venture within. Yet it was important to remember that someone in the group before me was a murderer, and I had to find out who that was - preferably without alienating the others and their powerful parents.

Well, one has to start somewhere, and since he evidently felt himself to be the leader of the group, Domitius Ahenobarbus was the obvious place to start. Turning my back on the trainees, I sauntered to the edge of the training ground where I had ordered two wooden training swords to be placed against the fence. With a sword in each hand I walked back and tossed one sword at Domitius Ahenobarbus. The sword came down low and to the left, so Domitius had to half turn to take it in his right hand. Before he could straighten up I hit him hard across the ribs with my wooden blade.

Wood the blade might be, but training swords are designed to build muscle and are somewhat heavier than the real thing. Domitius cried out with the sudden pain for like myself he was wearing just a tunic.

'I wasn't ready', he protested.

'You can be ready for a good meal, or to make love. When it comes to fighting, you don't have to wait. Sometimes the fight comes to you, even –' without pausing in mid-sentence, I slapped Domitius with the sword across the ribs again, '- when you are not ready.

Consider that Lesson One.'

The young man glowered at me and hefted his sword upwards, then yelped as I leaned in and rapped him hard across the knuckles. 'You have now lost three fingers', I observed. 'Picking your nose has become that much more difficult.'

Made savage by pain, Domitius stepped forward and made a wild swing at my head. A feint, as the direction of his eyes demonstrated, so I waited until he had checked his swing. Then stepped in, whacked his sword aside, and hit him across the ribs again. The next swing at my head was the real thing, and instead of ducking I moved inside the swing and blocked with the flat of my sword against his forearm. A dumb move because the sword flew from Domitius' hand and struck a glancing blow across my head that made me see stars.

Trying desperately to appear unharmed, I pointed with my blade to where Domitius' sword lay in the dust of the training arena. 'Pick it up.'

Domitius was cradling his forearm with his other hand. 'You've broken it', he complained.

'If I had used the edge of this sword instead of the flat, yes it would have broken your arm. If this was a real blade, you would be down to one arm. As it is, you've a bit of a bruise, no more. Now stop whining and pick it up.'

'So you can just hit me again?'

'Exactly so. Now if you don't pick up that sword, I'll put you over my knee and spank you with the flat of my blade. Would you prefer that? No? Then pick it up.'

Domitius stooped to pick up the sword and

predictably launched himself at me from a crouch, sword outstretched. I sidestepped the blade, gave Domitius a rabbit punch as he went by, and for good measure added a hard swipe across his buttocks as he went down. And stayed down. I went over, kicked the sword from his unresisting hand and turned to the rest of the group.

'Anyone else want to play?'

'I don't recommend it', commented Dextrianus to the others, 'I've seen him in action with the real thing and trust me, you haven't seen the half of what he can do.'

'My father shall hear of this.'

That remark came from a somewhat dazed Domitius as he sat himself up in the dust.

'A good idea. Why don't you come to my tent after lunch and we can compose the letter together?'

While on my leisurely trip to join Catulus' army, I had written in haste to the trainees' parents enquiring just how vigorously they wanted me to pursue their children's education in matters military. The father of Domitius Ahenobarbus had written back, 'Any child sired by me on my hellion of a wife is bound to be a plague on humanity. If you think it may do something to redeem the little monster, feel free to beat him like a donkey.' Domitius' complaints to his father would fall on deaf ears and from the way he was glowering, Domitius was well aware of this.

'Domitius Ahenobarbus, my congratulations. You have just been made sanitary supervisor for the group. What that means is that if my bed gets wetted again, or the bed of any other group member, we will have another training bout of swordplay that will make what you got this time feel like a few love-pats. Likewise if any kit gets damaged, goes missing, or should we suffer any other odd little incidents that can make life in camp so aggravating, then ... .' I waggled my sword suggestively.

'Why are you blaming me? You can't know it was me who pissed in your bed.'

'I don't care. My objective is not justice but dry bedding. And that's what you are going to ensure from here on in.'

'How am I supposed to manage that?'

'Not my problem. You intend to become a leader of men, so figure something out with your fellow trainees. Meanwhile, be grateful. We've only met for a few minutes and already you have been promoted to a supervisory role. Truly, you are blessed.'

'Now, if no-one else has anything else to add, let's break for lunch. Don't eat too heavily because we have a busy afternoon ahead of us. You are dismissed, gentlemen – for now.'

Liber V

'Young Ahenobarbus tells me that you gave him a beating at lunchtime', Catulus observed as we walked together back to his praetorium. Catulus offered his comment as information rather than complaint, from which I gathered that he was none too upset about the young man's misfortune. The commander went on to confirm this by remarking, 'Can't say that I like that young man much.'

I shrugged. 'He's a bully. He and his sidekick Lafranius have been making young Marcellus' life hell since he got here. He accused Marcellus of being a bed-wetter, and the poor kid has barely had a night's sleep in dry sheets since. Pissing in my bed was their way of extending the joke.'

Catulus gave this information little regard, as I had rather expected he would. Like most Romans he had an insouciant attitude to the fact that children tend to beat up, humiliate and generally torment those younger, weaker, or of lower social station than themselves. Such conduct is regarded as giving the young 'uns a valuable lesson in the way that the world works and toughens up the victims for later life. It's an attitude that many, probably including young Domitius, will carry into that later life.

'Do you intend to keep thrashing him regularly?', Catulus asked, again out of idle curiosity rather than any great concern. After all, if there was to be any reaction from the father, the main victim would be myself. Catulus was sufficiently well-established politically to have little concern for what even the powerful and influential Ahenobarbi thought of him. Besides, he had other worries at the moment – a few hundred thousand such worries, all of them at present making their way across the river towards his poorly-trained and demoralized army.

'Regular beatings will probably not be necessary. Today was setting up the ground rules in our relation-ship, rather as his attempt to sabotage my sleeping quarters was a similar effort on his part. He was the top dog in our pack of trainees, and my little demonstration was to point out that the pack has a new leader - and I'm it.'

We were briefly interrupted as a junior centurion came trotting up to Catulus, and the pair quickly plunged into a technical conversation involving the staggering of meal times to feed the camp's extra popu-lation while the kitchens were being kitted out for their expanded new role. I let the details pass me by and idly examined the hills to the north of the camp. What could someone with keen eyesight make out from up there?

'This group are not much of a pack.' Catulus told me as we resumed our walk. 'More of a collection of lone wolves. When they are not training or attending meetings with me, they each tend to go their own way. That's one reason why it was so hard to establish where everyone was when that Italian trainee, Minatius, was murdered in my tent. The other problem is trying to work out why anyone would do it in the first place. If it really was one of them – somehow I still can't bring myself to believe it.'

This lack of group identity confirmed what I had already established. At the time of the murder Domitius Ahenobarbus and Lafranius reckoned they had been preparing together for the staff meeting to come. I intended to find out later what they had really been up to, but for now it was enough that each vouched for the other's presence away from the command tent. Marcellus had been studying alone on his bed, as was apparently his wont when he had free time. Young Scipio Dextrianus had been out riding with a group of cavalrymen whom he had befriended in that easy-going way of his, and Marcus Antonius claimed that he had been gambling in the *canaba*, an admission shameful enough to make it probably truthful. Thus, apart from Marcellus – an unlikely assassin if ever I saw one – everyone had an alibi. How well those alibis would withstand scrutiny was another matter.

We had reached the command tent, and the guards snapped to attention as Catulus lifted aside the tent flap and like a gracious host, ushered me in. Blinking in the relative gloom, we proceeded to the scroll-rack at the back, where a clerk looked up sharply as we approached. 'I make sure that there's someone here all the time now', Catulus explained. 'Rather closing the stable door after the information has bolted, but I would be stupid not to do so anyway.'

'So he was standing right here', I noted.

'Minatius? That's right. How did you know?'

'He coughed up blood. You've had the rack cleaned, but it's harder to clean up the scrolls themselves. You can see the pattern here, here – and here.'

'And that stitching there the back of the tent is where the killer sliced open the cloth and let himself out. It was coolly done, I'll grant you, but at least it confirmed that we have a spy in the camp.'

'And you are sure that it was one of your trainees?'

Catulus nodded reluctantly. 'I can't see how, since they all have witnesses to their being elsewhere – but I also cannot see how it *can't* be. The Cimbri clearly are getting information from right out of this tent, some-times from my personal notes that I have not even shared in staff meetings, and only my trainees are free to come and go from this tent as they please. These days I don't dare to write anything down. In fact if I thought my shirt knew what I was planning, I'd burn it, but let's face it that's hardly the way to run an army. We have to stop the leak.'

Catulus was right. A barbarian horde might get away without paperwork, but a Roman army practically runs on the stuff. Somewhere in the command tent was a record of every man of the thousands in the army, with notations of his disciplinary record, his pay, health, the level of his training and his length of service. There had been a list of the watchwords for the coming week until Catulus had changed that and now personally gave it to the commander of the guard each evening. There were cavalry patrol schedules, food requisitions and supply projections, reports from spies and outposts, and a thousand other scraps of papyrus. And the damnable thing was that, as trainees for high command, not only were Catulus' young men given access to all this material, they were *required* to access it as a part of their training for the time when they too came to command the armies of Rome. Whoever had recruited the Cimbric spy had picked the perfect man for the job.

Walking back through the gathering twilight I pondered what motive might cause one of these young aristocrats - the chief beneficiaries of Rome and its empire – to betray the very state that had given them so much.

Antonius, well, I could nail at least two motives on that amiable young lout. For all their high social rank, his family were perennially short of cash and their care-free spending habits made it unlikely that the clan would be solvent any time soon. Also, just as he was vulnerable to bribery, the chances were high that Antonius had done something that might get him blackmailed. Indeed, should I so want, I could black-mail the lad myself, for some of his sexual indiscretions in my brothel could put a major crimp in his political career. The time when he had rented himself out to a wealthy Syrian so that he could afford to roger a girl he had thought he was in love with - now that juicy example was just one of several.

Lafranius I knew less about, but he was an Italian, and relations between the Italians and Romans were currently at an all-time low. The Italians fought and died alongside the Romans in equal number, but were denied the advantages, and above all, the legal pro-tection of Roman citizenship. I made a mental note to check whether Lafranius or any of his friends or family had recently had lands stripped from them by some greedy Roman aristocrat, or whether any female relations had been casually raped by some Roman magistrate who was well aware that his connections would save him from prosecution. That all these things happened I knew well, and I was also uneasily aware that some day the arrogant manner with which Roman aristocrats routinely abused their power was going to come back to bite them. Perhaps Lafranius had decided that the Cimbri might make better masters than the Romans?

Marcellus Porcellinus might seem a mild-mannered lad, but he was of lower social standing than the other trainees. For all that he shared his name with an illustrious family, his branch was an offshoot far from the central trunk of the family tree. In fact his parents had worked every connection they had to get Marcellus into this group of aristocratic trainees in the hope that he would form friendships that would be helpful in later life. Some hope. It was pretty clear that the other trainees despised Marcellus, and I would be surprised if he did not hate them right back. But did he hate them enough to want to bring down the entire Roman Republic along with his enemies? On the face of it, the question was ridiculous, but regrettably, teenage passions are seldom married to a sense of proportion. Also, Marcellus might draw comfort from knowing that even while the others bullied him, he had the secret power to destroy them all.

And then there was Dextrianus, the easy-going golden boy who seemed to have it all. Everyone liked him, everyone respected him, and he seemed to instantly become friends with everyone he met. That alone made me suspicious. No-one could have their life running that smoothly before they were nineteen, and I was grudgingly certain that further investigation would reveal something on the seamy side in young Scipio Dextrianus' life. Money, good looks, an aristocratic family that doted on him, powerful friends and casual confidence - it had to be a facade, surely?

My mind drifted back to a fragment of conversation we had exchanged while riding to the camp. Dextrianus had asked if I was a patron of the theatre, and winced when I admitted a liking for the slapstick comedies of Plautus.

'He's so Roman, Lucius. Just like so many things Roman, Plautus' plays are just an inferior rip-off of the Greek originals. Aristophanes and Menander, they did those plays first, and did it so much better.' Once on his hobby-horse, there was no stopping Dextrianus. 'Can you imagine Rome without Greece? There would be nothing but inferior statuary, basic architecture, a Roman's religion and philosophy would be barely above that of some stone-wielding savage, and we'd have no literature to speak of. Do you know that when Fabius Pictor wrote the first history of Rome, he did so in Greek, because at the time no educated man would dream of using any other language?'

Since my own ability with Greek was schoolboy stuff that barely enabled me to keep up a conversation with some of my business' eastern clients, I had kept discreetly silent. But a final thoughtful comment by Dextrianus now had me thinking.

'Rome without Greece – that's unthinkable. But Greece without Rome? Yes, I can imagine that. Without Rome, the state that crushed Sparta and plundered Corinth, where would Greece be today? What glories might the Greeks have achieved in the advancement of humanity? It's food for thought, I tell you.'

Food for thought indeed. One could attribute mean and sordid motives to an Antonius, revenge to Lafranius or Marcellus, but if Dextrianus were to betray Rome it would be through some soaring, idealistic and hopelessly impractical ideal. I sighed. There was nothing for it but to keep investigating. At least I was reasonably certain that I had ruled out Domitius.

In a Roman army camp the Porta Decumana is traditionally the gate which leads to the *canaba*, and I paused there on my evening walk to exchange greetings with a fellow tribune and a friend who were heading to town. The tribune was a veteran, and he and I knew each other from Rome where we shared a fondness for dice at the Samnite's Helmet tavern. After our meeting at the gate I spent a few moments renewing our acquaintance.

Eventually we agreed to go together to one of the few wooden buildings in the *canaba* -that same tavern where Antonius had allegedly been playing dice at the time that Minatius was getting murdered in Catulus' tent. I wanted to check the reliability of some witnesses, and also to get acquainted with the other tribunes, the men who commanded the individual cohorts of Catulus' army. Certainly I did not want to indulge in the tavern's wine, which resembled the real thing rather in the same way that a pig turd resembles a fine truffle.

However, I gulped down a few swigs to show willing. A few senior centurions drifted over and listened while the tribunes earnestly poured out their doubts and fears.

'We're not ready, Lucius, and that's a fact. The centurions have been training the men for weeks now, but veteran soldiers they are not.'

'No,' interjected another tribune sourly. 'Marius took the veterans, and everyone who knows that you're not supposed to hold a sword by the pointy end. We've got the sweepings of the gutter, the sick, and the lame. And had half the prisons of Italy were emptied into the ranks. Seriously, I'd swap my cohort for the same number of barbarians any day.'

'So what happens when the Cimbri finish crossing the river and come back downstream at us?' I asked, although I was not really eager to hear the answer.

'We lose', said my friend brutally. 'Catulus will march the army out to fight, because he's a Roman general and a Roman army fights in the field. Make no mistake, there's some good men in the ranks and given a bit more training, I reckon they would have a chance. But after that disaster with the camp on the east bank, morale is just too shaky. If the barbarians mount a headlong charge a lot of the men won't stand. They'll break and run, and take Italy's chances of survival with them as they go. If we go out and fight, it may be close for a while but eventually the men will break. They've no confidence - we haven't got them believing in themselves yet.'

It was beginning to dawn on me that the meeting by the gate was no accident. The tribunes were worried, and they had selected my dice-playing acquaintance to pass on their concerns to me. While I also was a military tribune in rank, not all tribunes are created equal. Some military tribunes are grizzled veterans who can throw maniples of legionaries around a battlefield with practised ease, and others are fresh-faced young aristocrats appointed for their political connections who have to be carefully monitored to keep them out of trouble. None of the young aristos, I noticed, were present at the meeting tonight. It was strictly professionals only.

Each legion has six tribunes, and Catulus' army had some fifteen in all, a number which included specialists who handled things like logistics and intelligence. The other tribunes regarded me as one of the 'funnies' – those who report direct to the commander on matters best dealt with outside the regular chain of command. It appeared that no-one was buying the idea that I was there to train Catulus' cadets. However, whatever the reason for my presence, I appeared to have the ear of their commander and the tribunes were eager for me to pass their concerns on to him.

Irritably, I took another swig of wine, regretted it, and looked about for somewhere to spit the stuff. Realizing there was nothing to do but swallow, I did so and prayed my palate would forgive me later.

'So what alternatives do we have?' I asked, when I could talk once more. 'There's no way that Catulus will retreat again. He's been pushed back from the Alps, and now pushed back to the west bank of the Adige, He's got to make a stand somewhere.'

'He's been buying us time,' said one of the older centurions, a *Pilus Prior*, by his emblems. 'Training an army takes time. If we fought at the Alps we would have been massacred. If we fought in the Po valley we'd have been heavily defeated. Give us a few days to get the morale back up after the loss of the eastern camp, and if we take the field then, we'll be narrowly defeated. Give us just another fortnight and with decent generalship we'll have the men able to fight the Cimbri to a standstill. Give us a month more training time, and maybe, maybe, we get a win. It won't be a pretty one, mind you, but we'll win.'

'And given a year, we'll conquer the world,' chipped in one of the others. 'Trouble is', he added morosely, 'We've got days.'

Everyone looked at me expectantly, and a sinking feeling developed in my stomach that had nothing to do with the wine.

'Guys. I'm a junior tribune. If you're not aware of it, I'm only here because of a minor scandal while I was under Sulla's command. They sent me here to train the young aristos who share Catulus' tent, which is hardly the most prestigious job around. If I go and tell the general how to fight his war, first he will laugh at me, secondly he will get annoyed with me, and thirdly, I'll have my bags packed and be leaving in disgrace for

Rome on the morrow. Go with Petraeus to talk to Catulus, and Catulus might listen. I'm not that important.'

'Bullshit', one of the older tribunes said bluntly. 'If you're a training officer, I'm a latrine attendant. Everyone knows that you're here to take over from Gratidus, and a damn good thing too. As an intelligence officer he should be a latrine attendant – if he could even find the pig-fornicating latrines.'

There was sour laughter, and another voice was raised above the chuckles. 'And it was Petraeus who suggested you might have a word with Catulus. You're one of them, tribune, for all you have a foot in our world. Top Romans don't listen to men like us, they listen to men like themselves. Don't underestimate the value of your advice. Petraeus says that Catulus admires you for your conduct in some trial at the law courts in Rome.'

The P*rimus Prior* chipped in, 'Well, to be really frank, 'admire' is not quite how he put it. His actual words were, 'He's a duplicitous villain with the morals of a sewer rat, but right now he's the man I need.' And I don't think he was talking about someone to find him a girl to relieve his stress, though maybe you can do that too, eh? You're a man of many talents.'

'Talking of which', I said seizing the chance to change the subject, 'Has anyone tried this Satula? I believe she is the best of the whores in the *canaba*.'

'Don't call her a whore to her face or she'll scratch yours off', one of the tribunes informed me. 'She prefers to call herself a lady for rent, and the price for entry to her basement is remarkably steep. She won't sleep with anyone lower than the rank of centurion either. Worth the money though. The lady has taste.'

'So why did she sleep with you?' someone else interjected, to general ribald laughter.

I rose from the table. 'Well, gentlemen, it seems I shall have to try the matter for myself. The past few days have been somewhat stressful for me also, and I can hardly recommend a girl to the Proconsul without having personally sampled the wares. Assuming she got my message, she's currently expecting me, so much as I enjoy being here, unless I've been severely misled by your unshaven faces none of you have the personal attributes I'm looking for in company right now.'

'With the other matter we've discussed, as I said, you over-rate my influence. There's not much anyone can do, but rest assured that whatever can be done will be done. But in the end Catulus is our commander and what he says goes.'

As I left someone shouted to my back, 'Enjoy yourself! You might never live to be with a woman again. Do as we ask or we are all dead!'

After the hurly-burly of the tavern, the tent of Satula was a complete change. Somehow in the dust and dirt of the *canaba* she had managed to set up her quarters as a cool oasis of elegant furnishings and blue silk. A silver beaker of river-cooled wine was awaiting my arrival, and to my delight this wine was the slightly smoky local vintage that I had been wanting to sample for some time. The wine did not disappoint, which suggested that the elegant, ivory-skinned woman who greeted me would not disappoint either.

'First things first', I muttered quietly as we kissed and I cupped one heavy breast in my palm. 'There's a man who needs to be discouraged from following me. Dark tunic, with a white stripe – you may have seen him lurking by the farrier's when I came in. Send a couple of your heavies to deal with him, if you would be so kind.'

Satula pulled back from me and raised a perfectly shaped eyebrow. 'Fatally?'

'Great gods, no! He's the camp intelligence officer. He probably imagines he's just doing his job. Get your boys to make it look like a standard mugging – perhaps that will teach him not to be outside after dark.'

We settled down together on the couch and Satula topped up my wine while she poured some for herself. She did so from an elegant vessel of chased bronze with a decidedly eastern appearance. Seeing me looking at the thing, Satula said, 'It was a gift from Bassianus the horse trader. It's almost certain that he's in the game, but I have not figured out his affiliation just yet. He's good.'

I nodded in acknowledgement. Satula was an extremely good spy herself, and I had benefited from her services before. She was also unshakeably loyal, since for reasons I could never figure out, she was deeply in love with Sulla.

'And the others?' I asked.

'The main barbarian contact at the camp is the

owner of that tavern you were drinking at earlier this evening. He's got an informal network of agents about the *canaba* who get paid for any interesting information or tips. He edits it down, adds any juicy tidbits he overhears from the soldiers who are drinking in his tavern, and sends it out with the boy he uses to gather firewood. The boy meets with Cimbric scouts in a grove not far from here. Do you want anything done about that?'

'H'm. Depends on the quality of the information he's feeding them. We'll have to stop it if he is leaking any good stuff.'

'It's just camp gossip, reports on the morale of the soldiers – which is terrible by the way – and reports on what supplies are coming in from where. Background stuff. The main Cimbric information source is within your camp itself – and that's at a very high level. Our tavern owner doesn't know who it is.'

'And you know this, how?'

'Oh, I read the reports before he sends them, and occasionally remove anything too compromising. I have an arrangement with the tavern owner's wife.'

'Is she expensive? Not that the money is an issue, but if she's seen with extra gold that could be a problem.'

'No, it's all good there. She's working for free. The deal is that I kill her husband when this is over – and she wants to watch.'

'And people wonder why I never married', I sighed. 'What about Marius?'

'Well, Gratidus, your intelligence officer, spies on

Catulus for the Marians but you knew that. I think Catulus knows too. Gratidus tried to recruit me also, and was not very subtle about it. I let him, naturally. He does not pay very much but it all helps. No other Marian spies that I know of in the *canaba*, because Marius probably thinks that if he has the camp intelligence officer then that officer has all the other spies he needs. Something of a miscalculation there, I say. Oh yes. Talking of other spies … .'

Satula rose from the couch in a single fluid motion and sashayed over to unlock a trunk beside her bed. Fully aware that her rounded buttocks showed perfectly through her near-transparent dress as she bent, she smiled back at me as she retrieved a small scroll. 'This looks like a love letter of some description but probably isn't. It was sent to me for forwarding to you.'

The letter was written in a semi-literate hand, starting with a crudely sketched picture of a dove, the symbol of Aphrodite.

'My love,
Three days after the full moon, and it will be a month since you left my side. I cannot wait any longer to be with you again, in that house, to be a worthy woman with a worthy man. Do not forget me for I yearn to be with you. We have so much to talk about, so much that we left uncertain when we parted. Do please hurry back to me, and know you are always in my thoughts.
Your loving Giselda.'

I laughed and tossed the parchment scrap aside. 'It's

nothing. A girl whom I was able to rescue from something in a predicament in Mediolanum. She was very grateful and eager to demonstrate some new-found skills. I fear that she has formed a somewhat over-optimistic idea of our relationship. Hopefully time will disillusion her.'

'So no reply needed?'

'She won't ever hear from me again.'

Satula nodded, and her hand slid beneath my tunic. 'Well', she breathed softly, 'if that concludes the business part of the evening …'.

Liber VI

A summer night is rarely quiet, and a variety of chirps and rustles from the side of the path kept my nerves on edge as Maphronius quietly clopped along under the stars. One of the first things I had discreetly enquired about after my tumultuous arrival at Catulus' camp was the whereabouts of the nearest shrine or temple of Venus. I had been expecting the summons in the letter and the drawing of Aphrodite's dove and the reference to 'that house' told me that my presence was indeed urgently required at the nearest 'house of Aphrodite'. The letter had specified the contact time, and as it was already 'three days after the full moon', it meant that my departure from the camp needed to be expeditious, no matter how miffed and suspicious the fair Satula became after I rejected her charming invitation. If 'Giselda' said that we had 'a lot to talk about', then the matter was extremely pressing.

A bright glow on the horizon informed me that moonrise was not far off, and against that glow I could see the sanctuary of Venus as a dark shape against the stars. We were on a hillside, and the path was altogether too exposed for my liking. Anyone hidden in the bushes would be able to see me coming from well over a stade away – which was doubtless one of the reasons why the sanctuary had been chosen as the site of our meeting. Ahead, not far from the sanctuary, was a small stand of trees, possibly a sacred grove where – sanctified as the place may or might not be, I planned to stash Maphronius while I did some reconnaissance on foot.

On a normal evening, say in the woodlands outside Rome, it might have been a pleasant ride. The night breeze was gentle and there was a certain majesty in the constellations towering overhead, the stars hard as silver pebbles. There was an earthy scent in the air and an undertone of sweetness in the breeze that followed me from the wheat field I had just passed. Almost under my breath I began to sing the haunting legionary love song 'Bona Barca Veneris.'

Almost at once a singer hidden somewhere in the bushes nearby joined me quietly in the chorus.

'Futuimus in amisso clavo,
irrumamus in tabulato,
manu turbati in ponte,
nullus erat fac-e-re.'

As soon as we finished the last drawn out word of the verse I stopped singing and urged my horse to step faster toward the grove where I promptly dismounted and dropped into the soft grass. From there I carefully loosened Maphronius' saddle strap, so that anyone trying to ride off on my steed would end up unceremoniously dumped on to the ground. Then I scrambled hastily towards the friendly darkness of the bushes at the edge of the grove. My intention was to scout the area and make sure that my contact was alone before we entered into conversation. Regrettably, this did not happen. Instead I was barely enveloped in the shadow of the bushes before the feel of a steel blade at my neck made it clear that this particular bit of cover was already occupied

'Oh, in Aphrodite's name, put that dagger away', I snarled, 'You can't see a thing and you might hurt someone.'

'Two years, two whole years without seeing the man who saved his life and this is how he greets me. The ingratitude of it, and the lack of fellowship it demonstrates would sadden a man less hardened than I to the unkindness of the world. But it still hurts, oh yes, I won't deceive you, it hurts none the less. Anyway, that was the back of the blade at your throat not the edge. Just a gentle lesson from your uncle Madric pointing out that what seems the best cover to you is the most obvious cover to everyone, and sometimes the second best cover is best after all. You should have tried that long grass over there.'

'Do you ever shut up?'

'What kind of spy would that make me? But if you like I can ride away now without saying another word. And you'll note that my horse is not in this grove. Obvious places, obvious places … you are so predictable, Lucius. I - '.

'Madric?'

'Yes?'

'Shut up.'

There was a pause as the Gallic warrior and I shared an embrace made clumsy by the fact that we were still both on our knees. Rising, we moved quietly to the shadow of the sanctuary to properly renew our acquaintance.

Madric had been among the band of desperadoes who had accompanied the priestess Momina to retrieve a sacred statuette from a temple in Tolosa. True, that adventure had made me fantastically rich, but on the other hand the same escapade had simultaneously robbed me of a decade of my life through sheer stress. At the end of it, Madric double-crossed me into going off to war with the doomed Roman army. That's the Roman army which the Germanic horde had wiped out at Arausio, not that Madric had been in the Roman ranks. Instead he had defected to the winning side at the first opportunity and had been an auxiliary warrior for the enemy ever since. It's all there somewhere in my memoirs.

'So how was Spain?' I asked. 'A good holiday destination?'

'Not so the Germans noticed. Turns out it was a mistake for them to go there after they beat you Romans. They should have gone straight on into Italy and conquered Rome right there and then. They are not used to the heat in those scrubby Iberian mountains. And the Celtiberians! Those I met were hard as flint, stubborn fighters with a scary cruel streak. They tell me that the menfolk are even worse, but I stayed away from them. No-one expects much effort from a Gallic axillary - we are mainly there to make up the numbers, so to speak. The Celtiberians live in little fortified hamlets that are hell to besiege – it's because they are on mountaintops, see? - and once you've taken them, there's nothing inside that's worth the effort.'

'So they came back. The barbarian horde, I mean.'

'Oh indeed. Compared to Spain, Italy's a land of milk and honey. This is not just a raid, you see. They plan on taking Italy from you, pillaging it from end to end and settling down forever among the ruins.'

'Well, Marius and the Battle of Six Waters will have shown you, er, them, that it won't be that easy. How did you do in that battle, anyway?'

'Escaping death and general massacre, you mean? It was a breeze. Information goes two ways - not that you would know about that, secretive sod that you are – I passed information to Momina, she passed it to Marius, and in return our little prophetess let me know where the safest place on the battlefield was. The left wing, it turns out, and it was not hard to get there because that's where the Germans put their Gallic levies. We broke and ran before the fight even started.'

'So now you're with the Cimbri.'

'It was not hard to join them. A bunch of us from the dribs and drabs of the beaten army made it to their horde. Marius might have beaten one chunk of the barbarian army, but the surviving chunk is still bigger than Catulus' and Marius' armies put together, so the Cimbri still reckon their chances of a home in Italy are pretty good. Me, I'm not defecting from them until someone can prove otherwise. You might own the deeds to your little farm in the Alban hills, but you never can tell - it might be me who's the one growing peaches there next year.'

Since we were clearly alone, I wandered back to my horse and retrieved a couple of gelatinized meat pies from the saddlebags. Then Madric and I sat in the shadows outside the sanctuary, munching away and gossiping like old ladies. Madric told me that Marius now feared and shunned Momina, but he could hardly get rid of her.

'She turned up one day at the provincial games, and got the attention of Marius' wife by sitting nearby and correctly calling the result of each gladiator fight even before it started. Say what you like about Marius – and I've heard you say a lot – you can't deny that he knows a good propaganda tool when he sees one. Your little priestess has been re-branded as an infallible Jewish seer. She travels in Marius' retinue dressed in the finest silks and he touts her to the troops as his direct connection to the gods. And as we both know, he might not even be wrong about that.'

I thought of Momina's ghostly appearance whilst I was in a drug-induced haze at that alpine village and nodded sombrely. There definitely was something unearthly about Momina. She and Marius had some-thing of a falling out last year, when Momina had privately predicted – with her usual accuracy, I hoped – Marius' ignominious death and post-mortem disgrace. However, no matter how uneasy she now made him, Marius could not do without Momina, for much of Marius' success was because his prophetess had kept the consul updated on German troop movements, morale and plans.

Of course, one reason for the little priestess' un-canny prescience was that she had been getting regular reports from Madric, the spy now sitting beside me chomping through his pie crust. The other reasons

...well, I preferred not to think about those.

Changing the subject, I enquired, 'What do you know of a Cimbric kid called Metus? A tall, blond skinny streak of piss who can get grown warriors jumping to obey his slightest command?'

'The son of Boiorix? Hmm, now you don't want to underestimate him, sonny boy. His dad trusts him with a lot of the diplomatic and espionage stuff, and he's remarkable good at it. For the same reason you are, I might add – you both look so innocent that by the time that people figure out the duplicity behind your sweet young faces it's already too late and they've been royally screwed. He acts all disingenuous and direct, and behind those blue eyes there's a mind like a steel rat-trap.'

Madric held up a warning finger. 'And that is pretty much all I know, and all that is second-hand. Remember that while you swan around with Catulus and the top rankers on the Roman side, me, I'm a dogsbody, a despised Gallic footsoldier with the Cimbri. The only reason I get to hear anything useful is because the average warrior gets kind of stroppy if he's not kept in the loop about what his commanders are planning, and often those plans are hashed out in open meetings. A man can learn a lot by just hanging around being inconspicuous.'

'Your spy? If you mean who is behind the leak of information from Catulus' tent, I have totally no idea. Your boyfriend Metus runs the espionage, I think that umm, a few weeks back he got visited by some hooded figure who rode in – camp gossip said it was a Roman traitor, but I've no idea. At the time I was running for my life and freezing my backside off in the Alps. Since I became a warrior for the Cimbri there's not been a peep about spies, which is totally fine by me. The less that people are thinking about espionage the happier I become. So if Metus is talking to one of your trainees, there's either a dead-drop or an intermediary involved. Possibly both.'

'Okay, I'd better be getting back. I killed a brace of rabbits while you took your own sweet time turning up, but the excuse of being out hunting only carries a man so far. Good seeing you again, Lucius.'

Still sitting on the steps of the shrine I waved a casual goodbye and slowly counted under my breath. I had reached twelve when Madric turned back and asked irritably, 'So are you not going to ask why I wanted to see you so urgently? Did you ride all this way just to ask about my lumbago? Man, you are a tough one to wait out – I've a mind to just ride off and leave you sitting there, really I have.'

'You'd get around to it at some point. I just didn't want to hurry you. We still need to discuss what you know about the Cimbric plans for the battle – you know, the one we will doubtless be having in the next few days. What are the Cimbric arrangements for the dance?'

'Well for a start, put yourself well to the rear. The Cimbri reckon the legions won't stand - and this time they want to make sure Catulus can't save his army. There were a lot of recriminations when the attack on the eastern camp failed – were you there? If you were, it's sort of obvious that you got across the bridge in time. They're still scratching their heads about why your guys suddenly decided to evacuate the eastern camp. There were legionaries sprinting across the bridge even before the first logs floated downstream. Got any ideas about why that might have happened? Who warned the legions, and how did that person know to do the warning? It's the kind of thing that gets our friend Metus looking for information leaks, which makes me *werry* nervous, because Metus is good at what he does, and I'm an information leak.'

I made a non-committal noise, and after a reflective pause Madric went on, 'So the plan is to encircle the army of Catulus, destroy it completely and then wipe out Marius when he gets here in a fortnight or so. Yes, we know about Marius' movements. If I was really curious, which I really am not, I could probably find out the colour of his under-tunic. There's scouts and spies watching every step his army takes.'

That Marius had problems with being spied upon did not concern me as much as Madric's earlier disclosure. I shook my head dubiously. 'Encircle our army? Not sure that will work. Given his recent set-backs, the first thing Catulus is going to ensure is that he has a good line of retreat. Everyone knows the morale of the legions is … shaky.'

Madric shook his head and his tone was slightly smug. 'Oh, yes, that's the reason I wanted to speak to you. I knew there was something important I needed to mention, so thanks for reminding me. Trouble is you gossip too much. It distracts a man and it made me completely forget what I was here to tell you. Catulus won't be in charge of the battle when it starts. He will be too busy dying.'

The following morning saw me rise early, my late night notwithstanding. Bright sunlight lit the interior of my tent and turned the oiled calfskin fabric milky white as I sat at my camp table absently rubbing my shoulder. The news Madric had given me was distracting enough that I had forgotten about the loosened saddle girth on my horse. After swinging into the saddle I saw the rising moon describe a swift arc across my vision until I landed on the grass with a thud and Maphronius' large head had swung around curiously to see what I was playing at.

Now I lifted a spoonful of oatmeal porridge into a sunbeam and was contemplating it thoughtfully when someone stormed violently through the open flap to my tent. This turned out to be Gratidus, the camp intelligence officer, whom I greeted with some consternation.

'My dear fellow! Whatever happened to your face? Here, do sit down, please. Have you seen a medic about that eye?'

'You little rat! How dare you!'

'How dare I what, exactly?'

'How dare you ... how dare you, everything! You come swanning into my camp and try to take over my job, you start having secret conversations with the consul, you subvert my influence with the centurions, and last night you … you …'.

'I, um, wasn't here last night. Not until just after midnight anyway, and then I went straight to bed.'

Gratidus glared at me, though his swollen, slitted eye rather ruined the effect. 'You are saying you had nothing to do with what happened to me in the *canaba* last night?'

'Is that where your face happened? It can get rough out there after dark, I'm told. Best to take a friend or better yet, two – if you have them, of course. Still your sacrifice was not for nothing, eh?'

As far as was possible, Gratidus' battered face registered incomprehension. 'What in Hades are you babbling about?'

I took a scoop of the porridge and passed the loaded spoon to Gratidus. 'Take a look at that.'

'I'm not interested in your mother-loving breakfast!'

'It's not my breakfast – it was going to be the Proconsul's. Now look at it!'

There was a pause, and then Gratidus said hesitantly, 'It's glinting. There's small, shiny stuff in there.'

'Ground glass, to be precise. Care to guess what it does to the insides of the person eating it?'

'Gods! It probably shreds the intestines, and if it gets into the liver …!'

'That was the idea. By now Catulus should be in his bed slowly dying, and that shit-wit Aemilius Scaurus is supposed to be in command to lead the army to its doom. Happily Scaurus has now unexpectedly left us and Catulus is as healthy as a flea.'

'Fortunately, rather than shredding your insides,

ground glass does almost nothing. Ever eaten outdoors on a windy day and got grit with your food? That grit is sand, and ground glass is no better or worse. Which is just as well, because Catulus has been crapping powdered glass for the past three days. It's fortunate that his orderly knows very little about poisons and gets what little he does know from popular misconceptions. Still as they say, it's the thought that counts. The orderly is now in the stockade awaiting your interrogation. Then you can report your discoveries to the commander. With the battle coming up and Catulus still healthy, the orderly would probably have soon switched to something more drastically effective. Therefore we can agree that you have probably saved his life. Congratulations.'

'I did?'

'Of course you did. A good intelligence officer makes effective use of informants and resources. I'm an informant *and* a resource, and you have just made effective use of me to foil a Cimbric plot to poison the consul. Excellent work, that is.'

Gratidus shook his head. 'I don't get it. Why are you helping me? What's in it for you?'

'Look, it's pretty well known that I'm Sulla's man. Sulla can't be seen interfering in the consul's campaign so I have to keep a low profile. At the same time, it's to everyone's benefit if Catulus' campaign goes well so if I can lend you a hand behind the scenes, why not?'

'After all, I might be here to tutor Catulus' trainees, but my former employment means that there's still sources and contacts who pass information to me. When something useful turns up, it's my duty to turn that information over to the army's intelligence officer and I have just done my duty. It's not Pythagorean theorems.'

I pushed back my chair, wincing as my shoulder gave another twinge. Still, it was some compensation that last night's beating had left Gratidus in even worse shape than I, although the intelligence officer was now looking at me with a kind of bewildered gratitude. Rising I gave the man a hearty clap on the shoulder.

Pretending not to notice Gratidus flinch, I remarked, 'Well, you clearly have business to see to, so to save you time tracking my movements today, here's advance notice that Catulus wants the trainees out taking a look at our prospective battlefield this morning. We're off to scout deployment positions and the optimal routes for getting troops to those positions, fall-back positions, points of tactical advantage, order of advance and so on and on. Have fun with the orderly.'

As I departed, I reflected that someone really should do something about changing the 'intelligence' part of Gratidus' job description.

'Well, what do you think? Give us a summary.'

It was five hours later, and by default my question was addressed to Domitius. Now that we had ridden over the ground where the fight would take place – and the battle would perhaps be as early as tomorrow – everyone had a good idea of the venue.

For some reason I could not be bothered to

discover, Lafranius and Antonius were at odds, and any attempt to question either of them got me back little more than a mumble and a surly glare. Young Scipio Dextrianus was loquacious enough, but his conversation had little of value. Rather to my disappointment, the young Scipio showed very little of the military genius of his famous forebears. Rather he possessed of the tactical vision of Oedipus – after that tragic hero had been blinded. Porcellinus was certainly not going to say anything that showed up the inability of Dextrianus, so that left me with Domitius Ahenobarbus. Despite our mutual dislike, it was clear that the scion of the Ahenobarbus clan had by far the best military mind of the group. He surveyed the battlefield, his fledging moustache writhing like an uneasy caterpillar as he contemplatively chewed his lip.

'It's not ideal. The way I see it, the battlefield is a huge funnel. The sides of the funnel are the river, here on the right, and those hills on the left. North – the direction the Cimbri are going to come down - is open and that means that they can deploy early and advance on a broad front. If we beat them – yeah, I'm an optimist and I believe the gods are on our side – if we beat them, they've got room to fall back and get cover from their cavalry as they retreat.'

Domitius turned in the saddle. 'If we have to fall back, we best do it early. Some of the units on the left might squeeze out through the side, using that gap in the hills back there, but most of the army will have to take the road running south. Over there, where the hills almost meet the river, that's the tube at the bottom of the funnel. If the army is beaten and if we fall back in good time, that gap right there is where a small rearguard can hold the Cimbri off while the Proconsul gets his army re-organized.'

Domitius paused, then resumed. 'If we don't fall back in time, then the entire army is a mighty big turd to squeeze through that one very small asshole. There will be a crowd trying to force their way through, with the Cimbri hewing away at their backs while they try to do it. The men will panic, break ranks and well, what happens next won't be pretty. Now you can call me a pessimist, or a defeatist or whatever. But you asked me what I see and that's how I see it.' Domitius shrugged and glared at me.

With a grudging nod, I acknowledged a report that accurately reflected my own thinking. Then I gestured at a small grove of trees on a ridge a few hundred yards from the camp. 'And that?'

The rest of the group remained mute, so Domitius took it on himself to continue. 'Of local tactical significance only. It might be a good command post, because it would have a good view of the battlefield, however…'. Domitius stopped as I held up a finger.

'However, indeed. Anyone else care to elaborate on that?'

After a pause and a shy glance at Dextrianus, Porcellinus offered, 'But on a plain like this in the middle of summer, um, thousands of men tramping around are going to raise so much dust no-one will get to see much anyway.'

Domitius grunted and continued, talking right over

Porcellinus, 'Relative to the battlefield, the hill and grove are a pimple on a dog's bollocks. It might anchor half a cohort, but it's of no other significance.'

I nodded, ending lessons for the morning. 'Well, I am going to take a look at that grove anyway. No need for you lot to accompany me - head off to your quarters until after lunch, when we shall be discussing winter camps – where to site them, when to build them, and how to avoid rheumatism while in them. ' I dug under my armour and removed the small wax tablet on which I had been taking notes.

'Porcellinus, take these to a clerk and stay with him while he transcribes this into a report suitable for the Proconsul.' I tossed the report to Porcellinus and was pleased by the way he smoothly transferred the reins of his horse to his left so that his other hand could snatch the tablet from the air. 'Good catch. You are dismissed, gentlemen.'

That grove which Domitius had so quickly dismissed from his tactical reckoning was that same grove where the treacherous innkeeper's messenger met with his Cimbric contacts, and I wanted to have a close look at the site for myself. Having background information never goes amiss, though attempting to acquire it can be fatal - as was almost the case today.

Much of the army had been out doing battlefield drills during the morning, the centurions wheeling their cohorts this way and that. There had been a squad of five cavalrymen exercising and putting their horses through their paces while I took my cadets around and though I had not paid them much attention, I had observed that they never seemed far away.

As I took Maphronius toward the trees the cavalrymen began to drift towards me. Samnite cavalry, judging by the plumed helmets and round pectorals on their armour. Possibly they wanted to ask what conclusions our group had drawn from our little tour of the forthcoming battlefield - but probably not. There was something in their attitude that made me uneasy. It was as though they knew a secret that I didn't, a kind of gloating anticipation in the way they carried themselves. With a sudden sick feeling clenching my stomach it occurred to me that I had seen exactly the same manner in a gang of street bravos in Rome as they prepared to close in on an unsuspecting victim.

Twisting in the saddle I looked casually around. The grove was several hundred paces ahead and the nearest infantry cohort was behind the cavalrymen coming up on my right. To the left was mostly empty plain until one reached light infantry who were performing skirmish drills a quarter mile away. Fleeing now would only invite the cavalrymen to give chase and to anyone looking on, it would appear as nothing more than some horsemen having a bit of high-spirited fun in an impromptu race. Gently I reached down and palmed my dagger, turning the handle so that the blade was out of sight, flat against the inside of my forearm.

The cavalrymen approached casually with two of them fanning out to vanish from sight behind my back. The leader, his sun-darkened features hard beneath a bronze helmet, reached out and caught Maphronius by the bridle. 'Tribune? A word, if I may.'

My smile was as pleasant and casual as I could make it. 'Going on patrol? You gentlemen are carrying a lot of gear for riders doing exercises.'

'No, we are deserting. There's just one thing we have to do first.'

Then things happened quickly. The leader's gaze flicked to somewhere behind my shoulder and I leaned forward, slashing with my dagger at the hand holding the reins, then twisting violently sideways as something bounced painfully off the armour over my ribs, and I was kicking Maphronius hard into a forward leap that left a spray of blood across my face as the leader jerked back his wounded hand. Then it was a frantic race toward the grove with dust in my face and the thunder of pursuing horses just yards behind.

It had been necessary to get into an obvious fight so that anyone casually watching would know that this was serious. Now the trick would be to stay alive until help arrived, and doing that was not going to be easy. Maphronius was a good horse but I was a lousy horseman, and the riders behind me had been in the cavalry business for most of their adult lives. Furthermore, there's a sort of protocol about this sort of thing. Two riders push their horses into a full speed sprint, forcing their prey to run even faster to keep ahead. Then, when the two fast riders fall back with their horses winded, the other two close in at their leisure on their equally exhausted victim.

The answer, insofar as I had an answer, was to belt

hell for leather for the grove, dismount and make my stand among the trees. Cavalrymen don't fight so well on foot and their lances are less than useful against a practised swordsman so I reckoned on having literally a fighting chance despite odds of four to one. (I'd made sure to slash the leader across the large blood vessels of his wrist and rather doubted his further involvement in the fight.)

The fatal flaw in this cunning plan was revealed when the hunt came within fifty paces of the grove and a dozen horsemen came hurtling out at a gallop. A glimpse of long blond hair beneath conical helmets and of trousered legs gripping the sides of the horses told me that we had run right into a Cimbric cavalry patrol. The enemy riders must have been sitting quietly in the grove, carefully taking note of our army's manoeuvrers. It was bold to the point of effrontery and the Cimbric scouts must have expected to be discovered at any moment. It was therefore no wonder that they reacted violently when a squad of Roman cavalry appeared to suddenly and spontaneously charge their position.

A huge rider on a steed which appeared to my terrified eyes to be the size of an elephant came bearing down on me, the rider's face contorted into a bestial snarl. Maphronius wisely deduced the total paralysis of the rider on top of him and at the last moment swerved hard to the left so that I actually brushed thighs with the man hurtling past. From behind came violent crashes and clangs which signified that the considerably outnumbered Samnites were making a fight of it.

A hurried glance over my shoulder confirmed that a savage little melee had broken out to my rear. Wishing both sides bad luck in their battle, I kicked an uncomplaining Maphronius towards the camp from which surprised shouts were starting to rise. Amazingly, no-one in the Cimbric patrol seemed much interested in me, which was just as well since my horse was already slowing down, flanks heaving as he gasped for air.

The gates of the camp were only a few yards away when half a squadron of legionary cavalry exited at a gallop, after which it seemed safe to pull up and let my blown horse recover. A deep, sharp pain in my side told me that the blow to my ribs had not bounced off as harmlessly as I had originally thought.

With my horse wheezing beneath me, I gingerly explored the damage while watching events unfold in front of the grove. At the sight of Roman cavalry exiting the camp the Cimbric patrol had disengaged, though they had little reason to stay in any case. Squinting against the midday sun I reckoned that four bodies and one horse lay crumpled on the grass with a fifth – the leader of the group – lying a short distance further off. He had joined in the pursuit after all, then.

Light-headedly, I watched the departing plume of dust that was all that remained of the Cimbric patrol and reckoned that they would be using picked horses which could easily outdistance the standard legionary nag. There was something else distracting me, a nagging question replaced by another – why was it getting dark at noontime?

I didn't even feel it when I fell off my horse for the second time in twenty-four hours.

Liber VII

'Are you sure about this, Lucius?'

'Fine, Sir. I'm absolutely fine.'

My reassuring reply was addressed to the right-hand Proconsul on the basis that of the two Catuli in front of me, this was more likely to be the real one. It was something of a guess because I had to admit to myself that since I had woken up in the infirmary yesterday my grasp on reality had been somewhat shaky.

A cracked rib, blood loss and severe concussion was the medic's diagnosis, combined with a reassuring prognosis of complete recovery if I remained in a dark room for a week. Hence my commander's reservations about my being out in the field on a bright summer morning with battle about to commence.

The cracked rib was from where the point of the lance wielded by the deserting Samnite cavalryman had bounced from my armour as I twisted to slash his friend's wrist. The blood loss was from that same twist, because the other thug behind me had been trying to decapitate me with his sword. He had missed, but the tip of his blade had put a tiny nick in my jugular. The cut was so small and the cursed blade so sharp that I didn't even realise that I had been injured (there was a lot else going on at the time) until my blood-soaked body had hit the ground - causing the concussion which was at present by far the worst of my worries.

It was not heroism that compelled me to be present for this confrontation with the Cimbri. I would much rather be in the medical tent with dim light soothing my headache while I sipped on meat broth to replace the blood I had lost. Unfortunately my carefully-laid plans had failed to take account of the fact that I might not be well enough to execute them, so well enough I had to be. Otherwise twenty thousand or so men might die today and Italy fall to the Cimbric invaders. Petraeus had dropped by the infirmary tent after breakfast just to make sure that I was absolutely clear on this point.

I glanced over at Catulus, who had temporarily merged into a single Proconsul for the moment. He was busily overseeing the deployment of the army and a stream of messengers constantly came and went with reports and orders. There had been a brief rain shower overnight and rather to the embarrassment of Domitius and myself this had flattened down the dust, making the grove we had so cavalierly dismissed from our tactical plans into a perfect observation post from which to observe the unfolding battle.

The Cimbri were already deployed and about a mile and a half away – mostly visible as a line of pale brown, bare-chested warriors from behind whom a variety of banners stuck out like random spikes. Some of those banners, I knew, were Roman standards captured from our armies in earlier engagements. Already faint shouts and war cries drifted down on the morning breeze accompanied by the flat blare of trumpets.

In comparison our legions deployed in grim silence broken only by the tramp of feet, the jingle of chain-mail and the occasional frustrated bark of a centurion at some legionary who failed to keep station. Catulus was deploying his cohorts in checkerboard fashion, blocks of five hundred or so men arranged with gaps between so that the cohort behind could charge up to relieve pressure on the front line. At the same time if – when – the Cimbri flowed into the gaps between the front cohorts, the men on the sides of those cohorts would turn to fight them, as would the men in the front rank of the cohorts behind. In other words, Catulus' plan was to trap the enemy in a series of little pockets in which they were surrounded on three sides and outnumbered.

Yes, outnumbered – even though the Cimbric army was around five times the size of the Roman. However, when you are in the front rank on the battlefield, it does not matter how many people are lining up behind you - there's still only so much space at the sharp end. Now consider that any Cimbric warrior who could afford to own one uses a long, round-tipped slashing sword. Which is great, not only for cleaving the foe in twain, but for also cleaving in twain any of your brothers-in-arms who are within four feet of you. This forces the Cimbri to stand well apart so as to have space in which to work.

Roman legionaries on the other hand stand behind their stout plywood shields and stab out their sword-arms with a simple forward thrust. The result was that every three slashing Cimbri would have to contend with five stabbing Romans, each of whom had better equipment, and armour which had evolved over centuries of fighting sword-slashing Celts to absorb and deflect the most damaging blows. Also of course, Roman armies are disciplined and fight as a unit against enemies who are largely amateurs fighting as a hobby.

Usually, therefore I'd bet a large sum on a Roman army defeating even this large barbarian horde, but these were not usual circumstances. Those slashing swords were handicapped against ranks of formed, disciplined legionaries. But should the legionary ranks break and a gap appear, then one warrior who got in amid the densely-packed cohort formation would cause disruption and chaos which his fellows could exploit so effectively that within minutes there would be no cohort left.

I knew that, the centurions knew that, and crucially, the legionaries knew that. They also knew that the cowards who broke and ran first were the ones most likely to survive the massacre that followed. So there was something of a dilemma facing every man on the Roman side – if they all stood and fought, they would win. If just a few men from each cohort broke and ran, then the only survivors would be those who ran first and ran furthest. So every legionary was looking at the soldiers beside him and the units alongside his own, and the question in every man's mind was – will they stand?

Catulus himself seemed to have no doubts. My eyes were having trouble adjusting to the morning sunlight, so the Proconsul had now become a blur against an intolerably bright backdrop. His voice as he gave commands was both loud and cheerful. This, I reflected rather sourly was very typical of the Roman aristocracy as a whole. Catulus was very well aware that the morale of his army was fragile and if his men broke, he would have the impossible job of trying to hold back the human tide – a job that would almost certainly cost his life. Yet the man seemed to almost welcome the coming challenge.

Put a meal with rancid butter in front of a Roman aristocrat at dinnertime and you would think from his reaction that it was the end of the world. Yet should that same aristocrat be faced with the actual end of the world, it was probable that he would respond with the same calm imperturbability and good cheer as Catulus was showing at the moment. Even the fact that the cohorts on the far left wing were not deploying to plan didn't seem to upset him. Instead he sent off messenger after messenger clearly and patiently explaining what needed to be done. In a way it was inspirational, I guess.

Scipio Dextrianus came alongside me. I noted that the youth had acquired himself another set of brightly polished armour - evidently shiny breastplates were some sort of battle fetish. Unable to stand the sight, I closed my eyes and over the pounding headache which was beginning to develop I heard Dextrianus anxiously asking if I was all right.

'Just as well those Cimbric scouts were there, eh?' remarked the lad with all too much good cheer.

I agreed somewhat sourly. 'Yes, our cavalry tried to kill me, and the Cimbri rescued me, but that's the story of the fledgling and the farmer all over again.'

'What do you mean?'

Looking over at the left wing I saw that the situation there was still something of a mess, so there was a minute or two before something needed to be done. I turned to Dextrianus and explained.

'There was once a little fledgeling that fell from his nest on a winter's morning. Since he was too young to fly back up the bird simply lay on the ground sadly going 'peep-peep-peep'. A passing farmer heard him and being a kindly sort of fellow, the farmer picked up the little bird. However, the farmer was also a busy man and all he could do was stop at the nearest pile of steaming cow droppings and carefully insert the chick into them.'

'The droppings were fresh from the cow and wonderfully warm. The fledgeling sat there comfortably, going 'peep-peep-peep' with great contentment. A fox heard the noise, plucked the bird from the droppings, and after quickly dunking it in a nearby stream had himself an early breakfast.'

'So, as with my experience yesterday afternoon, the point to note here is that it is not always your enemies who drop you into the shit and it is not always your friends who get you out of it.'

Absently I picked at the bandage around my neck and squinted at the hills overlooking the left flank. 'Be a good fellow and send Gratidus over, would you Dextrianus?'

I was still massaging my temples when Gratidus rode up. 'What do you want?' he asked ungraciously. 'You can't just send your trainees to fetch me as though I were some sort of miserable servant.'

'Gratidus, I believe you want to tell Catulus that you are taking my trainees to scout the hills over there. It will be excellent training for them, it's far enough from the action to be safe, and they'll have an excellent view of the battle as it unfolds. Make sure you get far enough up the hill to see over the crest. You'll find it's well worth the effort.'

'Did that hit to your head make you silly? Of course we've scouted those hills already. There's no ambush waiting there. Nothing but a few wild goats. A total waste of time.'

'You want to do it anyway, Gratidus, trust me. And make sure you look over the crest of the hill, okay?'

'No way. I've got better things to do. This battle …'.

Gratidus stopped, because my nose was almost touching his battered face.

'Listen to me very carefully, you pea-brained imbecile, because I'm done with the subtle hints. Now, you will do exactly what I say. Take the damn trainees. Go to the left wing. Ride up the hill and look over the crest. Got it? Do that one simple thing and I guarantee that you will be the hero of the army by sundown. Screw up, and please believe one simple truth, which is that before tonight I will take pleasure in killing you slowly, carefully and very painfully. Am I making myself perfectly clear about this, Gratidus?'

Gratidus gulped and paled slightly under his bruises.

'Yes. Very clear.'

'Go now. And hurry.'

Once Gratidus and my trainees had cantered off on their mission, I nudged my horse over to where Catulus and Petraeus were involved in a complex discussion involving the deployment of the baggage train which Petraeus had ordered to prepare to depart the camp at a moment's notice. Already teams were at work dismantling the camp gate sand loading the shaped logs onto waggons for reassembly at our next stopping point - wherever that might be.

Catulus did not disagree with this, because win or lose the army would be on the move after the battle, either retreating or following up against a retreating enemy, but nevertheless the Proconsul was annoyed at not being consulted. There were issues to resolve about how the train should fit into the general order of march. Messengers were waiting to carry the final decisions back to those affected.

The discussion concluded, Catulus saw me and waved me over to join him. 'It's annoying that Scaurus and his cavalry decided to abandon us the other day. Most of my senior officers were in his camp and now they have vanished down the road with him. A strange feeling to be commanding a battle almost single-handed, though I can't say Scaurus himself is much missed. Confidentially speaking, I'll admit he was not my first choice of second-in-command. I had to have him for … well, reasons.'

I nodded, knowing full well that the 'reasons' were that Scaurus' hugely influential daddy had wanted an important command for his son and Catulus had decided it was politically worthwhile to go along with this.

'Still', Catulus went on, 'It's excellent that we no

longer have to worry about that cursed spy. So it was
the orderly all along, eh? I owe those young men
sharing my tent an apology for suspecting them
although of course we never let them know that they
were suspects in any case. Seems that I dragged you
over to my army on something of a wild goose chase,
after all. Well, you don't need to do any more
investigating for me. Gratidus tells me that he has
everything in hand.'

While Catulus nattered on, I kept a pleasant and
attentive smile in place and enjoyed the cool morning
breeze on my face. Apparently the orderly had con-
fessed to everything – sneaking into the tent to steal
documents, killing the young trainee who had discovered him, and on one occasion even hiding in the
room where battle plans were being discussed.

'Amazing. And because he was my orderly, people
were accustomed to seeing him come and go from my
tent and on those few occasions when anyone did
question him, he simply said that he was obeying my
orders. Such a pleasant young man. Who knew that he
was from Picenum? Or that his family were captured by
the barbarians? Of course, the traitorous fool should
know that service to the Republic comes before helping
his family. That should be plain, no matter what the
Cimbri threatened to do to his children. But still, if it
was wrong it was understandable, and I certainly pray
that I should never be faced with so invidious a choice.
Nevertheless, if a man must choose between family and
country he should choose country every time. That's
obvious.'

'Oh, excuse me, my dear Lucius, it looks as though the Cimbri have stopped their advance for some reason. I have to dress my lines.'

The Proconsul kicked his horse away, yelling for messengers. Indeed, the advancing mass of Cimbri had come to a restless halt, as though that huge army was waiting for something. The legions that had been advancing to contact halted in their turn as their tribunes awaited instructions as to how they should respond to this new development.

That's the thing about battles. They tend either to start because two front-line units engage in an untimely scrap and both sides then feed more units into the melee until there's a full-scale engagement, or we have a situation like today where each commander deploys, manoeuvrers and counter-manoeuvrers in a dance that can take up much of the day.

While awaiting developments I dismounted gingerly and leant my aching body against a tree to get some rest. The advantage of being among the walking wounded was that no-one actually expected me to do anything constructive so for the moment I was essentially a spectator.

Around dawn this morning an unsigned letter had appeared on my breakfast tray. Later I planned to investigate how it had gotten there, but for the moment the contents of the letter were sufficient food for thought. The missive was from Satula, who had – obviously – been informed of developments in the camp.

My dear boy,
How horrible to hear of your near-descent to join the shades in the Underworld. I trust that you will return to health soon – after all, blood loss is soon recovered through healthy eating. Just rest those ribs, and perhaps regret that you failed to exercise other parts of yourself while you had the chance. Caerus has taken revenge for your scorning his gift!

I made a note to find out how Satula had discovered the details of my medical record, and mentally invited Caerus – the Roman God of Opportunity – to perform upon himself a physical act of which Satula would doubtless have approved.

Our treacherous innkeeper is no more. I suspect that it will be reported he has absconded, fearing the worst from the coming battle. We had a long conversation before he left us and he firmly denies that the Cimbri were in any way involved with those Samnite cavalry wanting to kill you. This therefore is probably the case, because I was most insistent in my questioning and I doubt that the man could have lied. His wife has taken over his duties.
Nevertheless, the money found with the Samnite corpses suggests that someone paid those men to kill you, and paid them very well. You have enemies, my boy, but doubtless you knew that already. You will of course eat, burn or otherwise dispose of this letter

after reading, and when Sulla writes enquiring after your health – as doubtless he will - please pass on in your reply the salutations of his faithful
Satula

Thereafter I might have slept. Concussion does funny things to one's sense of time. In any case, I was awakened by Catulus exclaiming, 'That's Gratidus! He is back soon – and in a great hurry. Where are the cadets he took with him?'

Our commander was back on the knoll, watching with sympathy as I struggled from the grass into the saddle. Sure enough, our intelligence officer was re-turning, belting through the ranks on a thoroughly winded horse. The heads of infantrymen turned to watch him as he passed, the soldiers well aware that his urgency probably presaged bad news.

'Consul … the Cimbri! They are almost upon us! They ...they …'. Gratidus fell to gasping for breath.

'Yes indeed, my dear fellow. We know', said Catulus in a kindly voice as he waved an arm at the enemy army poised a quarter of a mile away. The commander shot me a puzzled look, but then Gratidus recovered his breath and went on.

'Not … them. There. Gap in the hills. Back there. They are coming through, thousands of them. More coming over the hills, light infantry. We were almost killed. They went round us, lots of them. Ten thousand, maybe more.'

Catulus' head shot up, and he gazed at the gap in the hills with mounting horror. 'Those hills? The gap in those hills, behind on the left flank? Oh Gods. Messenger! I need messengers! We are outflanked, Gods curse it!'

'Maybe the situation can be saved, Sir.' This from Petraeus, who was squinting across the battlefield. 'The units on the left seem to be responding appropriately. Perhaps it was fortunate after all that the soft ground prevented them from deploying in a timely manner.'

'I sent the cadets … to inform unit commanders, warn them of the peril. They should be back here after that.'

'Excellent work, Gratidus', said Catulus absently, 'I shall see you are rewarded for it.'

The first ranks of the Cimbric force that Gratidus had seen over the crest of the western hill were now appearing in the gap between the hills. However, instead of the exposed backs of soldiers who had marched past them, the newcomers found that three cohorts had wheeled to face the new threat and another two cohorts were waiting alongside the hill to the south, ready to take the attackers in the flank should they advance further.

'How did the Syrian archers get there?' asked Catulus with some bewilderment. The Cimbric light infantry had come swarming over the hill to the north of the gap, ready to support the heavier-armed warriors swarming through the gap itself.

These Cimbric light infantry found themselves caught on the open hillside by our Syrian auxiliary archers, who had smartly deployed into a skirmish line supported by legionary cavalry which threatened sudden death to any Cimbric light warrior who ventured on to the plain. For the moment the Cimbric attack over the hill was stalled and taking casualties from bowfire.

'The archers? That was me, Sir', said Petraeus smoothly. 'I moved them across to that flank this morning. With the infantry being so slow on that side, I thought they would need missile cover as they deployed.'

'Good man, good man', said Catulus chewing his lip. He sighed. 'We still can't fight the battle on two fronts though. We haven't the manpower to sustain it. We have to … dammit, who told the Ninth Campanians to retreat?'

We watched one of the allied cohorts pulling back, while the unit beside it wheeled sideways to cover the gap in the line. A crowd of Cimbri surged forward to take advantage, but their advance was swiftly discouraged by several squadrons of heavy cavalry that trotted forward, ready for business.

'The Umbrians are going too', observed Gratidus. And indeed, almost as though the withdrawal of the Ninth was a signal, the Umbrian units alongside the riverbank neatly folded into line of march and started heading back for the camp. The Cimbri there watched, confused and unable to advance for fear of being caught between the river and the units to the right.

On the left flank the Roman infantry were dis-engaging so smoothly that it might almost have been practised (as it had been, extensively, all yesterday. Petraeus and his centurions had made good use of the information I had given them).

Catulus was furious. 'Who gave the order to break off from the battle? I gave no such order!'

Tentatively I ventured a suggestion, 'Um, you did say that our situation was untenable, Sir. Perhaps the local commanders can see that and are using their initiative? After all, they have just been updated on what Gratidus and the trainees saw over the hill.'

A messenger pulled up breathlessly beside our little group. 'Sir, commander of the second legion says he needs to pull back now. He's lost support on his flanks. Has he permission?'

When a Roman squad reaches camp someone brings up the pack mule and within moments a tent is unpacked, gear unloaded from packs, and where there were eight men standing around before, there is suddenly a small but comfortable encampment.

This was rather the same process but in reverse and on a much larger scale. The Roman army was neatly packing itself away as it changed from an army in battle array to an army in line of march. Units slid past one another in smooth formation, each part covering for the next as a column began to form, already marching back towards the road by the river. The Cimbri, presumably holding back their charge because they were still waiting for chaos to erupt on the left flank, waited in some confusion - and all the while the gap between the armies widened. A formidable rearguard of mixed cavalry, infantry and bowmen discouraged unexpected initiatives on the part of the enemy. Overall it was as smooth a disengagement as I have ever seen.

'Curse it all to Hades!' howled Catulus in frustration. 'If my blasted army is going to retreat, I will at least be leading that retreat. Trumpeters, sound withdrawal. Signifer, take the standards and join the column - there between the legionary cavalry of the second and the Tarentine levies. You .. you ...and you, come here.' Catulus signalled to messengers while giving Petraeus a poisonous look. 'You and I, we need to have a talk later.'

The *Primus Pilus* was stone-faced. 'Of course, Sir.'

By now it had dawned on the Cimbri that their outflanking manoeuvrer had failed. As I rode down from the grove, a look across the plain showed that the stand-off by the gap remained. The Syrian bowmen had driven the Cimbric light infantry back up the hill to the north of the gap, and in the gap itself the warriors at the head of the Cimbric column hesitated. It was a reasonable hesitation, for to advance meant getting hit head-on by the cohorts waiting for them, one from the front and the other from the side, while on the other side, the Syrians had only to turn sideways to perforate the Cimbric column's exposed flank. Any advance would end in a massacre.

In the main Cimbric army the question doubtless being debated by the leaders was whether, given that they would now be attacking only from the front, it was worth doing so, as the Romans were well on their way to an effective disengagement? The problem for the Cimbri was that the gap between the two armies had now widened to half a mile so the warriors would have to advance at a trot until they got within charging range of the Roman rearguard. That rearguard would then fall back to catch up with the rest of the army and the Cimbri would then have to make another trot-and-charge.

In the end the Cimbri settled for following the Roman army at a brisk walk. This bothered Catulus, though by now I was too preoccupied with a pounding head to worry too much about it. We had gotten the Roman army off the battlefield intact, as I had promised the tribunes. Now a week's sleep seemed a good idea, and once the legions got over the pass that was what I planned to do, even if they had to carry me in a litter.

For the moment even sleep in the saddle was temporarily impossible, as almost the entire army's remaining cavalry came thundering past me, having been peeled from the column by Catulus and sent to cover the retreat of the western cohorts and the archers covering the gap. These troops were now heading for the retreating Roman column at the double, with the Cimbric outflankers finally pouring onto the plain where they were met with shouts of derision from the rest of their army.

Once it became clear that the legions were going to march through the pass in good order, Petraeus relaxed so comprehensively that only now was it clear how much pressure he had been under. He rode his horse alongside mine.

'We did it, Lucius.'

I would have nodded, but I was pretty sure that the top of my head would slide off if I tried. Petraeus pointed with his chin. 'Look at Gratitdus.'

Word had clearly spread through the ranks that our intelligence officer was the man who had discovered the Cimbric outflanking manoeuvrer in the nick of time, and his speedy return with the news had saved the army. It was possible to locate his presence at any moment by the local cheers and shouted congratulations from different points along the column. Even Catulus allowed himself a sour smile as Gratidus rode towards us, men occasionally breaking from the ranks to group around his horse until chivvied back into the column by exasperated centurions.

'The hero of the hour.' I muttered.

'Oh, come now,' reproved Catulus, overhearing. 'You must admit it was an excellent idea of Gratidus to go scouting those western hills, even if his main concern was probably to take your trainees off your hands for a while. Evidently the man has good instincts. Much as I hate to retreat, it's astonishing to see that our withdrawal has actually improved the morale of the men.'

Well yes, I thought ungraciously. Yesterday the army knew you were going to lead them out into a battle where everyone was going to die. For some reason people were feeling a bit down about that. Today it looks as if we are going to live after all. And also it is clear that the army has comprehensively outmanoeuvred the enemy on the battlefield and left the Cimbri looking like fools. Right now the men are probably feeling that the Cimbri are not so terrifying after all. Perhaps some are even thinking about the next meeting and how, when that happens, they might actually win....

'Gratidus!' called out the Proconsul, and our hero swung his horse about at the call. He trotted over, my trainees following him like a gaggle of goslings after a mother goose. Out of the corner of my eye I saw Petraeus regarding me with sardonic amusement, and I discreetly gave him the finger.

'Gratidus, the Cimbri are following our column but not closing with the rearguard. They have no chance of stopping the army before it is over the pass and out of the valley. At that point our rearguard will block the pass, so what do the enemy hope to gain?'

Gratidus looked gravely thoughtful. 'I am not sure, Sir. With your permission, I would like to take some men and scout the land ahead of our line of march. Just in case there are any more surprises.'

As Gratidus rode off, Catulus nodded approvingly, 'A good man that. It appears I may have under-estimated him.' Behind me Lafranius, the Italian trainee, snickered quietly. I later discovered that Gratidus had spent the ride out to the gap cursing me, cursing the trainees, and cursing life in general. Nevertheless he had obediently ridden up to the crest of the hill, looked over and nearly died from shock – not surprising since he had almost ridden into the arms of the Cimbric light infantry swarming in their hundreds up the other side of the hill.

It was now four hours after that moment, and the army was stopped, stretched out in a long column alongside the river with the pass safely behind us. Three cohorts backed with bowmen were safely blocking the road and daring the Cimbri to come any closer. Catulus had ordered a late lunch and men were sprawled along the banks of the Adige, cooking, relaxing and chatting with the peculiar febrile tension of those who find themselves alive when they did not really expect to be.

I had persuaded a fatigue party to reap rushes from the riverside, and had arranged these into a crude bed over which I had spread a cloak. My plan to get a month's sleep was eventually disturbed by the clop of a horse's hooves which stopped right beside me. Opening one bleary eye revealed that indeed there was a horse's hoof about a foot from my head. Looking up from the hoof I located a horse's foreleg, chest, and finally the face of Petraeus looking down at me from a great height.

'Gratidus is back. You had better come and hear this. It's not good.'

Groaning I arose, wrapping myself in my cloak as I did so. Even in the midsummer sun, I still felt cold.

'Right across, you say?' Catulus was asking Gratidus as I stumbled to join the command group.

Gratidus nodded. 'The stream runs along the side of a ridge right up to the Adige. I'd say there's a thousand men on that ridge, and they block the road entirely. It's a narrow ridge, and they are jam-packed on it, but they've removed the culvert across the road so they have a natural moat and rampart.'

Dextrianus moved alongside me and brought me up to speed in a whisper. 'Now we know why the Cimbri were following and not trying to catch up. They were happy enough to let us get to where we are, and then block the way we came in by. Ten miles ahead the hills narrow the road against the river again, and there's an enemy force there, blocking us in. We're trapped on this stretch of road.'

There was an embarrassing silence and Dextrianus and I realised that everyone else had paused their discussion to listen to his summary. The young Scipio raised his head and looked at the Proconsul.

'What are we going to do, Sir?'

Catulus seemed serenely unworried, almost cheerful. That whole Spartan aristocratic ethos again, I supposed. 'What are we going to do? Why, we will finish our lunch of course, have a nap and then march the army over to take a look at this new problem.'

Liber VIII

Afternoon sunlight slanted over the hills to our right as the attack cohort shuffled into formation. On the ridge the Cimbri yelled defiance and hurled the occasional spear – a pointless exercise as the cohort was commanded by a veteran tribune who was forming up his men just outside spear range.

One Cimbric warrior elbowed aside enough of his fellows to allow for a run-up through the tight-packed ranks of warriors on the ridge, yet as that man opened his stance for a throw, no less than three arrows abruptly sprouted from his naked chest. The men around him threw up their shields as they had on earlier occasions when tested by our Syrian bowmen, and so close-packed were the men on the ridge that for a moment that clump of men looked like a single huge creature with scales of red, blue and green. The warrior who had fallen vanished from sight.

There was a pause, and then on a shouted command the Syrian bowmen launched several hundred arrows from behind the attack cohort. These were launched almost vertically, arching as thin dark blurs against the blue afternoon sky, taking a trajectory which forced the Cimbri to throw their shields high against the arrows dropping straight down upon them. Beside me, Catulus grunted with mild satisfaction.

As the arrows began to drop from the apogee of their flight, the attack cohort hurled itself across the stream, the ranks carefully spaced to allow each line of men to cross without losing formation.

155

'Knee deep mostly, never more than thigh', Petraeus observed to my trainees. 'Look there, see how the cohort is losing formation on the left? There will be slippery rocks underfoot at that point. Centre looks good though.'

The cohort looked like a steel carpet of armoured men as it rippled across the stream and up the natural rampart of the ridge on the other side, the dark purple plumes of their helmets nodding in the sunlight. The Cimbri met them with a roar, and a wall of shields and spear-points dropped into place to meet the Roman attack.

'No pilums?' murmured Dextrianus as the bang of sword on shield and the clash of weapon on weapon echoed back across the narrow valley. 'Shouldn't they hit the enemy with a shower of spears at close range before they draw their swords?'

Petraeus had taken over my duties as instructor while I was recovering from my injuries. 'No time. The idea is to get over that stream and up the embankment on the far side as fast as possible. The men would be throwing uphill and their pilums would have limited range and effect anyway. Better to close quickly with the enemy, especially as there's a stream and ridge to cope with. Carrying pilums would get in the way and screw up the cohort's formation even more. As it is, because they're in formation, they can rotate men out of the line – watch.'

At that point I had closed my eyes hoping that the darkness behind my eyelids would ease my thumping headache, but I could imagine what the trainees were seeing. At the battle-line on the ridge, the first rank of legionaries would be tiring, because even a trained soldier can only swing two pounds of sword at the end of his arm for so long.

As he prepared to rotate out, the legionary would launch a savage slash at the warrior in front of him, turning his body to the right as he did so. When his left, shielded, shoulder was pointed at the enemy he would step back and sideways, while the soldier beside him stepped across to cover the gap, and a man from the second rank moved forward on his left to step into the fighting line. For months the centurions had been drilling that manoeuvre with the men, and now, with the ridge raising each rank slightly above those behind, the trainees had a perfect view of Roman military teamwork in operation.

'That way, we keep fresh fighting men on the battle line', explained Petraeus unnecessarily. 'The Cimbri can't do that.'

'They don't have to', observed Lafranius ruefully. 'They're holding.'

I lifted my head and looked over at the fight. The stream was invisible beneath the hundreds of men standing in and beside it, but those men were not moving forward. The Cimbri on the ridge were not moving back so much as a step, for all the ferocity of the Roman attack.

'Give it a slow count of a hundred, and pull them out', Catulus instructed, and Petraeus signalled for a trumpeter to come over.

157

The Roman trumpet had a clear, almost musical tone, a marked contrast to the off-key farts of the Cimbric battle horns. Yet in sheer volume, the triumphant Cimbric horns easily overwhelmed the single Roman trumpet as the attack cohort responded to the signal, and the Cimbri rejoiced at the Roman retreat.

Yet it was also a successful withdrawal, for the cohort stepped out of the combat backwards, always facing the enemy, and taking their casualties with them.

'Good discipline on both sides', muttered Domitius. 'Someone must have really drilled it into the Cimbri that no-one is to take a step down from the ridge. You'd have hoped that they'd follow up and we could pull them into the stream and chop up at least some of them.'

'Doubt we inflicted even a dozen casualties', observed Lafranius. 'They just had to put their shields edge down and slash at our men's heads while we poked at groin height. Still, not too many in the cohort were harmed either.'

'Armed men fighting each other don't do too much damage if both sides know how to defend themselves', remarked Petraeus. 'That's what shields and armour are for. It's when a side breaks, and cavalry get loose among panicked men fleeing a battlefield, that's when armies are destroyed. Or when a German wearing only a pair of trousers finds that he can easily catch up with a running infantryman carrying twenty pounds of chain-mail.' The chief centurion gave me an apologetic look, knowing that it was not so long since I had seen exactly that happen to thousands of doomed legionaries at the fatal battle of Arausio in Gaul.

Just before the stream, a rank of legionaries stood and presented shields to the enemy on the ridge as their comrades turned and, finally abandoning formation, straggled back to the ranks of the main army. Catulus nudged his horse forward, and went to congratulate the men on their effort.

Antonius gave a shrug and a sigh. 'Well, that's it. The valley is too narrow to attack the ridge with more than a cohort at a time. And we've seen that a cohort on its own can't hack it. What now? We've got the entire Cimbric army behind us, and we can't go forward.'

Porcellinus squinted at the hills, dark against the setting sun. 'Can't we go over?'

Lafranius scoffed. 'Those hills are swarming with Cimbric light infantry by now. No way can the legions hope to keep any kind of formation – in some places you'd have to climb with hands and feet. Look at those rock faces. It would be a slaughter. Might as well just march the army into the river and be done with it.'

'So what do we do now?'

'We start making camp.' This from Catulus who had rejoined out little group. '*Primus Pilus*, get the men started on digging a trench and a rampart, and get the cooking fires started. I want to see some tents going up.'

'We're digging in for the night, Sir?'

'Great Jupiter, no. We have to get across that stream. I want the Cimbri to *think* that we are digging in for the night. Look at the crowd on the ridge.'

Obediently, we looked.

'They're packed up there as tight as spectators at a play in the forum. Standing room only. Now, they'll have been on that ridge since morning, waiting to bottle up either the fleeing remnants of our army, or the entire thing in battle order. Either way, the Cimbri always planned to finish off my army right here. Well, that means that there are men on that ridge who have been standing waiting for us for the last eight hours. Now they've met us and as soon as they see that we are standing down you can bet they'll want to do the same also. There's some tired legs up there and our recent test of their strength will have helped to tire them out further.'

Petraeus studied the ridge thoughtfully. 'So you'll want to try before dusk, right?'

Catulus nodded.

'Why?' asked Lafranius rather plaintively from behind me. 'Why not wait until it's dark and they can't see us attacking at all?'

'Sentries. They'll know when we storm the ridge anyway. The secret is in stopping them from stopping us. Watch and learn, young man.'

So we watched as the Syrians and Italian auxiliary units started digging the ditch which surrounds every Roman marching camp. As they dug, other workers threw the excavated earth back to make the beginnings of a rampart. Light infantry units dispersed into the woods and began to drag in firewood, and the legionaries went rooting through the baggage train to find their pack mules and set up tents.

The Cimbri on the ridge watched this for a while

and after about half an hour I heard Petraeus murmur, 'It's working.'

Sure enough the packed crowd on the ridge was thinning out as warriors slowly made their way to a rough camp situated in a field between the ridge and the hills. It was a pretty tight fit there also, but the stream was not as tight against the ridge nearer the hills, and this gave the warriors more room to spread out. Of course, having more room on the ridge allowed ambitious spear-throwers to take a run-up and hurl their spears at our trench-diggers, so squads of legionaries came out to provide shield cover for the diggers.

Even in total, these small groups of legionary shield-bearers were less than a fifth of the size of the cohort which had failed to take the ridge earlier so the Cimbri showed no alarm at their presence. The Cimbric camp was a lot closer to the ridge than the closest legionaries, so the ridge must have seemed secure.

The sun set behind the western hills, and the summer afternoon was just deepening into dusk when Catulus murmured to Petraeus, 'Now.'

In the middle of the developing Roman camp a standard dipped twice, a signal that immediately started a silent rush for the ridge by the veteran legionaries guarding the trench diggers. The attack force had hardly gone ten paces before there were shouts of alarm from the Cimbric sentries on the ridge and a confused reaction from their camp. Still, the legionaries were at the stream before a tide of warriors burst from the camp and headed for the ridge with plenty of time to be in position before the Roman attackers reached them.

At this point the Syrian trench diggers stopped pretending to dig and snatched up their bows. Within seconds the first volley went high into the twilight sky, and as they had been conditioned to do during the afternoon's skirmishing, the Cimbri flung up their shields to meet it. This slowed the Cimbri and made the race a lot closer because the attacking legionaries were fewer and faster than a cohort, and they knew the best places to cross the stream.

Then even as the first arrows thudded into the upraised Cimbric shields, the Syrians did something that had not done all afternoon and fired a new volley on a flat trajectory. This created considerable chaos at the arrival end because the arrows landing on the Cimbri from above arrived at the same time as the second volley which was fired straight into their chests. Looking over, I saw that some of the archers were still lobbing their arrows high, as if they were stones fired from a siege catapult, and others were shooting directly at the enemy wherever they saw a man exposed as he tried to use his shield as an umbrella.

At that moment there came a further outbreak of chaos to the west. Not all those light infantry who had gone to collect firewood had returned. A substantial number had remained in the woods and these now launched an attack on the Cimbric camp. The attack was doomed to failure, of course, but it further confused the Cimbri who consequently sent fewer men to join the scattered defenders on the ridge. By now these had worked out that the only way to avoid the hail of arrows was for one man to stand with his shield above him while another stood in front of him blocking arrows from that direction.

Complacently Catulus remarked to the trainees, 'We needed daylight so that the archers could see to do their work. Mighty Apollo may wield a bow, and may he forgive me for saying so, but in war the bow is a coward's weapon - a filthy thing fit only for use by Greeks and orientals. But by Apollo, and Diana also, I wish we had another thousand bowmen right now. Look at what they're doing to them.'

'Them' were the front ranks of the Cimbri rushing to re-occupy the ridge. The archers were concentrating a withering fire on the front ranks which had slowed almost to a standstill. Not so the hundreds of men pushing behind them, and the mass of their bodies actually pushed over some of those who had slowed to protect themselves from the hail of arrows. The people on the ground tried to get up before they were trampled and their efforts slowed the Cimbric advance even more.

Meanwhile, the legionaries had crossed the stream and angled for the river portion of the ridge furthest away from the Cimbric camp.

'They're up', Domitius observed with satisfaction, and sure enough, the first Romans were now on the ridge and wheeling into formation, trotting along the narrow ridge towards the Cimbri. These were selected veteran soldiers, men who had chopped down barbarians before and were confident in their ability to do it again. Their front rank presented a wall of shields spiked with swords and the men behind the wall briskly started killing the first Cimbri they met.

Still, the barbarians could have pushed the legionaries off the ridge by sheer weight of numbers were it not that the sheer weight of numbers was now on the Roman side. An iron tide was flowing from the Roman camp towards the ridge as a full legion - which had only pretended to down arms and set up for the night – now proceeded toward the ridge at an implacable jog trot. This time the front ranks did stop just before the stream to unload several hundred pilums at an enemy now fighting on two flanks with most of the ridge already lost. As before, the pilums did little damage, but they were a demoralizing reminder to the Cimbri that they were now fighting on two fronts – and losing on both.

As dusk fell the ridge was once again packed from end to end, but now it was occupied by men in chain-mail and the only Cimbri in sight were pale corpses flung down to lie beside the stream. A Roman advance guard was already clearing the way south to where the hills opened up to a wide plain alongside the Adige, and the Cimbri had abandoned their camp. Confused noises from the woods indicated where they were still fighting it out with our light infantry as they retreated.

'Get the men over the ridge to the plain and we will set up camp there for the night', a smug-looking Catulus ordered Petraeus. 'And then you and Turpillius

Panderius are going to join me in my tent for dinner.'

The consul wheeled his horse to join the column of march, waving to acknowledge the cheers of the legionaries whom he approached. As he turned in the saddle to face us once more, Catulus' smile mutated into a snarl. 'Do not expect to enjoy the meal, gentlemen.'

The Little Bear constellation had rolled well to the west across the night sky by the time that a thoroughly chastised Petraeus and I headed for my tent for a soothing beaker of wine. Once we got there, Petraeus collapsed on to my cot bed while I dug out the beakers and sat myself on the camp chair.

'Well,' I remarked. 'That was unpleasant.'

'Gods, what would the man have done if we hadn't saved his army and his life – despite his best efforts to lose both?'

'Well, I think then we would have received an actual lashing, rather than a tongue-lashing.'

'But we did nothing wrong!'

'Um, preparing an alternative plan of battle and actually executing it in the field without telling your commanding officer might be considered a touch insubordinate in some circles. Especially if that commander was there at the time and believed that he was in control.'

'Okay, well yes. We did that. But our defence was that we had prepared the army for all sorts of scenarios, including one where we needed to retreat suddenly and in good order. And that's what happened. We suddenly needed to retreat so local centurions and the occasional military tribune did as they needed to do without waiting for orders from the top – orders that would have been too late in any case.'

'The trouble is that you did it all too well. There's no way that the army could have disengaged so smoothly unless you had spent almost a week practising. Even before you knew of the outflanking manoeuvrer by the Cimbri, you were planning a disciplined retreat - Catulus knows that. He is stubborn, no military genius, but no fool.'

Petraeus nodded gloomily and swigged his wine. 'He managed the taking of that ridge perfectly. I'll give him that.'

'Face it. You are guilty whether we look at it up, down or sideways. Just the fact that you had the baggage train packed and ready to move the moment Catulus left the camp shows premeditation. And Catulus clearly did not believe for a moment that bad deployment on the left wing just happened to co-incidentally leave the units there perfectly positioned to deal with the outflanking Cimbri coming through the gap in the hills.'

I frowned indignantly. 'A more interesting question is why I get lumped in with you in your near-criminal behaviour. I'm just the tutor to the trainees. I had absolutely nothing to do with any of this!'

'Officially, no …', began Petraeus, but I cut him off.

'Officially, I've been doing nothing but teaching generalship to my cadets, recovering from my various escapades, and wandering around the camp. Catulus has no proof - none at all - that I've been meeting my informants or that I even knew of the Cimbric battle plans, let alone that I passed them on to you. Yet he came down on me like a ton of bricks. I've done nothing.'

'Officially.'

There was a pause, and then Petraeus asked, 'Why did Catulus make you "Tribune in charge of Funny Business'? What does it mean anyway?'

'Oh, the cadets pissed in my bed the day I got here. Yes, the bed you're sitting on right now. Don't worry, I changed the mattress. So I beat up young Domitius Ahenobarbus and made him Hygiene Officer for the group. Any similar stunts and he's the one who is punished, whether or not I discover who actually did the deed.'

'And did it work?'

'That bed is dry, isn't it?'

'So now you are Tribune in charge of Funny Business. I assume this means you take the blame for anything that goes down in the camp that Catulus reckons is the result of hidden scheming or behind-the-scenes manoeuvrers? It's all become your responsibility, whether you are officially involved or not?'

'Exactly.'

'Sounds fair to me. Let's face it. You are generally behind all the hidden scheming and behind-the-scenes manoeuvrers in any case.'

'It's unjust!'

'Tell that to Domitius Ahenobarbus.'

167

Moodily I stared into my beaker, the wine black as ink in the lamplight. 'Ungrateful sod. Catulus, I mean.'

'Don't you ever get tired of it?'

'This concussion, or working wounded generally? I've been pretty much beat up since that fight at the fort at Sarni. Jupiter, that seems so long ago now.'

'No, I mean your shadow war. All the deception, the double-crosses, the deceit and distrust. H'm interesting how all the nasty words in spycraft start with the letter 'd'. Anyway ... don't you ever yearn for a clean, simple world where all you have to do is locate your enemy and kill him?'

'And that's what you call my shadow war?'

'What would you call it?'

'Yours is the shadow war, my friend. I fight the real war.'

'How so?'

I raised my wine beaker and waved it gently in the lamplight. 'See what happens here? I move my arm and the shadow follows. Up, down, and there goes the shadow. I need my shadow to move right and look, there it goes.'

'Now, suppose I come to Catulus tomorrow and tell him that the enemy plan to occupy a hill on our line of march tomorrow. What will he do?'

'I suppose he will send cavalry and light infantry to occupy the hill before the enemy get there.'

'And if I tell him that a large enemy force is marching up alongside the river?'

'Well, we've lost most of north Italy now and Catulus is determined to meet up with Marius before we next fight the Cimbri, so he will take the army west away from the river. We're clear of the hills now so he can do that.'

'In other words, I supply the information and the army moves in response, no? I tell my arm to move and the shadow moves in response. Watch – I move left, my shadow follows. I see the enemy plan an outflanking move and our army moves to block it. Finding out what is going to happen, when it's going to happen and who is going to make it happen - that's the real war. Then like the shadow moving to follow my arm, the army moves in response. That's the shadow war.'

Clearly Petraeus did not like the idea. He finished his wine and rose from the bed.

'I don't think it is like that at all', he said stiffly. Then bidding me a formal farewell, he went into the night to seek out his own tent.

Liber IX

Another perfect summer afternoon. I had left the cadets in the care of a riding-master who was taking them through the subtleties of leading cavalry into a charge. A wing of Gallic mercenaries doing drills of their own had volunteered to be the victims of these attacks, which were guaranteed harmless as the horsemen following my trainees were completely imaginary.

Having some time to myself, I had packed a picnic lunch and headed for the hills. My concussion had gradually faded away, leaving nothing behind other than a slight ringing noise in my ears – and even that I only really noticed when I focussed my attention on it. Two weeks of healthy eating had restored my energy levels to where they had been before that Samnite assassin on horseback had nearly succeeded in cutting off my head, and generally I was feeling considerably restored and rather cheerful about life. Even my ribs were healing fast.

For a start, no-one had tried to kill me for at least a fortnight. The army was retreating across northern Italy towards the city of Placentia, a fortress town established some two hundred years ago when the Romans took it from the Gauls who had taken it from the Etruscans. For the moment the Cimbri were letting us go, possibly with the intention of meeting the combined Roman armies of Catulus and Marius and demolishing both while Placentia - and the rest of Italy – changed ownership once more.

According to Madric (whom I had met just yesterday), the Cimbri had tired of the frustrating game of trying to nail down Catulus' army and were instead waiting for him to make his stand with Marius. Meanwhile the Cimbric horde was proceeding at its own speed towards what everyone was agreed would probably be the climactic battle between Rome and the barbarian invaders.

Until that final confrontation it was time to slow down and smell the roses, or in this case the fragrant Dianthus flowers blooming enthusiastically in the meadow behind the trees where Maphronius and I were encamped. It was a scene rather reminiscent of that where I had first met young Dextrianus, with the exception that the sausage I was currently enjoying was an excellent mix of spiced ham and ground mutton with just a hint of garlic. This, a sheep's milk cheese and a loaf of pan-baked bread constituted my lunch, while I had a carefully-wrapped box of date cakes saturated with wild honey that I planned on sharing later.

In front of me a grassy hillside sloped down to a paddock. Beyond that was a thatched farmhouse, the solid walls gleaming with fresh whitewash. A dirt road curved from the homestead around a stand of trees and out of sight. All that this peaceful rural scene lacked was the farmer and his sons at work in the field of ripe barley that lay golden in the sunshine behind the house. I could almost imagine that the farmer was sitting in the shade of the apple orchard, his waggon parked beside him while his wife emerged from the farmhouse with fresh bread rolls and water still cold from the well.

Instead, the paddock was long emptied of livestock and the doorway of the farmhouse gaped wide, missing the door which instead lay flat in the yard. Doubtless, as he prepared to flee, the farmer had taken the hinges off the door and buried them somewhere safe. Doors and even entire farmhouses can be rebuilt, but things like window frames and hinges need specialized work and there was no guarantee that the blacksmith would be alive when everyone returned.

One thing was certain – the barley would not be there to reward the farmer who had so carefully cultivated it through the spring. At present a line of auxiliary foragers was moving steadily across the field, mowing it flat as effectively as a plague of locusts. A line of laden waggons showed where the foragers had already reaped the bounty of other farms along this pleasant little woodland valley. There was after all a hungry army to feed, and no point in leaving nature's bounty for the approaching Cimbri.

This particular forage party numbered almost a three hundred men, and they had been busily looting the valley all morning. This was the last farm they would strip of anything remotely useable to either themselves or the enemy and then the laden convoy would slowly trundle back to where Catulus' army was setting up camp some five miles down the road.

I yawned, stretched, and went to see if Maphronius had finished eating the bucketful of grain I had commandeered from the waggons earlier, and casually patted the horse's muzzle as he gave me a friendly nudge of greeting. All the while I kept my eyes on the wooded slope across the valley. The Cimbri there were getting increasingly sloppy about remaining concealed, which suggested that they were not going to wait for the foragers to finish stripping this last field before they launched their attack.

In a way there was something poetic about it. The farmer was going to lose his crop to the Roman foragers, and the work of an entire season would be wasted. The Romans in turn were going to lose the results of a day's work to the Cimbri who intended to become the end beneficiaries of all that labour, and all for the minor effort of cutting down half a cohort of unwary auxilia.

Certainly there were guards. A squadron of cavalry, currently leading their horses behind the foragers to glean any spare grains of barley, and a half-century of spearmen divided equally on to the meadows of my hillside and that on the other side of the valley. My estimate was that they would last approximately thirty seconds against the barbarian tide about to wash over them. If Madric had been correct, there were just over a thousand men tucked away in the trees and behind the hillcrest.

My picnic had been laid out on a tablecloth of pure white linen upon which I had been sitting cross-legged. Now I stooped and shook out the last of the crumbs. Wrapping the cloth around one arm, I strolled to the side of the clearing away from the farmhouse and there carefully hooked the tablecloth around a low-hanging branch and tied it in place. I had brought along a length of string for the purpose since there was no sense in tearing such fine material. Returning to Maphronius, I pulled a small leather flask of cinnamon-spiced mead from my pack and settled down to await developments.

The barbarians came down the hillside in a silent rush. One moment the meadow was empty and the next there was a huge mob bounding downhill with no other sound than the thud of their boots on the soft grass. The spearmen of the guard made no attempt at resistance. Instead, as soon as the first Cimbric warrior emerged from the trees, the spearmen turned and hastily bolted for the shelter of the waggons, yelling as they ran for the foragers in the field to do likewise.

The line of waggons was between the farmhouse and the field, some twenty waggons in all, parked in a semi-circle. Already the waggoneers were pulling the waggons closer together and anchoring the line on that reassuringly solid farmhouse. The speed with which they operated demonstrated the assurance of long practice – getting ambushed while in the field was every forager's nightmare so every precaution was taken in case that nightmare came true.

Seeing that they were discovered the Cimbri broke their silence and the valley resounded to their yips, whoops and full-blown war-cries as they rushed down the hill toward their prey. Thoughtfully I took a swig of mead and watched as the last of the foragers tumbled to safety between the waggons, which now sprouted a hedge of spears to fend off the wave of Cimbri only a few paces behind.

What had been a peaceful rustic scene just two minutes before was now a lively little battlefield with the Cimbri packed twenty deep against the waggons and flowing around to where a stubborn Roman rearguard was forming in the gap which the waggons had not covered. Javelins flew, but otherwise the melee reminded me of nothing so much as the crush of housewives pushing to get into a market hall the moment it opened. The key difference was that the product this crowd was after was Roman blood, and it was clear that the foragers' makeshift defence was not going to last much longer. There were just too many Cimbri.

About now ... I turned to look up the valley and sure enough there a line of lancers was silently fanning out into attack formation, unit banners fluttering brightly in the breeze. They proceeded at a gentle walk, a trot, and then broke into a slow canter as the clarion note of a trumpet finally split the afternoon air.

The Cimbri in the front ranks fighting the foragers were too busy to pay much attention, but the reaction of the men at the rear was almost comical. A man would look over his shoulder, do a double take at the sight of steel-tipped death bearing down on him, and then turn to the comrade beside him and violently attempt to draw his attention to the peril.

Once it had dawned on at least most of the rear echelon that they were about to be cut down by a cavalry attack from behind there was little consensus on what to do about it. One group voted with their feet and abandoned their comrades as they sprinted for the trees. Others yanked fellow warriors into a crude shield wall which would in fact have had a good chance of standing off the cavalry had it formed in time.

However by then the cavalry were in full charge, and they hit the confused knots of men like Hades on horseback, knocking bodies aside and spearing them as they hit the ground. The foragers took heart from the weakening of the attack in front of them and launched a counter-attack of their own and even as the cavalry broke off from slaughtering the Cimbri gathered around the waggons, the standards of half a legion of infantry appeared at the top of the valley.

That was enough to break the Cimbric morale. Now none of the attackers had any ambition other than to gain the shelter of the trees – a somewhat difficult feat as the cavalry had broken away from the waggons to chase down the first men who had left the fight. Now the same horsemen closed ranks and charged downhill again. It was slaughter, plain and simple.

No-one had been paying much attention to the hillside on my side of the valley because the paddock was something of a barrier to an easy escape. Now fifty or so desperate men decided to try it, scrambling over the wooden fences and running more or less directly at me. The Roman cavalry were too busy with their bloody work to pay much attention.

The warriors were getting closer now, mouths open as they gasped for air, shields and swords long discarded in their flight. Maphronius would appear as a gods-sent escape for the first man to see my horse, so I was stepping over to loose his reins when I was nearly bowled over by a rush of horsemen galloping through the clearing. There were only two dozen or so riders, though my world was a brief chaos of noise and colour as they hurtled past and directly into the ranks of despairing Cimbri on the hillside.

Some men turned to run downhill once more, a few formed defensive clusters, and some simply sank to their knees in surrender. Whatever the choice, the result was the same – within a minute the warriors on my side of the valley were bloody bundles lying dead in the grass. Looking past the farmhouse I could see the same result on the other hillside, with bodies lying heaped one upon the other and none of them Roman. The ambushers had been wiped out almost to a man.

Dispassionately I surveyed the jumbled bodies. The returning farmers, I knew, would bury them in the field and the Cimbri would pay for ruining this year's harvest by fertilizing the next. To me personally the idea was enough to put one off barley for a while, but then, no-one objects to crops fertilized with manure, do they? Certainly I had seen enough Roman soldiers killed by the Cimbri for the sight of the bodies strewn before me to rouse no emotion beyond mild satisfaction. Had they won, the Cimbri would not have left one of the foragers alive either.

Taking another swig of mead, I turned thoughtfully to retrieve the tablecloth with which I had signalled the lancers to prepare their charge. This brought into view a man who was dressed in shiny armour but helmetless so that his blond hair clashed with a red, sunburned face. He was smiling with such warmth that one hardly noticed that the smile came nowhere near his hard blue eyes.

'Cornelius Sulla!' I exclaimed happily, then corrected this to a formal 'Sir!' and was about to salute when Sulla bounded across the clearing and took me in a bear hug.

'Lucius, Lucius! The idea was for you to spend a quiet few weeks with the army of Catulus, not to go about almost getting yourself killed every few days. You really must ...'. There was a pause, and then Sulla gently let go of me. 'Er ... how are the ribs?'

'All the better for seeing you, Sir. I've got honeyed date cakes in my saddlebags if you'd care for a quick bite ? I can update you on developments while your men clear up down there'

Sulla looked down into the valley, where the reapers were straggling out to resume work on the barley field, and the cavalry were methodically looting the corpses on the hillside and then dragging the bodies into loose piles. Already crows were starting to circle overhead. How did they always know?

'So you'll remember to tell Catulus that you decided to push ahead and join up with his army earlier than planned? And you came upon the Cimbri attacking the forage party completely by accident?'

'It was just another example of the Gods favouring Rome', Sulla assured me solemnly. 'Why don't you want the credit for setting this one up?'

'Because I don't want the Cimbri to know that we discovered that they were planning an attack on the foragers. Word will get back to them and they'll start looking for a spy in their ranks. Catulus is determined to believe that the spy in his camp was his orderly – now executed. He hates the thought that any of the young aristocrats in his care might be involved in betraying Rome to the enemy. But one of them is, and this ambush is further proof. Someone told the Cimbri where our forage party would be working and they set out to kill the foragers.'

'And then someone told you what the Cimbri were planning so you messaged me to hurry up and 'stumble upon' their attack. It had to seem accidental so that the spy in Catulus camp does not tell the Cimbri that they have a spy in their camp.' Unlike Petraeus, Sulla had no trouble keeping up with the complexities of the shadow war.

'All of the trainees but Lafranius knew where this foraging party was headed – because Catulus happily told them in yesterday's briefing. Lafranius wasn't there because he has been down with a nasty stomach bug and is confined to his tent with a bedpan. I had some-one watching the tent and it's reasonably certain that no information came in or out.'

'You slipped Lafranius an emetic, just to rule him out of your investigation?'

'There were other ways of ruling him out, but this idea appealed to me. He recently beat up Porcellinus, and I'm rather fond of that young man - though I have to admit that the lad will never be a warrior.'

'So. Antonius, Porcellinus, Dextrianus or Domitius Ahenobarbus – which is the spy?'

'Not Antonius. There's two dozen men who will swear that Antonius was gambling in the *canaba* at the time that young Minatius was murdered. One of the witnesses was a tavern-keeper who stuck to that story even under torture. Talking of which, I'm sorry about Satula.'

'Why? She was just a whore.'

'A good spy, though. She liked you.'

'Good spies don't end their careers with a bread-knife in the stomach. She should have been more careful.'

'If it had been Bassianus, Gratidus, or even myself she would have taken more precautions. Who was to know that the tavern-keeper's wife suddenly decided that she loved her husband after all? I swear I'll never understand how married life operates.'

Sulla grinned. 'Keep your relationships with the opposite sex on a purely financial basis, and you'll never have to figure it out. On the bright side, you'll be meeting your boyfriend Marius and his little priestess again soon. He and Momina are two days behind me with their army, so this whole thing ...', with a sweep of his arm Sulla encompassed the valley, North Italy, the barbarian horde and the fate of Italy. 'This whole thing is going to be over soon. One way or the other.'

As the sun set I was back in camp, waiting for the trainees who had been instructed to report to me before dinner for a quick debrief on their cavalry exercises of the afternoon. As it happened, only Porcellinus turned up. I looked at him with weary cynicism.

'Where are the others?'

Porcellinus shrugged. 'Delayed. They said to tell you that they'll be with you shortly, apart from Lafranius, who is still not well enough to be away from the latrines for long.'

I nodded, and gestured to the back of my tent.

'Crawl under there – and go to the kitchen commissariat. They will be checking food supplies and working out what we have plenty of that we can trade with Sulla's army in exchange for what we are lacking. Get over there immediately, and make yourself seen. Learn about supply logistics while you are at it.'

Porcellinus looked at me blankly, but I wasn't going to explain. Instead I instructed him, 'You have not been to this tent this evening. Trust me, the guard outside will have no memory of your being here - so forget that you were here at all. You were told earlier this afternoon not to attend the cavalry debrief, but to go to the stores instead. Now go - and don't be seen going!'

A few minutes later, a small delegation marched into the tent of Catulus. The commander was at his field table working on a scroll, and looked up with some surprise. 'You seem very serious, gentlemen.'

'Serious? We are disgusted.' said Domitius Ahenobarbus. Beside him, a rather pale-looking Lafranius nodded and Antonius echoed firmly, 'Disgusted'.

Catulus sighed and put aside his stylus. 'What's going on?'

'We have noticed that Panderius has been favouring Porcellinus over the other trainees. It has got so

181

unashamed that it's hard to ignore the fact that there's a romantic relationship between them. Then this evening ….'

Domitius cut in across Lafranius' little speech. 'This evening, Panderius told us that our cavalry debrief was cancelled for everybody but Porcellinus, who needed 'special instruction'. Well, we were curious as to what form this special instruction was going to take, so I will confess that we followed him to Panderius' tent.'

'And …?'

'From the sounds that emerged from the tent, it was clear that fornication is happening within. We can all three testify to that.'

Domitius stepped forward to stand over Catulus on his camp stool. 'Sir, I must protest about this in the strongest possible terms. Some men have younger lovers, it is true. But for the morals of one of our fellow cadets to be corrupted in this way … it is un-speakable. Panderius is totally unsuited to be an instructor and with respect Sir, you should have known this. Once a brothel-keeper, always a brothel keeper, but I and my fellow cadets will not stand idle while one of our number is the target for his unnatural lusts.'

'Where is Scipio Dextrianus? Is he with you on this?'

'Most certainly. He is even now outside the tent where this horrible copulation is taking place and remains there as witness to the ongoing debauching of one of your trainees. You must come at once, Sir.'

'And if I arrive and find that the two are sitting quietly studying cavalry tactics?'

'If you hurry, we can catch them in the act.

Otherwise, well, the four of us can testify to what we have heard, no matter how firmly Panderius and his lover attempt to deny it.'

Catulus frowned. 'Very well, let us proceed.'

It took careful timing, but Petraeus, the commander of the second legion, a junior centurion and I all turned up just as Catulus and the trainees prepared to storm my tent. Standing in the middle of the group, I waited until Catulus was about to grasp the door flap before I spoke up.

'Commander! We were just going to have a drink. Sulla gave me a rather good wine from the Veneto and my friends and I were going to sample a beaker or two. Would you care to join us? Wait, are those the cadets? Gentlemen, didn't you get my message? You are supposed to be at the commissariat observing the redistribution of supplies.'

Carefully contrived astonishment crept into my voice. 'What's the matter? You all look as though you have seen a ghost.'

Catulus gave Domitius a long, steady look. 'Explain.'

'I … I … he.'

Turning to me, Catulus asked tightly. 'Where is Marcellus Porcellinus?'

'I don't know. I imagine he is at the stores, which is where the others are supposed to be right now. What in Hades is going on?'

'Have you and Porcellinus been in that tent this evening?'

'I can't say about Porcellinus, but I've not been in my tent for an hour or so. I was at the stores and sent a messenger to tell the trainees to report there, and then I went to see Petraeus. Is Porcellinus missing?'

Catulus turned to the guard on my tent, who had been standing like a statue the whole time. 'Is this correct?'

Doubtless thinking of the substantial bribe he had been given, and of the fact that he didn't like Domitius at all, the guard replied stiffly, 'It is as the tribune says, Sir.'

'Why, you …!' began Domitius, but Catulus shut him up with a curt gesture before turning back to the guard.

'Listen to me carefully – because I assure you that your life depends on it. Have you ever heard the sounds of copulation coming from this tent, this evening or any other time?'

The guard had not been briefed on this bit and his astonishment and denial were transparently unfaked. 'Eh? No. Not ever.'

Petraeus was looking from one face to another with absolute bewilderment. 'What's going on, Sir?'

'*Primus Pilus*! Please do me the favour of going to the commissariat and locating Marcellus Porcellinus. Then bring him back to my tent, if you would be so kind. Cadets, come with me. You too, Panderius. I am afraid your drink with your friends has to be postponed.'

As we straggled silently behind Catulus, I could see that the commander was putting together the pieces of the student plot to get rid of me. First, they would arrange that Porcellinus arrived for lessons ahead of the others. Later the others would claim that Porcellinus had been told to come alone in the first place. Then the cadets would storm over and report to Catulus that I was taking indecent advantage of the most vulnerable member of their group. Catulus would hurry to my tent where he would catch Porcellinus and I alone together.

True, the pair of us would be decently dressed and discussing horsemanship but there would be four witnesses prepared to swear blind that I had been practising a different kind of horsemanship a few minutes previously. Then it would be the word of a junior aristocrat and a brothel-owner against the word of the scions of some of the greatest families in Rome. Even if he doubted their story, Catulus would have no choice but to discharge me.

Except I had not been in my tent, Porcellinus was down at the stores, and both of us had witnesses to that effect. My fortunate change of plans had ruined the entire conspiracy and my motive for changing the evening's lesson – that I might have a drink with friends - was all the more credible in that it reflected somewhat badly on me.

This was a teachable moment I reflected, as Catulus began to tear into the cadets with ever mounting incredulity and fury at their impudence. Someone – probably me – should have explained to the class that before committing to a course of action one should do basic checks. Such as ensuring that the person one was accusing was actually present at the scene of the crime. Of course, the students had seen Porcellinus enter my tent from the front and had not seen him immediately exit from the back. Therefore they had assumed that Porcellinus had remained in the tent, and because he was there they had further assumed that I was still present also. Ah, assumptions, gentlemen – so many disasters begin with a false assumption.

Things got even worse for the trainees when Petraeus turned up with Porcellinus and the *optio* in charge of the stores. That rather bewildered *optio* confirmed that Porcellinus had been counting cured legs of ham in front of half-a-dozen witnesses at the precise time that he was allegedly getting rogered in my tent.

That rather put the lid on it. Having been on the receiving end of a Catulan tongue-lashing, I almost felt sorry for the little group as Catulus laid into them methodically, viciously and without mercy. Just to add to the fun about five minutes in, young Lafranius' bowel control gave out and he had to make an undignified dash for the commander's privy.

As the intended victim of the trainees' plot, it was my job to give a prize-winning show of incredulity, anger and astonishment as the entire iniquitous scheme was slowly unravelled before me. Any impression that my performance would have warmed the heart of the most accomplished Thespian was promptly demolished once the thoroughly-chastised students had been contemptuously dismissed and Catulus helped himself to a beaker of the Veneto wine that I had promised to Petraeus and his friends.

'So', asked Catulus, 'how did you arrange that?'

'Sir?'

'The students plan this elaborately-contrived accusation, which falls as disastrously flat on its face as can possibly happen. All because you just happened coincidentally to change your plans at the last moment, and change them in a manner which left no possible doubt of your innocence. With anyone else, I would believe it. With you, my dear Lucius, not a chance - not the slimmest, faintest shadow of a chance. So I ask you again, how did you arrange it?'

'Um ...'.

'You do know that if I had sent the students back home in disgrace and once the reasons for their dismissal became public, no other army commander would want them either? And with no military background, combined with a reputation for collusion in false accusations, these men would struggle in any elections, even with their powerful families helping them. This would lead to some very disappointed and angry fathers when the sons got home – and a Roman father has the power of life and death over his sons. No wonder those young men were terrified - until you stepped in.'

'I thought the situation was still salvageable, Sir.'

'So thanks to your intervention the trainees still have their reputations and a career. They have to thank your persuasion for saving them by getting me to allow them to stay in the camp. And for a Roman aristocrat the debt of gratitude is the one debt that they must always repay. So I let those young men off the hook at your request and you now have the cadets locked in your grasp for as long as you want them. Well played. And for the last time – how did you do it?'

'Well, I er ... may have gotten wind of their intentions. Forewarned, forearmed ... you know the expression.'

'Lucius, remember how recently I explained the role and responsibilities of the Tribune in charge of Funny Business? Well, this is about as funny as business gets. So if you don't want to be in charge of a firewood-gathering detail right in front of the Cimbric army's line of march every day for the next fortnight, you had better give me some details.'

'Well, as an intelligence officer, old habits die hard. So when there's a troublesome group that one needs to deal with, one applies the standard solution.'

'Which is?'

'Plant a spy. I've been getting inside information on those trainees since the second day I arrived.'

Catulus sipped his wine and looked at me with a mixture of fascination and disgust.

'Looking at their alibis and motivation for the murder, it was clear that young Antonius had both the most solid alibi and the greatest vulnerability to blackmail. He is also desperately short of cash, so when I promised him a bribe and threatened him with blackmail, he rolled right over. With a carrot, a stick and a ready source of information, I already knew what the trainees were planning yesterday evening, and well ... they walked right into it.'

Liber X

'So let's see these ambassadors', Sulla muttered to Catulus as the proconsul's lictors cleared our way through the ranks of curious soldiery who had gathered along the via Praetoria.

Marius had insisted that the meeting with the Cimbric ambassadors take place outside, rather than within his tent, so that everyone in his army could witness his meeting with the enemy's embassy. That way there would be no morale-sapping rumours of secret deals or false claims of what had been discussed. It was populism in a good way, and the sort of thing at which the shrewd Marius excelled.

Also, perhaps with the disastrous battle at Arausio in mind, Marius had held off negotiating until his fellow commander was present for the talks. At Arausio, the barbarians had been negotiating in the camp of one consul - Mallius – when the other consul – Caepio - had attacked the Germanic army, perhaps out of pique that the enemy had chosen not to negotiate with him. Therefore, little as Marius probably wanted Catulus to be there, it was best that on this occasion Rome pre-sented a united front. Accordingly messengers had been sent asking Catulus to please present himself at the Marian camp as soon as was humanly possible.

Naturally Sulla was not going to miss the fun, and he invited me to come along also. Catulus agreed to my being there, not least because he was aware that Marius could hardly stand the sight of Sulla, and thanks to our past history, the consul came close to apoplexy whenever he saw me. On such happy malice was the relationship between our two generals founded, and I was quite prepared to go along with it if it meant that I got a front-row seat at the making of history. Naturally, as members of Rome's top aristocratic families, the cadets joined our group - uninvited but simply assuming their natural right to be there.

There were six of the Cimbri, who stood in a bored-looking group disdainful of the watching Roman soldiers and scorning the camp chairs placed for them to sit upon while they were waiting. To a man they were tall, blond and clad in magnificent armour, and certainly I was not alone in observing that the embossed silver cuirass sported by one of the group had clearly been looted from the corpse of a Roman officer in some previous battle. It was also pretty sure that this choice of armour by the Cimbric delegate was not accidental. Just by silently standing there the warrior proclaimed that the Cimbri had repeatedly beaten Rome in the past and could do so again.

'Not this time, sonny boy', muttered Sulla, and I guessed that he had seen the cuirass and read from it the same message as I had.

'Magnificent horses', observed Dextrianus from behind me. Indeed, even to my less than expert eye it was clear that these beasts were equine aristocrats – tall, graceful and with powerful muscles rippling across their haunches as they shifted their hooves, uneasy at the close confines of the Roman camp.

Once Catulus' lictors had completed the protocols, Marius emerged from his tent and the two commanders embraced in a stiff gesture of fraternity which was purely for the benefit of the audience. After a swift glance which encompassed Sulla and me, Marius ignored us completely and brushed by to effusively greet our cadets. Very much to the chagrin of the bully Lafranius, Marius spent several minutes talking to and making much of young Porcellinus, whose relative Claudius Marcellus was one of Marius' senior commanders.

During all these greetings, the Cimbri were ignored as pointedly as Sulla and I had been – the message being that Marius considered relationships among his own as being far more important than the need to be polite to his enemies. You would think that Marius had not seen the cadets for years, whereas in fact he had invited them to dinner at his tent just a week ago when our two armies had finally joined up just north of Placentia. Thanks to Antonius I knew that the tricky subject of the murder of Minatius had not been discussed at the dinner, and by unspoken mutual agreement none of the parties concerned had mentioned me at all.

Again, the Cimbri refused the offer of chairs, and Marius was certainly not going to sit and allow the Cimbri to tower above him even more than they did already. So this meeting would be conducted standing. Given the extent of their intelligence network, it was certain that the Cimbri knew that Marius suffered badly from varicose veins. Making him stand for the duration of the meeting would cause the Roman commander some mild discomfort to repay him for his impoliteness in ignoring the Cimbric delegation until now.

As the meeting shuffled into order, I noted with delight that the Cimbric interpreter was none other than the fat little man whom I had last seen being hauled by ropes up the walls of the fort at Sarni. Oh my. So I knew now that the interpreter's character of a somewhat ridiculous windbag was actually a persona adopted by one of Metus' senior agents. Once I came to think of it, there was no way that the son of the Cimbric leader would trust the ambassadors to give an unbiased account of their meeting with the Romans so the interpreter was there as much to observe as to translate.

The interpreter started the meeting with a long account of the battles that Rome had fought with the Cimbri, starting twelve years ago when the Consul Papirus Carbo had perished along with his army when he treacherously tried to ambush the Cimbri along the banks of the Danube. Then there was the defeat of Junius Silanus in Gaul, and the later battle of Burdigala when another Roman Consul, Cassius Ravalia, had lost his life. Then of course, there was a lengthy account of the Battle at Arausio (where Lucius Panderius had very nearly also lost his life, and with that 'nearly' he had been considerably luckier than the 80,000 Roman soldiers who had died that day).

It was a depressing tale for any Roman to listen to, which of course was why the Cimbric delegation had chosen to lead off with it. As the interpreter ploughed on with his story of one Roman defeat after another Marius yawned with feigned boredom and unashamedly scratched his buttocks. Catulus stood by calmly and spent the time examining his elegantly manicured fingernails.

When the interpreter appeared to be winding down, Marius interrupted, observing casually, 'Yet for all your alleged prowess at war, it seems to me that the warrior Cimbri have been rather shy of fighting another battle recently. Could it be that they are tired of war? Did their best and bravest die in the battles you have just described at such length? Perhaps it is because our first clash was over a decade ago and the Cimbri who knew how to fight are, dare I say it - becoming elderly? After all, it is now, what, some twenty years since your people started your migration from the shores of the North Sea?'

The translation of these questions led to an impassioned diatribe from one of the ambassadors, a fellow whom the Romans called Claodicus. I knew of the man, as I knew of all of the Cimbric leaders as part of my job. I already knew, as Claodicus was currently reminding Marius through his interpreter, that the Cimbric leader had been present at Arausio where the enemy had certainly proved that their fighting skills had not diminished with time.

Beside me Sulla murmured softly, 'Our translator is editing as he goes along. Tactful. Claodicus actually started his little speech by calling Marius the ulcerated scab on a diseased donkey's testicles.' I recalled what Claodicus probably knew - that Sulla and several of the other Romans present had learned reasonably good German over the years, so doubtless word of the insult would reach Marius eventually.

'It is not as if the Cimbri have not the will to fight, it is more that we have not been able to get you Romans to stop running and instead face us in battle', declaimed the interpreter. He made an eloquent gesture towards Catulus who grinned back at him unashamedly.

'If you Romans were any good at fighting, you would stand and fight us!' declared Claodicus.

'If you Cimbri were any good at warfare you would have been able to make us', retorted Catulus in reply, drawing a chuckle from the assembled soldiery. (Marius later stole that line for himself in a later war.)

The amusement of Marius' soldiers was genuine, and I knew that the men in Marius' army had considerable sympathy for Catulus. They of all people knew how hard it was to manage a fighting retreat in the face of the enemy without taking substantial casualties, and if there is one quality that veteran soldiers really appreciate in a general it is frugality with the lives of the soldiers under his command.

Naturally this did not stop the Marian army from ribbing Catulus' men as 'the best long-distance sprinters since Pheidippides' [the famous runner who completed the first Marathon], and Catulus' men were now actually eager to stand and fight. It was quite a different army from that which had edged so reluctantly on to the field at Tridentum, and a testament to the relentless training and drills the centurions had subjected them to in three weeks that had followed.

My attention had drifted away from the rather pointless back-and-forth between Marius and the

Cimbri until it was jerked back by Sulla digging an ungentle elbow into my ribs. The negotiations were getting serious.

'We stand on land which the Celtic people took from the Etruscans as a prize in war. So has it always been. The victors make their claim and the defeated accede to the terms of their conquerors. We, the Cimbri, have defeated Rome not once but time and time again.'

'Yet we are merciful – we, the conquerors leave to you Romans your Latium, your conquests in Africa and Greece, and even the south of Italy. Yet this land here in the North, which the Celts took from the Etruscans and which we have taken from you – this is now our land by right of conquest.'

'Liguria, Transpadane Gaul, Cispadane Gaul, Venetia and Istria are now no more. They are now the Cimbric Fields. Our land, now and forever. All that you need do is acknowledge this and there will be peace between our peoples. No more Roman soldiers need die needlessly at our hands as they have done time and again already. You, now, have the choice. Make a lasting peace that will allow these men here to return home safe to their families, or force them to die pointlessly on the battlefield as so many of their friends and relatives have done already.'

'We offer peace, not in exchange for lands we wish you to give us but for lands which we have taken already, lands which are ours by right of conquest, and lands which we all know you cannot take from us anyway. It is time, Romans, for you to accept reality. Do that and tonight we can feast together and tomorrow these men here listening can prepare to return to their homes.'

Clearly, not only Marius understood the uses of popular appeal. I knew, as did Catulus and Marius, that the Cimbri had no intention of stopping until their pillaging armies had reached the toe of Italy. However, the men of the Roman army did not know that and the Cimbric embassy was dangling the prospect of an amicable end to the war in front of their noses. When Marius – as he must – snatched that prospect away, the Cimbri knew that his men would resent him for it and fight less hard. I awaited Marius' reply with interest, for whilst I despised the man from forehead to toenails, he was genuinely good at this stuff.

Marius seemed thoughtful as he replied. 'There is truth in what you say. Almost every man in this army has lost friends or relatives at your hands. Your warriors have killed them. Tell me, you Cimbri, what do you call a man who leaves the deaths of friends and relatives unavenged? Do you even call him a man at all? This here is an army of men, and not just any men, but men of Rome and Italy. We don't give up Italian land because some barbarian tells us to, and especially not when we, as men, have a score to settle with those barbarians.'

'You know where we are, you know that by next week we shall be north of Mediolanum. By then half of those lands you so arrogantly claim will be - as they always should be and will always remain – a part of Italy.'

Marius paused to milk the maximum effect from the

murmur of approval which arose from the soldiers on the walls then continued, 'You claim we Romans won't fight, yet here we are, and there you are. We are now advancing and you are now retreating.'

One of the Cimbri started to say something but the interpreter was talking even before the man had finished. 'We fight when and as we want. Just as you Romans have united your armies, so we await the arrival of our brothers the Atrebates, in order that they might share the honour of your final defeat.' Two of the Cimbric delegation exchanged swift glances which told me firstly, that these men understood Latin, and secondly that the interpreter's words were no part of whatever sentence he had been translating.

Marius pretended not to understand. 'Your brothers? But you have no brothers.' As an afterthought he murmured, 'Nor mothers either'. Then enlightenment appeared to dawn. 'Oh, do you mean the Atrebates?'

The Cimbri did not reply, but merely glared.

Marius spread his hands placatingly. 'Why did you not say so? Come, we have made our peace with the Atrebates already, and stand here more than prepared to make the same peace with you - whether you wish for it or not.'

There were chuckles, shouts and even hoots of derision from the assembled Roman soldiery. Whether or not the Cimbri understood what Marius meant, the rest of his audience clearly grasped his meaning. One of the younger members of the Cimbric delegation bypassed the interpreter altogether and asked in accented Latin, 'Land? You gave up land to them?'

Marius looked as smug as the cat that got the cream. 'They have all the land they need.' A roar of laughter from the soldiers greeted this reply.

So it was true then. Madric had told me that many of the Cimbri were in outright denial about the defeat of the Atrebates at the Battle of Six Waters. Certainly the Atrebates had all the land they needed - for a corpse needs only the grave in which it is buried.

Yet many of the Cimbri simply refused to believe that it was so. They had been invincible for so long and had beaten the Romans so often that it seemed impossible that over a third of their combined army could have suddenly been wiped out by Roman arms. These Cimbri – mostly the younger warriors – believed that the story of a massive Roman victory at the Six Waters was a clever propaganda effort by the Romans aimed at lowering their morale.

Many of the survivors of that battle who had made their way to the Cimbric army had been roughly handled or even killed by Cimbri who accused them of being Roman agents. Madric himself got around the problem by pretending that he had not been at the battle. He had disingenuously claimed that he had been home visiting family and had then decided to enlist with the Cimbri instead of returning to the Atrebates, and so he had no idea of what had or had not happened to his former employers.

Sulla was frowning thoughtfully, and indeed my own brow was furrowed. We were both probably working on the same problem – why had the interpreter brought up the Atrebates on his own account without waiting for the official delegation? My own conclusion was that Metus, as the Cimbric spymaster, was well aware that the defeat at Six Waters had actually happened, and he wanted the fact to be acknowledged and out in the open within his army. Therefore he had instructed his agent – the interpreter – to make sure that the Atrebates were mentioned, and in a context where the reaction of the Roman audience would make it plain that whatever had happened to that tribe the Romans evidently no longer considered them a threat.

One of the older Cimbric delegates shrugged and laconically observed, 'Atrebates or no Atrebates. The Cimbri still outnumber your combined army three to one.'

'And yet we advance and you retreat.'

'You advance to your doom.'

'Indeed. We shall probably all perish from frostbite if you retreat far enough north.'

'Stop it!' protested one of the younger members of the delegation. 'We can see what you Romans are doing. You wish to provoke us into fighting before the Atrebates join us, a provocation that so many of our people have already fallen for. You Romans are scum. Instead of fighting like honourable men you try to undermine us with lies and lying falsehoods. You fight like women.'

Marius chuckled. 'Would that be like the Celtiberian women who beat you out of Spain? We understand that their menfolk lay abed while the women fought and sent you packing.'

'No, you are less than Roman women, who shall all

soon become whores grateful to be servicing true warriors instead of their degenerate menfolk.'

At this point Catulus yawned, covering his mouth with an elegant hand. 'Come now', he drawled. 'If our discussion has come to this, there are some children belonging to the camp's cleaning women who can take up the conversation. I believe that they can muster a piquant turn of phrase. But if the adult part of the conversation is done, then I have more important things to do than listen to childish insults.'

The older Cimbric delegate rapped out a single sentence and the interpreter drew himself up to deliver it.

'So do the Roman commanders reject the peace which the Cimbri have offered and insist on their men dying on the battlefield?'

Marius replied in measured tones. 'The Romans – and the Italians – say that you can take your peace and ram it up your backsides with a tent pole.'

'Oh, I say', muttered Catulus in a pained voice and clarified the Roman response to the delegation. 'What my esteemed fellow commander has so eloquently explained is that - we'll fight.'

And that was that for the day.

Dinner that night was in honour of a special guest, so I had prepared soft-boiled quail eggs in a pine kernel sauce followed by medallions of roast wild boar with broad beans and chervil root, with a dessert of honeyed cream cheese and figs. Not bad overall for a soldier on campaign, I reckoned, especially as in order to prepare the meal I'd had to commandeer one of the ovens in the field kitchen for the afternoon.

Not unexpectedly, the kitchen staff had raised not a peep of objection – not once they were informed that the dinner was for the delectation of the famous 'Martha', as the army called that prophetess whose predictions had helped Marius to win his victories. I had been a bit concerned that Marius might be keeping the little priestess on a tight rein, and she would therefore be unable to visit me as she had proposed. As it turned out that was not the case – Momina had simply announced that she was going out for dinner and had then casually strolled out of Marius' camp, detouring to the stores where she dug up the vintage urn of Rhaetic wine which we now shared.

'Really, this wine deserves better than to be swigged from a leather cup while I'm sitting on a camp stool', I remarked. 'It deserves its high reputation – sweet, yet not cloying, light on the palate, but still rich in flavour. What was it doing in legion stores?'

Momina's cheeks dimpled in a grin. 'It's for the entertainment of visiting dignitaries. I decided that you count as one.'

'And what did our consular dickhead Marius have to say about that?'

Momina shrugged her little shoulders carelessly. 'Marius is really not sure what to do about me. So he will pretend it did not happen. Whenever I do something that he doesn't like, he either pretends not to know I did it or he makes out that I did it with his permission, or even on his instructions. His guards do keep a close eye on me, however.'

Those would be the guards who had accompanied Momina on her arrival, and whom she had solemnly thanked for escorting her. Then she had dismissed them for the evening and they had trotted off like well-trained hounds.

'Marius' guards, or your guards?'

'Well, I did help them out on a few occasions. Perhaps we should say 'our guards' since I take care that their loyalty to me never conflicts with their loyalty to Marius. Anyway, Marius is tiptoeing around me more carefully than usual since I briefed him yesterday on how his conversation with the Cimbric delegation would go. The Cimbri stuck to their script almost verbatim, the little dears, and I had anticipated a bit of improvisation by that interpreter. You do know that the funny little fellow is one of Metus' top agents?'

'I figured it out. So Madric told you what to tell Marius?'

'Mostly, yes. The rest was common sense. Poor Madric spends a lot of time listening at tent-flaps, and the rest of his time riding out to tell us about it. Thanks for that deer by the way.'

Madric had become the unofficial supply commissariat for his little group of Gallic warriors. They ate a lot better than their Cimbric fellow soldiers because Madric had proven himself to be a highly capable hunter. Because he so regularly rode back to camp with partridges, deer, rabbits and the occasional plundered sheep he was basically allowed to come and go as he pleased. Generally it pleased Madric to ride to meet his Roman spymasters and exchange information for his catch of the day - a catch that we supplied to him from camp stores to give to his grateful fellow warriors.

Madric's last hunt had allegedly yielded a deer, which in fact I had supplied to him at Momina's request. In response to her thanks I shrugged and replied, 'Given the value of his reports, our payment to Madric was cheap rather than deer.'

Dodging the grape that Momina hurled at me, I changed the subject. 'How do you like being the Jewish Martha rather than Momina the Greek?'

The priestess shrugged. 'I have had many names in my time.'

And what 'time' was that? I privately wondered.

'Time is more flexible than you imagine, Lucius. It isn't actually something that goes straight from past to future. It's sort of bendy and occasionally ties itself into knots. Really, I wouldn't wonder about it too much. You'll get a headache, trust me.'

'You are …'.

'… doing it again?'

'Yes, stop …'.

'Saying what you were about to say?'

'Yes, and telling me …'.

'What you were thinking?'

This time it was my turn to hurl a grape at Momina. She casually caught it in mid-air and popped it into her mouth. The trouble with that was that she was raising her hand to catch the grape even before I had touched it. Momina could drive a man to drink, so it was just as well that she had brought along a good vintage.

Scowling slightly, I buried my nose in my cup as the priestess went on. 'It was Marius who decided I should be Jewish, even before I suggested it. He thinks it gives me greater prestige with the soldiery. The Romans venerate the Greeks of old, but they don't think much of modern Greeks. They call us 'Graeculi' - lesser Greeks. Jews on the other hand they consider odd and eccentric but with a definite talent for regularly producing prophets. The fact that I'm nothing like a proper Jewish prophet doesn't trouble the soldiers because they've never met one. All they know is that I steer Marius in the right direction and so long as that happens they don't care about the rest.'

'Oh, and talking of steering people in the right direction, that reminds me. It's been really wonderful coming over and enjoying your cooking – the boar was fantastic – but that's not the reason for my visit. Since you are making puns, here's one for you. When you are out in five days' time with those students of yours, be a dear and watch for deer. It's important.'

'Why?'

Momina replied, 'You'll see, dear' or 'You'll see deer.' I'm still not sure which.

There was no time to ask because Momina was gathering her colourful two-part gown about her and preparing to depart.

'I have to leave, sorry Lucius. After his delegation to Marius was so unsatisfactory, the Cimbric king has decided to visit the Roman camp in person early tomorrow. I have to warn Marius so that he can prepare a suitable reception. It was a lovely dinner – please do invite me back again soon.'

I stood courteously and prepared to usher my guest from my tent, noting gratefully that she had decided to leave the rest of the wine with me.

'Before you go, I've one last question which may test your priestessy powers … .'

Momina grinned. 'Awww, you know that's not much of a test, Lucius. Who better than you to know who the spy is? And as for the murderer of that poor Italian boy – you knew who it was even before you left Sulla's camp. So stop being silly. And remember - watch for deer.'

Boiorix, king of the Cimbri,was an impressive sight. He had arrived unannounced, and was clearly surprised to find Marius and Catulus waiting for him at the gates of the Roman camp when he trotted up on his horse, accompanied only by a bodyguard and his son Metus.

Both Catulus and Marius sat on curule chairs, wearing not armour but Roman togas. Behind them stood Momina, wearing a purple robe and holding a spear wreathed with slender branches of oak. The men of Marius' army were in armour, lining the ramparts of the camp as they strained to listen to the parley between the leaders of the two opposing forces. I had elbowed my way to a central position at the gate and so had a perfect view, looking down upon the conference at back of Marius' head and Catulus' large and growing bald spot. Metus was looking up, and when our gazes locked for a moment he gave me a friendly grin.

Boiorix was older than I had expected, a man in his sixties but still very much fit and vigorous. He swung himself easily off his horse and strode to tower over Marius and Catulus in their chairs. The Cimbric king's armour was of gleaming silver and as he advanced on the Roman generals he took off a helmet shaped like the head of a snarling wolf. His bodyguards retained their tall helmets, each shaped like a different animal's head, so that it appeared that behind the king an impassive menagerie of fantastical animals sat on horseback, their lances pointed at the sky.

Marius indicated a comfortable-looking leather-backed chair that had been set up facing him, and after a glance at Metus, Boiorix settled himself into the offered seating. I knew what that glance signified. Boiorix had intended his arrival in person to discombobulate the Romans and force them to negotiate unprepared. Instead, the Romans were very clearly ready and waiting. The look which the king had given his son said more clearly than words, 'They knew we were coming. Find out who told them and do something about it.'

Mentally I decided that it was past time that Madric left the Cimbric army and rejoined the Romans. His job was done in any case, and it had become far too dangerous for him to remain.

Now that the three army leaders were comfortably seated in the morning sun, none of them seemed in a hurry to speak. Boiorix had a look of faint amusement on his face, though from where I stood it was impossible to see the expressions of either Catulus or Marius. It was Metus who broke the silence, stepping forward to say, 'Leaders of Rome, I present to you my father, King Boiorix of the Cimbric people, descendant of Tauranis, beloved of the gods, and victor at Arausio,Tridentum, and other places too numerous to list.'

In reply Marius offered a formal, suitably laconic greeting. 'Marius of Rome, and the men of the Roman and Italian armies greet you.' Though translation was evidently unnecessary it was Momina who did the honours, rendering Marius' words into apparently fluent German. Then, with a mischievous smile, she added something that made Boiorix sit bolt upright and look at her with startled astonishment. Marius turned in his chair and gave Momina a look of sour discouragement. She winked at him.

Boiorix lifted a hand and a rider of his bodyguard dismounted to join him. Removing a helmet that resembled a snake about to strike, the man introduced himself. 'I am Ietbatus. Henceforth I shall be the voice of the king.'

Marius acknowledged the translator with a casual wave of his hand. 'When I wish to be clear, my trans-lator, the Seer Martha shall speak for me and also for the Gods of Rome.'

Boiorix pushed out a lower lip and nodded in reply, all the while regarding the purple-clad seer with vague suspicion, as might a man who tries to recall where he has previously seen a half-remembered face. If Marius' intention had been to throw the Cimbric king off balance, it seemed that he had succeeded.

Boiorix looked at his interpreter and nodded. In response the man launched into what was obviously a prepared preliminary. 'I shall be brief. This is an informal meeting after all. Firstly, you Romans claim that you have destroyed the Atrebates in battle. Prove your claim or admit that you have lied.'

Marius shrugged. 'There is nothing I wish to say.'

'Then ...', the translator began, but Marius interrupted him by holding up a hand. 'I shall let these men speak for me.'

The gates behind Marius were opened and I heard the rattle of chains. I could not see what was happening right below me but there was a stir in the Cimbric bodyguard, and Boiorix pushed himself up from his chair. A murmur from the men lining the ramparts confirmed my suspicion that the king was seeing none other than the surviving leaders of the Atrebates. After their defeat at the battle of the Six Waters these men had attempted to flee eastward through Gaul. They had been captured by the Sequani tribe and handed to Marius.

'Ask these men whatever you wish', said Marius, still comfortably seated in his chair and clearly enjoying himself.

'Res ipsa loquitur', replied Boiorix impassively. And the matter did indeed speak for itself. I noted mentally that there was an impressive degree of linguistic ability being shown off below me, with Momina displaying an unexpected mastery of German and the Cimbric king showing that he had at least some grasp of Latin.

In German, Boiorix rapped out a brief query to the Atrebates and listened stone-faced to the reply. Once that was done, the king nodded to Marius who signalled for the captives to be taken away once more.

'Those men will not be harmed', Boiorix instructed Marius through his interpreter. 'If through the will of the Gods we do not crush you completely on the battlefield, the fate of those men will determine future negotiations. And should you be crushed completely, as you shall be, how you treat those men shall determine your fate if you are captured.'

'I take no orders from you', replied Marius evenly. 'It is the fate of captured enemy leaders to be strangled on the Capitoline Hill once the general who has conquered them has celebrated his triumph. Should you not wish to join them, I suggest that you arrange to die on the battlefield.'

'You rejected my delegation which offered you peace. Is it still your determination to destroy yourself and Rome's last army?'

'It is our determination to destroy your army in battle, if that is what you mean.'

Boiorix smiled, as though Marius had walked into a trap he had prepared. 'Then name a place and there our armies shall meet.'

'At the Raudine Fields.'

I wish I could have seen Marius' face at that moment, for it was not he who had spoken but Momina and her voice carried clearly to the soldiers on the ramparts as she continued, 'There you shall meet, and there the Cimbric horde will be destroyed.'

An excited babble broke out among the soldiers, and Boiorix nodded thoughtfully. 'The place beside that Vercellae which is about two days north of Mediolanum? A good choice. It is a wide plain where we can fight like men without cowering behind hills or alongside rivers.'

Boiorix did not look at Catulus as he spoke but it was clear at whom the barb was aimed.

Marius was squirming in his chair but Momina had put him on the spot. He could not publicly contradict his infallible priestess, especially not in front of his soldiers, but clearly that was not the battlefield he would have chosen. I guessed there would be hell to pay when Marius and Momina next met in private.

The Cimbri on the other hand were clearly satisfied. Having got what he wanted, Boiorix stood and gave Marius and Catulus a stiff nod. 'Morning, five days hence? Even if your army is reluctant and fearful, you should be able to get there by then. Then we shall meet again - for the last time.'

Marius could only nod. 'So be it.'

Liber XI

On a misty July morning six riders walked their horses cautiously across the broad expanse of the Raudine plain. The horsemen were myself and the cadets taking an early opportunity to scout the battlefield. We were riding cautiously because the Cimbri had doubtless been there already and we did not want to meet any of them coming back for a second look.

While the ground beneath our horses was dry and dusty, mist had spilled from the river to lie across the entire plain. Scipio examined the droplets forming on his armour and complained, 'It's Quintilis [July] Jupiter bless the month, so why is it so accursed clammy? We might as well be riding through the mists of the Underworld.'

'Well, that's why the village back there is called Vercellae', said Porcellinus. 'You have to expect things to be a bit damp.'

Vercellae is a generic name for where reed beds meet a river, and particularly for the settlements of workers who use the reeds to make rush matting and other items. We had ridden past such a hastily abandoned hamlet on our way in, although with my current interest being physical geography rather than etymology I had not stopped to enquire the name of the place.

'It's an even worse site for a battlefield than Tridentum', remarked Lafranius as he twisted in his saddle to look around. 'We'll be forming up on that slope, yes?'

'Yup', I nodded.

'Well, look at it – the slope goes back, gets steeper and eventually becomes a series of rocky ridges. Our army will have to enter the battlefield from the side, and then wheel left to face the plain. At least at Tridentum we had a way out, narrow as it was. Here, the army will be trapped between those bluffs and the Cimbri on the plain. There's no way out, no way at all.'

'Indeed.' I agreed gently. 'And if Rome loses this battle, even assuming there was a away out, where were you thinking of going?'

There was a pause as the students digested this. To ensure the point was not lost I pressed it further. 'There will be three Roman armies here the day after tomorrow. The army of Marius, the army of Catulus, and the much smaller force commanded by Sulla. Combined, these 50,000 men represent Rome's entire military might. If we lose this battle, we lose our armies, we lose Italy and we lose Rome. There will be nowhere to run. So we make our stand here on the Raudine Plain, and the sight of the ridges behind us will make the situation as clear to the average legionary as it now is to Lafranius. Here we fight and here we win or die. There are no other options.'

'So you don't think their king was serious when he claimed that the Cimbri would settle for north Italy? Think about it. After all, the Cimbri had Rome at their mercy before at Arausio, and they went to Spain instead of pillaging their way down the Italian peninsula. Maybe north Italy is all they want – a homeland for themselves?' Dextrianus was almost pleading with me.

I shook my head. 'Nope. The Cimbri now know full

well that either Rome must perish or they will. Leaving Rome to recover when they had their boots on our collective throat was a mistake, and well they know it. Romans never forget, and if you want a reminder of that, you could ask the Carthaginians – except there are no Carthaginians any more to ask. They came close enough to defeating us in two wars that we made sure to utterly wipe them out in the next one. *Carthago delenda est.*'

'And that's what the Cimbri have in mind for us. They won't be safe in Italy while there is a house standing on the Aventine or a temple left on the Capitoline Hill. As long as there is, Rome will keep fighting and the Cimbri know it. So sorry Dextrianus, it's us or them.'

'So we line up here –', Porcellinus gestured at the broad grassy slope with an expansive wave. 'And the Cimbri advance across the plain here – from the west? Is that the arrangement?'

I nodded. 'The Cimbri like the idea of us being trapped against those ridges almost as much as Lafranius here doesn't. They won't interfere with our deployment.'

This drew a disgusted snort from Domitius. 'They're barbarians! Since when did we start making gentlemen's agreements as though this were a combat between schools of gladiators? I'll meet you here, we shall fight at this time, and then what – a half-time break with sweet wine and olives?'

'It's rare but not unprecedented. That's what the Romans did with the Horatii', Porcellinus chimed in to remind his classmate. 'The Horatian brothers of Rome agreed to fight with the Curatii of Alba Longa to decide the fate of their cities. In Greek history, battles were often fought at a pre-arranged time and place.'

Domitius bridled at being corrected, and Antonius promptly nudged his horse forward so that he rode between the two. This caused me to hide a smile, because I had started paying Antonius a small subsidy to shield Porcellinus from the malign attentions of Domitius and Lafranius. Then, over time, the naturally generous spirit of Antonius had made him genuinely protective of his young charge and an unlikely friendship had developed between the two. The boldness of Porcellinus in correcting Domitius was an outgrowth of this, for fearless as Domitius was, he had nevertheless to think twice before tackling someone of Antonius' substantial brawn.

It was Dextrianus who startled me out of my self-satisfied reverie by exclaiming, 'Hello, where did they come from?'

Deer. I had forgotten about the deer and now here they were, a herd of some fifteen animals. They were standing a stone's throw away and regarding us with wary curiosity. Domitius gave Dextrianus a disgusted look.

'And you've just seen them? Aphrodites' buttocks, man – if those were Cimbric cavalry they would be all over us by now. I thought you were keeping watch on that side. Great job, sleepy head.'

'I was watching,' Dextrianus protested. 'They just appeared – one moment the plain was empty and the next, there they were. It is as if they sprang from the earth.'

'Sure', sneered Domitius, but with Momina's words clear in my memory, I was not prepared to leave it at that. There was something about those deer that needed investigation.

The deer watched cautiously as my horse walked forward and then suddenly, as if on a prearranged signal, the herd turned and fled. I watched them thoughtfully as they galloped away, noting that they had gone several hundred paces before they were swallowed up in the morning mist. Time enough surely for even the unmilitary Dextrianus to have noticed them beforehand. Indeed, since I did not trust my students entirely, I also had been monitoring our environment and I was reasonably sure that the plain about us had been empty just a few moments before.

'Very well gentlemen, it seems that at present we do not have the alertness required to do exercises in the field. Time for you to return to camp and arm yourselves with wax tablet and stylus. By the time of my return you should each have drawn up your proposed order of battle for the Roman army. Our commander will be briefing us on the army's actual deployment this afternoon, and the cadet who gets closest to the actual Roman battle plan earns a flask of my honeyed Apulian wine – the one from the consulship of Geta and Flavius.'

The prospect of a quality wine matured for fifteen years was appealing to even the refined aristocratic palates of my class, so the group cantered away happily exchanging badinage as to which of them would win the prize. Personally I grieved for that flask of wine as I might for a dear friend and I mentally offered its loss to Bellona, the Goddess of War, in the hope that my sacrifice might not be in vain.

Now, the deer were moving northwards so they must have come from here … and my, my, there's another of them. Why are you not with your friends, little fellow? And where were you hiding?

The mist had closed in again so that it seemed that the world about me was a wall of grey. Yet before the view faded into greyness there was nothing but hundreds of yards of earth, grass slightly yellowed by the summer heat, and puddles of fog nestling between the low hillocks of the plain.

The nearest patch of fog was quite extensive and I rode Maphronius warily into it, with tendrils of mist swirling around the sorrel's fetlocks. To my surprise the fog kept rising as we went on, first to the horse's chest, then to my waist, and finally I was completely submerged in a blanket of white. The steady clop of Maphronius' hooves changed to a slightly squishy sound and I realized that we were in a depression that was probably a small, shallow lake in the winter months.

It was a somewhat eerie feeling riding alone, hidden from the world and entombed in the mist together with who knows what. It was a definite relief when we came out the other side and I was again on dry grass – grass that would almost certainly be soaked with blood before sunset two days hence. Mentally I shook off whatever ghosts had accompanied me out of the slough and turned my horse towards the Roman camp. There was much to do before battle commenced, and none of it would be pleasant.

The next morning I rode into the Gallic village of Twin Pines with thirty cavalrymen at my back. This was mainly because the previous afternoon had been spent riding out to meet Madric and doing a last extensive debrief with our spy. I had wanted to formalize Madric's defection back to the Roman side that day but as I had rather expected he would, the Gaul had objected vigorously.

'Tomorrow's the day you get your foolish head cut off in the Cimbric camp. Do you think I would want to miss that? Someone has to take back word of your untimely end and it seems that fate has given me the job. Once that show is over, I'll rejoin the Roman army – there's a few Cimbri that I have a personal grudge against, and fate willing, I shall meet them on the battlefield.'

Madric's obstinacy had complicated my life somewhat and had necessitated this visit to the Twin Pines. As we pulled up our horses in a swirl of dust, the village headman stepped out to meet us.

'Ah, the Romans. Good of you to pay us a last visit before you die. They tell me that this will be soon.'

'And greetings to you. Since we are dispensing with

formalities, I shall come directly to the point. There's a Roman spy who has been using your services to relay information to the Cimbri. That spy made arrangements to meet with his masters today. I want to know when and where.'

The headman looked incredulous. 'And you expect me to tell you? Just like that? Even if I knew what you were talking about – which I don't – I'm hardly going to be threatened into revealing the information by a little boy on a red horse.'

I looked at Domitius, who had accompanied me on my ride. Catulus has decided that it would be 'educational'.

'Threats? I have no recollection of any threats being uttered. Did you hear any threats, Domitius?'

'Nossir', said Domitius, stone-faced.

'So here's what we will do. Instead of threats, let's bar the doors of that house over there. Your house, I believe?' I cocked an enquiring eye at the headman who was looking at me with increasing alarm.

'Optio, get to it. And you -' I indicated a nearby cavalryman – 'get me a decent brand from that fire over there.'

'What are you going to do?' demanded the headman urgently. 'My wife and children are still indoors.'

I wetted a finger and held it up. 'It's an east wind. So, ah, here's my torch. Let's put it to the thatch … like so … here … and here. Oh look, the flames have caught nicely. I always thought thatch was a fire hazard.'

Behind me there was a hiss of swords as the cavalry drew their weapons to hold back protesting and outraged tribesmen. Maphronius shied away as the flames flickered near his face, and a cavalryman dismounted to hold back the distraught headman who had tried to fling himself at the barred door.

Cries of alarm could be heard from within, followed by frantic hammering on the other side of the door. The villagers yelled abuse and a clod of earth sailed through the air to hit a cavalryman on the back. Smoke was billowing into the sky, for it was remarkable how swiftly the fire had taken hold. Fortunately the building's central position in the town square meant that nearby houses were in no danger. (I had checked that earlier.)

'The flames are spreading rapidly', I informed the now almost incoherent headman. 'But I wouldn't worry about your wife and children burning alive. The smoke from the fire will kill them first – any time now, I would estimate.'

'Curse you! Let them out. I'll tell you, alright? Open that door!'

Beside me Domitius stirred uncomfortably. He was clearly unsettled by the sudden brutality inflicted on a village which had been peaceful just minutes before. When the cavalrymen opened the door and a choking wife collapsed on the threshold, the young aristocrat visibly relaxed.

'Let's have your information, chief', I said cheerfully 'And if you don't come up with the goods, well, it will turn out that your wife and children have had just a temporary reprieve. Your home is toast unfortunately, but the village has plenty of other houses we can cook your family in.'

The cavalry formed a defensive ring about us as I dismounted, took the headman by the arm and dragged him to the privacy of a nearby hut. Behind us there was a stir as the villagers set about tackling the fire.

You left it accursed close', the headman grumbled. 'For a moment there it looked as though you were going to kill them for real. My grandfather built that house, I'll have you know.'

'Boo hoo. Now here's the agreed price for the building, pocket it, and if I were you I would hide it very carefully. That's the first instalment. You get the rest when you have given us the time and location of the meeting of that triple-cursed spy and his Cimbric handlers. And close your mouth Domitius, gaping is very unattractive.'

'It's not treason,' the headman snarled at Domitius. 'This … this monster here told me he actually would burn my babes if we didn't go through this charade. He's a demon, a pig and under that smiling mask he's rotten and depraved and – and probably like you too, Roman. Okay, you want to know the meeting place. It's to the east of here by the spring of Taunis, where the road forks near the forest edge. The meeting is at noon with everyone remaining on horseback. Is that enough for you? Eh?'

'Oh absolutely, my good fellow!' I clapped a hand on the man's shoulder and slipped another purse into his eagerly outstretched hand. Despite his protestations, the man had not been that hard to persuade. Gold is funny that way – show it to the right sort of person and their inhibitions melt like ice in sunlight.

I said earnestly, 'What I recommend now is that you take your family off on a short trip, a pilgrimage or whatever, so that you are away from the village. When they find that their spy has been betrayed you are the first person they are going to come looking for. If all goes well for Rome, by this time next week that won't matter, but until then …'.

The man spat, narrowly missing my sandal. 'I'll take your gold, Roman, but not your advice. I can look after myself. Now get out of my village. I've a home to re-build and a wife to comfort.'

Once out of the village I signalled the cavalry to turn east, and we headed that way until we reached a path forking off to the south. After a while that path turned westward, and I kept the horses moving at a steady walk. With at least two hours until noon we had all the time in the world. Once we were out of the trees the path widened into a trail, and I gave Maphronius free rein, letting him clip-clop along while I tilted my head back to enjoy the morning sun on my face. After all, as Madric had ghoulishly pointed out, today might be the last time I felt that sunshine - or anything else. After a while Domitius urged his horse alongside mine.

'Um … Tribune, I believe we are heading west right now. We've been doing so for a while.'

'Indeed. This track should go north-ish in a bit to get around that hill in front of us. But then it straightens out again. Don't I keep telling you lot that you have to learn the local landscape intimately?'

'I know the local geography well enough to know

that the Spring of Taunis is that way', Domitius jerked a thumb over his shoulder. 'If we ride hard now we can still make the spy's rendezvous before noon.'

'The spy isn't meeting his handlers at the Spring. Just alongside the hill you might see a grove of chestnut and pine trees – over there. In the middle of those trees is a charcoal burner's hut and that's where the meeting will take place. The headman lied. I know it comes as a shock to an innocent young man like you, but it happens. People lie.'

We rode in silence for a while, and then Domitius asked with some frustration, 'Well if it was a lie and you knew where the meeting was happening all along, what was the point of that whole performance in the village? It was charade upon charade.'

'Keep your voice down. There's no need to broadcast what you know to the entire valley, and I would very much rather no-one else knew. Actually I would prefer that you didn't know either, but Catulus insisted that you come along. He reckons you have the best military mind of all his trainees and seeing how one of his intelligence agents operates will be useful experience for your future. So you have to figure things out for yourself. It's not that hard.'

We had taken the horses almost halfway to the grove when Domitius came alongside me once more. This time he spoke in a murmur. 'You always knew where the meeting was going to be. However once you catch the spy, the Cimbri will want to know how you did it. Because of the way you threatened the headman they will think they know how you knew and stop looking.'

'Bullseye.'

Domitius looked thoughtful. 'It will go hard on the headman though, because the Cimbri will never believe that he lied to you. Not when you proceeded directly from the village to the correct meeting place. They'll believe that he gave up the spy - especially if they find the gold you gave him.'

'Well, I did tell the man to take a short trip for his health. Perhaps he will heed my advice.'

'I doubt it. He's probably sitting in his village chuckling at what a fool he made of you.'

'Play the game and you take the risks. That man thought he was one of the players, but it turns out he was one of the pieces. Sad, yet as I've just said ....'

The grove was shady and so dark that it took a while for my eyes to adjust. After a few moments I found the charcoal-burner's hut, with Dextrianus and four cavalrymen waiting alongside. As soon as he saw me, Dextrianus kicked heels into the ribs of his horse and hurried over.

'What kept you? According to the note that you left me, you should have been here a long time ago. We got a new message soon after you left – the spy isn't going to be at this rendezvous. He has gone directly to the Cimbric camp. Domitius, you are to take the cavalry and ride hard down the main road, intercept everyone you meet going toward the Cimbric camp and round up the lot. Our man may well be among them so we'll sort through your catch later. If you see one of the cadets, arrest him and head back to the camp immediately because that will mean that the spy was one of us after all.'

Domitius gave a slight snigger and looked at me smugly. 'So in the end there's no meeting, eh? Such complicated charades and all for nothing. Oh dear. Well, that's the game I suppose. Dextrianus, while I'm on the road what are you and our brilliant tribune going to be doing?'

'There's a back trail to the Cimbric camp and it's highly possible that the spy has taken that. It's not the sort of trail that you can follow with dozens of cavalrymen. Even six of us will be a bit slow, especially now that the spy has such a good start.' Saying this, Dextrianus gave me a slightly reproachful look. 'We should have been moving long ago. Good luck Domitius, and we can compare notes back at the tent tonight. Two silver pieces say that I'll be the one to nab our man.'

'I'll take that bet and pay up with pleasure if it means the traitor is caught. Good luck, Dextrianus! Tribune.'

After a curt nod to me, Domitius wheeled his horse and signalled to the cavalry. They left the grove at a gallop amid a thunder of hooves and a cloud of dust that afterwards slowly settled back onto the floor of the clearing. Dextrianus watched the horsemen go with his lip curled into a slight expression of contempt.

'I didn't leave you a note', I said mildly. 'You didn't give me a chance to tell Domitius that.'

'Idiot. I'm not surprised he fell for my little deception. But you, Lucius - may I call you Lucius after all we have been through together? - I rather doubted that you would be taken in by my rather crude improvisation. Still, it is my experience that most people are over-rated. They are all human in the end.'

Now that my eyes had fully adjusted to the gloom I was not at all surprised to see that the four riders with Scipio were Samnites. Nor, as Scipio raised his hand, was it any surprise that a dozen riders clad in Cimbric cloaks slowly moved out of the trees all around me.

Dextrianus gave me his most winning smile. 'Now Lucius, I hope you don't mind, but I think that you should accompany me to the Cimbric camp. My friend Metus has so very many questions he will want to ask you. And in case you haven't figured it out yet, yes, I am the spy you have been looking for.'

'Scipio Dextrianus, the spy? Impossible!'

That had been the reaction of Catulus when I gave him the bad news last night. Gloomily, I had taken a swig of the rough camp wine that the Proconsul had offered me earlier (seriously, a Roman aristocrat and commander of an entire Roman army and this stuff was the best that he could do?) and reflected that the evening had still much further downhill to go.

'Indeed. Actually I was reasonably sure of it the week before I arrived at your camp, and I've been certain pretty much since the Ides.'

'Sure of it so long ago? But that's impossible. You had not even met the lad.'

'And we met because he volunteered to come and find what was keeping me on the road, no? That's because the last thing he wanted was an investigator looking into the murder of Minatius, so he had arranged for me to die before I even got here.'

'It's that bright armour he so loves to wear. It was twinkling all the way up the hillside when he came to meet me – and he was leading not just Campanian cavalrymen but also a much larger unit of Cimbric horsemen. They were following further back.

If Plan A had worked Dextrianus would have returned to camp with the tragic news of how I had perished when we ran into a Cimbric cavalry unit. That's what the bright armour was for - Dextrianus wanted to make sure he was impossible to miss, both at a distance and when it came to close quarters. He wanted the Cimbri to know not to attack him. You'll recall he was wearing the same sort of brightly polished armour at the battle of Tridentum for the same reason - so that the Cimbri could pick him out and avoid killing him by accident.

'But didn't he save you in that fight at the fort in Sarni?'

'Only after he had fought his way all along the ramparts to kill me. Trouble is, it was night and he was no longer wearing his distinctive armour, so the Cimbri were trying to kill him also. In the end we had to save each other.'

'Then, during the night he somehow got word to Metus, and our young Cimbric spymaster made the unfortunate discovery that his top spy was about to be killed along with the rest of the garrison. The place was about to fall so Metus had to make up an excuse for us to surrender instead. He did it remarkably well, I do have to say, even though I could see tribesmen sniggering at us as we made our 'escape' in that diabolical German clothing.'

'So why didn't Dextrianus kill you then?'

'Oh, he tried. That same night he came sneaking up to where I was sleeping in a grove, dagger drawn. He was rather peeved that I was awake but he made up a cock-and-bull story about hearing suspicious noises on his side of the trees. As if, under those circumstances he wouldn't have been carrying his sword. Daggers are for assassinations, swords for combat. But I pretended not to notice so he reckoned he had got away with it.'

Catulus was still not convinced, because he didn't want to be. 'Yet how could Dextrianus have killed Minatius? Five cavalrymen testified that he was out riding with them when the murder happened.'

'Five Samnite cavalrymen. Not the same cavalrymen who tried to kill me a fortnight back, but men from the same unit.' I rubbed my neck thoughtfully. 'Almost did too. I'm pretty sure that young Dextrianus has convinced the entire unit to turn traitor. It might be a bad idea to deploy them anywhere crucial when our battle starts.'

'They're in the reserves anyway. This won't be a cavalry action. I still can't believe it's Dextrianus though. Anyone can take circumstantial evidence and bend it to fit their prejudices. And you were prejudiced against the lad even before you met him. Why is that?'

'Because of his name. Scipio Dextrianus. He started life as a left-hander.'

'What? Lucius Panderius, I can't believe that you of all people believe that stupid superstition. There's nothing sinister about being left-handed. Why, my own uncle is a lefty, and to base your allegations ... where are you going?'

'Indulge me please, Proconsul. Could you pick up that stylus from your desk and follow me?'

We walked together to the rack of scrolls where Minatius had been murdered. Carefully I positioned myself so that I faced the rack just where Minatius had been standing before he was killed. 'Now', I said, 'as Minatius reached up for a scroll he was stabbed between the ribs under his left arm. Here's me reaching up, so use the stylus to stab me just where Minatius was stabbed.'

After lifting an arm. I waited, listening to Catulus shuffling around behind me. Finally I felt the pressure of the stylus against my ribs. Without turning my head I said to Catulus, 'You're holding the stylus in your left hand, aren't you?'

Catulus gave a little grunt of frustration. 'I have to. You are too close to the scrolls for me to do it any other way. Unless I turn - like this - with my back to you and stab you backhanded with my right, which is ridiculous.'

'Yet look at all the other ways you can kill me with a dagger in your right hand. So, we can agree that the only reason that Minatius was stabbed here, between the ribs, was because the killer was naturally left-handed and acted without thinking.'

'Ah.' Catulus was near convinced, but his legal mind

was still looking for loopholes. 'The other cadets? Some of them might also be natural left-handers, since after all, not everyone who is trained out of left-handedness gets called Dextrianus. Some families prefer to keep that private.'

'Indeed. Which is why, almost as soon as I got here I tossed a training sword to Domitius, throwing it low and to the left. He almost ruptured himself twisting to take the sword in his right hand anyway. Later I tossed a scroll to Porcellinus while he was riding with his left hand off the reins. He transferred the reins to his left hand and caught the scroll with his right. Neither of the two had time to think about it, so they are natural right-handers.'

'And the other two?'

'Antonius actually has a solid alibi. He really was gambling in the cabana – over a dozen witnesses saw him – legionaries, tradespeople, and the tavern keeper's wife. I and Satula checked their stories carefully and they match.'

'Finally, Lafranius. A few days ago, he was smitten with a vicious attack of diarrhoea. As a result he missed the briefing when foraging parties were being deployed. Yet the Cimbri knew to prepare an ambush even though we had Lafranius so well quarantined that the only person who entered or left his tent was a carefully-screened slave who changed the honey buckets full of excrement. So he's not the spy and therefore not the murderer. Dextrianus and his Samnites though, went riding that day.'

'So with all that evidence, why is Dextrianus not

already in chains?'

'Because when you know who the spy is, you can modulate the information that goes through him and the enemy think they know what you are thinking. For example, that's why they found Tridentum so confusing. They thought they knew your battle plan and you didn't stick to it. If we had arrested Dextrianus, they might insert another spy we really don't know about.'

'Well we have to arrest him now. He was at the briefing this afternoon. He knows the complete Roman order of battle – where every single unit is going to be. We can't have the Cimbri knowing that. The fellow must be stopped – Gods, if it's not already too late.'

I studied Catulus thoughtfully. Time to break the bad news. 'Actually Dextrianus is going to deliver the battle plan to the Cimbri tomorrow. He's arranged a rendezvous. Fortunately, the battle plan they will get from him is completely false. However, the Cimbri will still end up in possession of the complete plan, as arranged between you, Marius and Sulla yesterday. Delivered by their other spy.'

'What! How ...who?'

I took a deep breath. 'You're not going to like this …'.

Liber XII

'You're not going to try to run away, are you?' asked Dextrianus anxiously. 'I mean, it won't work, but everyone will get upset and some of the Cimbri might kill you.'

My reply was understandably unsympathetic. 'I believe that killing me is going to happen anyway. Do you think Metus is going to offer me a mug of honeyed ale while we chat about Roman battle deployments? Red-hot irons followed by a messy death seems a lot more probable, no?'

'Ah, yes. But that will only happen after we reach the camp and I want you alive until then. I'm sure you want to stay alive as well, because being dead is very final. Until we reach the camp there's always hope, you know. Maybe we will run into an unexpected Roman cavalry patrol or father Jupiter will destroy me with a lightning bolt.' Dextrianus paused to lift his face and admire the fluffy white clouds in the midday sky.

'The point is, just don't do anything stupid, okay?'

My hands were free, though the Samnites had confiscated my sword, and Maphronius was trotting obediently behind another rider who had him on a leading rein. Just to make sure I didn't try anything heroic like leaping off my horse when we passed along a hillside path, my feet were loosely secured by a rope running from ankle-to-ankle beneath the horse. As Dextrianus had assumed, I had mentally run through my escape options and indeed it would be stupid to try anything.

'In the end, it's quite convenient that you turned up', Dextrianus mused. 'I assume that wretched headman at Twin Pines gave me away? You always were depressingly good at finding and cutting off my couriers. Now that we have stopped pretending, I can tell you that your activities have caused me a good deal of inconvenience. That supply convoy a week ago, for instance. It was you who changed the route at the last moment, wasn't it? Three thousand Cimbric cavalry spent two days getting to that ambush position and a wasted day waiting for a convoy that never came.'

'You can help me explain to Metus why that information I gave him didn't pan out. And of course, there was that failed ambush of the foraging party. It took the golden tongue of a Sisyphus for me to persuade my allies that Sulla just happened to turn up at the wrong moment, along with his legion. One problem might be just bad luck, but the thing is that none of the intelligence I have been giving my allies has been working out too well at the moment. People in the Cimbric camp are getting … restless. Now that I have you, you can explain to the Cimbri that you are the villain who has been throwing sand into the system.'

'Aww, so the Cimbri's top spy hasn't been earning all the gold they're paying him, then? Shame. Pass me a lyre so that I can set your troubles to music.'

Dextrianus seemed genuinely affronted. 'Gold? Lucius, you really do have a tradesman's mind, don't you? Of course they are not paying me, in gold or anything else. I'm doing this for Rome.'

'Eh?'

'Rome, you dunderhead. The city – that's what I'm trying to save, from the Cimbri, sure, but also from itself.'

'Um ... actually, last time I looked Rome was doing pretty well apart from the Cimbri – whom you are helping.'

'No! No, it wasn't!' Dextrianus's denial was vehement. 'Have you looked, really, looked at Rome lately? The place is corrupt, the senate is rotten to the core, the people live from bribe to bribe, and everything sort of keeps working because of the money we extort from helpless provincials. That's not Rome – that's a monster, a sick parody of what the city should be.'

'And you propose to save Rome by destroying it?'

'Not destroying it. By pruning back the empire that's destroying the city. Rome was never meant by the gods to be an imperial power, and imperial power is rotting the city, and ruining the world. We need to go back to Rome as a mid-sized Italian state, big enough to defend itself, but no threat to the neighbours. Then Rome will be the place it was always meant to be, where the people vote in democratic elections, guided by a senate which has the best interests of the people at heart. All that money flowing in from Rome's conquests and conquered provinces – what good has it done? The people want more, the senators want more, and now greed and selfishness define us. It doesn't have to be this way – we just have to stop it.'

'By 'we' you mean your traitorous self and the Cimbri?'

233

'You are wrong about the Cimbri, Lucius. All they want is an end to their wanderings and to make the north Italian plain into their homeland. And once we have the Cimbri settled there, Rome's adventures in Gaul and Spain will come to an end because the Cimbri will act as a buffer between those states and Rome. Gaul has a developing culture and the Phoenicians have started new intellectual developments in Spain. We should stand back and watch how these countries mature into real civilizations, not conquer them simply for the loot and slaves they can provide.'

'And Greece! We've ruined Greece, the land which was the wellspring of Mediterranean culture. We've enslaved their poets and killed their great thinkers. Archimedes at Syracuse is the perfect example – Greek thought destroyed by the Roman sword. Now the last great refuge of Hellenistic thought – the home of the ideas that are driving civilization forward, make no mistake – that last refuge is in Alexandria, at the Library.'

'What do you think will happen if boors like Domitius conquer the place, as some Roman inevitably will? At best the Library will be allowed to fall into decay and ruin. More probably the priceless scrolls will be looted so that some semi-literate moron can let them rot in a private library that he keeps just for the prestige of the thing. I'm telling you, Rome as it now is represents a canker on the body of the world – a poisonous growth that needs to be cut back before it destroys civilization.'

'So after this, with the Cimbri to the north and the

free Samnites and other Italians to the south, Rome will be trapped, and turned inwards. Then we Romans will be forced to really examine ourselves and the false path we have gone down these last two centuries. With the senate purged and purified ... '

'... and led by yourself?' I interrupted.

'Well, initially yes. Rome needs a dictator who can make the hard choices, a man who understands that some blood must be shed now to forestall rivers of blood later. Give it a hundred years, Lucius, and they'll raise statues to me in the forum. I'll be recognized as the man who re-founded Rome as the city it should be, not the depraved monster it has become. Athens never needed an empire that stretched from Asia to the Atlantic, yet still that city was the light of the world. That's what Rome should be. Will be.'

Well, I thought to myself. That explains the Samnites. Samnite and Roman had been butting heads for centuries until the Cimbric threat brought them both into an uneasy alliance. Now Dextrianus offered the Samnites a vision of a weakened Rome that was no longer an existential threat to their nation. No wonder he had readily gained so many Samnite recruits for his cause. It was certain that neither Samnites nor Cimbri believed Dextrianus' idealistic nonsense for a moment, but both parties had seen in him a useful tool for their own purposes. It was sad in a way, for despite everything I rather liked Dextrianus.

Meanwhile, unaware that he had temporarily lost my attention, Dextrianus was twittering on. 'So you see Lucius, what I'm doing is for the best. As a Roman patriot you can see that I have to sacrifice you for the betterment of your city. You'll be a soldier dying for Rome, just not in the way that you might have expected.'

I shook my head sadly. 'You do realize that your reign as the Cimbric puppet of Rome would last as long as it takes the Samnites, Campanians and Marsi to get together with the Cimbri and wipe Rome off the map? And that's assuming that the Cimbri don't stick with Plan A and just rip through Italy like an emetic before they settle in the ruins? Personally, I would take Cappadocia.'

'That's because you are thinking like a Roman again. The Cimbri are in some ways more civilized than we are. I've been promised that they have no intentions of conquering … wait, Cappadocia?'

We were riding through a meadow where the grass came to our horses' knees, and now Dextrianus, who had been declaiming from behind me, nudged his horse alongside. 'What has Cappadocia to do with anything?'

'You know the place? It's a tidy kingdom in Asia Minor, between the Galatians in the highlands to the north, Pergamon to the west and the Taurus mountains which sit between the Cappadocian plain and the Seleucid empire. It's much safer than Italy is going to be for a while.'

'Well, so what?'

'So they don't really have a hereditary kingship because they have only recently got out from under the control of the Seleucid empire. There's always something of a struggle to decide who is going to rule the place. The people of Pontus – which is a really powerful and well-organized kingdom by the way – the Bithynians, the Armenians and the Seleucids all want their own person on the throne and the power struggle has been destabilizing the entire region.'

'What the place needs is an outside candidate, someone acceptable to all parties yet not favouring one over the other. A Roman, for example, installed with the consent of all those with a stake in the Cappadocian kingship.'

'That's nothing to do with me.'

'Think about it,' I urged. 'You don't think that the Cimbri are without allies in this war, do you? The Samnites are not the only people who are looking at the approach of the Roman juggernaut. The Pontics really would prefer that Rome stayed west of the Adriatic, the Seleucids are having enough trouble holding their crumbling empire together without having to fight the Romans for it, and Egypt knows it cannot stand alone. The man who saves the east from the Roman menace, well, Cappadocia is the least of the rewards he can expect.'

'I don't want Cappadocia. My mission is to save Rome.'

'Ah, okay.'

We rode in silence for a while, until the sight of cooking-fire smoke rising above the trees ahead told us that the Cimbric camp was not far off. Possibly because he knew the fate that awaited me there, Dextrianus rather shamefacedly pulled back and waved to a messenger to report news of our impending arrival.

Looking at my hands, I was unsurprised to see that they were shaking. After all it had been one thing to carefully plan my way into the Cimbric camp, accepting all the while the extreme risk that it entailed. It was something else entirely to be now actually taking that risk, knowing that within an hour I might either be dead or desperately wishing that I was. I felt sick.

There was a small delegation awaiting us outside the royal tent. King Boiorix himself, no less, his son Metus, a group of nobles among whom I noticed the obnoxious Claodicus, and standing at the king's shoulder, none other than the Syrian horse trader Bassianus. Bassianus and I exchanged nods, though I noted the Syrian's frown as he observed my tied ankles. Ordinary warriors pressed around to observe the spectacle, causing the king's bodyguard to exert a certain degree of force to keep the throng at a distance. It took a small effort for me to stop myself from looking around the crowd to see if I could spot Madric's face.

It was Metus who stepped forward to greet us, his blue eyes alight with amusement. 'Ah, my two favourite spies. You have found each other then? I trust you bring me good news?'

At a nod from Bassianus, a servant darted from the crowd and began to untie my ankles. Silently I held out my arm, hand with palm upwards and after a long hesitation one of the Samnite cavalrymen placed my sheathed sword in it.

Dextrianus looked at me blank-faced with shock as I belted the sword back on, ignoring the chuckles of the Cimbric nobles who were evidently in on the joke.

Metus intervened smoothly. I noticed that his Latin had improved markedly now that he had no audience to whom he wanted to play the barbarian.

'You didn't know, Dextrianus? Lucius here has been one of us from the beginning. Those cavalry, who you thought were protecting you on your way here, they were actually to make sure that you and your Samnites did not do anything precipitate – as you and they tried before Tridentum. Just as well that on that occasion we had scouts posted in the trees with orders to preserve our man's welfare.'

'He's a Cimbric spy? He can't be. Tell them, Lucius.'

Metus answered instead. 'He found out about you early – and told us that it was you who killed that young Italian cadet. We needed someone in the Roman camp who was, frankly, less sloppy than you are Dextrianus. One thing about Panderius here, he is a professional. Clearly you never suspected his role at all.'

'But … but why?'

I nodded at Bassianus. 'He represents the eastern powers I told you about. A consortium of Pontus, Bithynia, the Seleucids and Egypt. He's my actual paymaster.'

'So you are doing it for gold? After what you said earlier …?'

Regretfully I shook my head. 'Why, no. I told you as clearly as I could. I'm doing it for Cappadocia - that's my payment. Once this is over and the Cimbri have won, you can send your first diplomatic mission to me, King Lucius the First of Cappadocia.'

'Once you've earned it', added Bassianus slightly

sourly. 'You've not done that yet.'

Dextrianus was looking at me with an odd expression of horror on his face, 'You ... you, you're a traitor!'

'And one who is about to earn his payment', I said and reached up to place a reassuring hand on Dextrianus's shoulder. At the last moment the little knife I had palmed from my belt flicked out and I drew the razor sharp blade quickly across the young man's throat.

Dextrianus's eyes bulged as he grabbed at the gaping wound, and Maphronius skittered aside from the drops of blood that spurted between my victim's fingers. Behind me there was a brief commotion as the Cimbric cavalry disarmed Dextrianus' Samnite riders. We sat quietly waiting until after about half a minute Dextrianus's body slumped sideways in the saddle and landed with a thump in the dust. His horse stepped back and nuzzled the corpse. There came a sort of collective sigh from the watching warriors.

Metus was watching me with puzzled interest that was slowly turning to anger. 'What did you do that for?'

Mentally I took a deep breath. Here we go – either the Cimbri would buy what I was about to sell, or my body would soon join Dextrianus' in the dust. Trying to appear relaxed, I looked about the Cimbric camp, noting that the buildings were a mixture of crude huts and captured Roman tents. There were quite a few womenfolk around also. I returned my attention to the royal party, who were looking just slightly impatient.

'Because you have just confirmed to the Romans

what Gratidus has suspected for some time. That I'm the spy. We can't afford to let that information get back to Catulus.'

'Gratidus? What has that clown to do with anything?' This from Claodicus, whom I ignored. My attention was on Metus, who was looking thoughtful. King Boiorix said nothing, but his gaze travelled from one to the other of us as though he were watching a ball game.

'You underestimated Gratidus. I underestimated Gratidus. The man acts the incompetent buffoon, but he's a demon, an agent of Eris herself, the goddess of discord. Dextrianus -', I indicated the corpse with a contemptuous jerk of my thumb – 'Dextrianus was nothing. He was the tool by which Gratidus told you exactly what he wanted you to know. No more and no less.'

'He told us where to find the unguarded Alpine passes', objected Claodicus.

'Passes that Catulus did not have the manpower to hold anyway. Marius had stripped him of veteran troops and his green levies were too few and too raw. Gratidus persuaded Catulus to let Dextrianus reveal the unguarded passes so as to gain your trust. Did you not wonder that Catulus pulled his army back to Tridentum in such good order? He never expected to stop you at the Alps.'

There was a thoughtful silence. Then looking at Metus I said, 'Nor was it such a good idea to let Dextrianus know how you planned to take down the bridge at Tridentum. I slowed him down as much as I could, but he still managed to alert the camp in good time. I almost managed to persuade that fool Scaurus that Dextrianus was talking nonsense, but his cursed *Primus Pilus* over-ruled me.'

'At the actual battle - or rather non-battle – at Tridentum, Dextrianus wanted me dead before I could tell you of Catulus' plans for a clean withdrawal. He succeeded well enough though, by wounding me so badly that I couldn't tell you that your outflanking move had been discovered. Thereafter all Gratidus had to do was ride up the hillside and 'accidentally' find your men heading for the pass. In reality, thanks to Dextrianus, Gratidus knew it all along.'

'Think of your other issues lately - the convoy ambush that failed, the foraging party that just happened to be protected by the apparently co-incidental arrival of Sulla's men – you have been played gentlemen. Led by the nose by the perfidious Gratidus.'

Metus nodded thoughtfully. 'This may be true. Yet I have problems believing that Gratidus is anything other than the idiot he appears to be. No-one is that good an actor. What if the person who has foiled our attempts is not Dextrianus, whom you have so conveniently silenced, but you yourself, my dear Panderius?'

This question I was prepared for, not least because Metus had nailed the truth exactly. Fortunately the summer sun was reaching midday so the beads of sweat on my forehead had an innocent explanation.

'Look at the back of Dextrianus's saddle. There, where the stitching is new.'

I dismounted and walked over to the slain man's

horse, and held the beast steady with a grip on one of the saddlebags while they sliced open the saddle. A murmur came from the crowd as a small metal cylinder was extracted. A grim-faced warrior handed the cylinder to Boiorix, who silently passed it over to his son. Metus unscrewed the cap from the cylinder, and shook out a small scroll and a roll of gold coins. Metus read from the scroll.

'Let whosoever reads this know that the bearer acts for me and in my name. Do as he wishes as if I myself had commanded it. '

'The scroll is signed Q. Lutatius Catulus, Proconsul of Rome. That's his seal, no doubt of it.' Metus shook his head, and looked down at Dextrianus's corpse. 'Could I have been so wrong about you?'

The Cimbric princeling turned his gaze upon me, his eyes hard and unfriendly. 'You were maybe a bit too eager in killing our friend here. These is much I wanted to ask him. Even more now after your revelations.'

I shrugged, knowing that Metus' reputation as a spymaster had taken a hard hit. 'Dextrianus could have told you nothing of value. He was Gratidus' creature and did as his master ordered. Mostly, I believe Gratidus kept him in the dark about what was going on, precisely because he foresaw an eventuality like this where his man might be revealed as a Roman agent. However, if you want the Roman battle plans that he was going to give you, I would guess they're in his saddlebags somewhere. I wasn't at the meeting where

243

the generals prepared their strategy but Dextrianus was - and I'll bet he took extensive notes.'

I stepped back from the horse and waited while warriors rummaged through the patient animal's packs. The little wax tablet with Dextrianus's notes was duly unearthed, which came as no surprise to me - I had slipped it into the saddlebag just moments beforehand. Despite the number of eyes that were on me, inserting the tablet had gone without a hitch, mainly because I had been standing with my back to half the crowd with the horse between me and the other half - and anyway everyone had been oohing and aahing over the dis-covery of the little metal cylinder I had patiently sewed into Dextrianus's saddle last night.

A small table was produced and the king and his council bent over the tablet. I hovered at the back of the group, none of whose members paid me any attention. Eventually Boiorix spoke for the first time. 'It's bold. Using the cavalry like that – not something we would have expected.'

'Quite a gamble though', one of the more elderly nobles interjected thoughtfully. 'If we have spearmen – here - that manoeuvrer falls apart and opens up an entire flank. And the legions of Catulus as the Roman spearhead – what's that about? Why wouldn't Marius use his veterans?'

'He would', I said causing a number of bearded faces to turn towards me. 'That plan is totally fake. It's intended to interfere with your deployments and is just unrealistic enough to cause division and argument in your ranks.'

'Says you', remarked Claodicus. 'I suppose you've seen the 'real' battle plan?'

'Better than that. I have it here.' Walking over to Maphronius I took a thick sheet of rolled parchment from behind the saddle. 'Handle it with care gentlemen, I'm supposed to deliver it to Sulla before tonight.'

'The real battle plan?' Sulla demanded incredulously. 'You showed them this?' He held up the scroll in one hand. 'This actual document? The one which shows every one of our deployments down to the maniple, our fall-back strategy and … everything? What in Athena's name, Lucius? What were you thinking? Gods curse you man, I should have you crucified.'

I nodded. 'It had to be the real thing. You can't fake that sort of document, not with the careful notations drawn up by the clerks and that degree of detail. It was totally convincing because it was real.'

Sulla looked at me, his face suddenly hard and unreadable. 'So now the Cimbri know our plans – down to the last detail.'

'It saved my life, for what that's worth. The plan I produced was completely different from Dextrianus's version. Both could not be right, and my document was so much more impressive than a schoolboy sketch on a wax tablet. It was further proof that I was trustworthy and Dextrianus was a double agent.'

'How did you get Scipio Dextrianus to draw up those false plans anyway?'

'Oh, not important. I told the entire class yesterday to draw up their version of the Roman order of battle. The only one I kept was Dextrianus'. Fortunately with a flask of excellent wine at stake Dextrianus did a pretty creditable job – partly because he consulted some of the senior centurions and one legionary tribune. Metus, of course knew Dextrianus's handwriting intimately and had to agree that Dextrianus's battle plans bore no relation to reality. So the real plans basically confirmed my allegations.'

'But Lucius', said Sulla with dangerous patience, 'The Cimbri know our battle plan. The real one. This is not a good thing. The reason that the Cimbri now trust you as a valued spy is because you couldn't have done a better job for them if you had actually been spying for them. You have done exactly what Bassianus wanted you to do when he recruited you all those months ago. How in Saturn's name did you persuade Catulus to go along with this … this suicidal folly?'

'Um, I may have forgotten to tell him the bit about me handing over those plans to the Cimbri. In my defence, he did say something like 'Very well, I'll leave it in your hands', when I started to outline my plans for Dextrianus. He was a bit squeamish when I started talking about cutting the throat of one of his fellow aristocrats, richly as Dextrianus deserved it. If you don't mind, I'll stay here at your camp while you ride over to discuss things with him. You have a lot to prepare for before tomorrow and Catulus might get a touch excited if I'm within range.'

Sulla nodded acknowledgement of the understatement of the year and went to the tent flap to bellow for an orderly to get his boots. Returning to his camp stool, Sulla steepled his fingers and looked at me steadily.

'And now Lucius, you will tell me exactly what you are playing at. No fucking around or I quite seriously will have you killed. Not a soul would blame me.'

It was at moments like this that I could use a beaker of wine. Not just any wine – one of those Greek raisin wines from Miletus that pours a calming fog into your mind a minute after you've consumed it. I'd been near death several times today, but never closer than I was at this moment.

'Well, sure. The Cimbri know our battle plan. But I was the trusted spy and advisor who sat in on their subsequent strategy meeting. They know our plan, but we also know theirs. Hades, some of it I devised myself.'

'You're going to love this …'

Liber XIII

'As hosts for this battle it's our duty to prepare to receive our Cimbric visitors in style', commented Sulla cheerfully. He seemed remarkably chipper for a man who had been awake for much of the night, cloistered with Catulus in his Praetorian tent as the pair re-worked the Roman battle-plan in view of newly-received information. Now, for all that it was not long past midsummer, the pre-dawn light barely gave the Roman army enough to see by as the troops stumbled to their assigned positions.

After our early awakening we had all been given a substantial breakfast of figs rolled in wheat pancakes buttered with honey. Also there were small loaves of bread with hard yellow cheese which many legionaries had stuffed into bags on their belts. This was lunch, to be eaten in the field by those not otherwise engaged at the time. It would have been nice to report that the condemned man – me – ate a hearty breakfast, and I had tried. Regrettably pre-battle nerves had me throwing up the lot behind my tent a few minutes later.

Catulus had been serious with his threat of con-sequences for his 'Tribune in charge of Funny Business' and even I had to admit that my current predicament was the result of business about as funny as things could get. Catulus had rather nastily pointed out to Sulla that I had leveraged my current position to maximum advantage. Should Rome win the forth-coming battle I could justifiably claim that this was partly due to my devious machinations. Should Rome be defeated, well, then I would be King Lucius of Cappadocia. Despite my plaintive protestations that this win-win situation was merely a serendipitous side effect of current operations, Catulus had decided to get me somewhat more vested in a Roman victory.

'You're leading the cavalry charge, Panderius', Catulus had curtly informed me (once he was able to look at me without risking apoplexy). 'And I'm assigning you a special bodyguard. Their duties are to protect you so long as we look like winning the battle - and to cut you down like a dog should we start losing. In fact I'll extend their orders so far as to allow them to execute you should you appear hesitant to engage at the signal. This is a hint that you no longer enjoy my full confidence and trust.'

Sulla beamed. 'Ah. I call that the Panderius Effect. Somehow, the more time that people spend with our Lucius here, the more they come to dislike and distrust him. Strange for someone who seems so open and honest at first sight.'

(Later Sulla clarified for my benefit. 'It's dumb to let your superiors know that you're a lot smarter than they are, but if you have to do it at least convince them that you're loyal. You're terrible on both counts. Too clever by half and unsympathetic with it.')

In one way, being assigned a murderous bodyguard was not particularly troubling, since I was fairly certain that Rome would win the coming clash. The only thing capable of keeping any 50,000 veteran Roman soldiers from victory anywhere and at any time is the jaw-dropping incompetence of the average Roman general.

For example that gibbering imbecile Caepio and his half-wit colleague Manlius had between them helped to massacre an entire Roman army four years ago at Arausio - but incompetent leadership was not an issue today.

Whatever his flaws as a person (list available upon request), Marius was a highly competent commander who wiped away better generals than Caepio and Manlius every time he visited the latrines after dinner. Catulus was cautious but sound, and Sulla as a commander combined effortless competence with a terrifying go-for-broke exuberance. He'd obviously enjoyed putting together the revised Roman battle-plan, which partly accounted for his good cheer on this foggy morning. He had given me a friendly wink when Catulus announced his plans for my 'bodyguard' and I was still trying to figure out if that wink was sadistic unconcern or something else.

Even had Sulla and Catulus stuck to the original Roman battle plan, I reckoned we would - probably – win. But it would cost us thousands of lives and the defeated Cimbri would be able to pull back and try again. And after that battle, even if they took twice the casualties of the Roman army, they'd still outnumber us next time around.

The Plan B of Sulla and Catulus would vastly reduce the projected number of Roman deaths and just as importantly, the Cimbri would be wiped out, both as an army and as a people. This slaughter of tens of thousands of Cimbri was something I could contemplate with equanimity. I'd seen acre after acre of Roman dead after Arausio where the Cimbri took not a single prisoner. The 80,000 souls who died that day called from the Underworld for vengeance, and today Rome and I would answer that call and lay those ghosts to rest.

The army would be deployed along the slopes leading back to the bluffs on the south-west end of the Raudine Plain. One reason for Sulla's early start was that his compact little force was deployed on the far right of the Roman battle-line, which meant entering the plain from the east and marching along below the bluffs until it arrived at its position. Normally in battle the right wing was the place of honour but Marius, with his usual weaselly appreciation of politics, had assigned Sulla this position because it meant that his rival for glory would be well removed from where the actual fighting was intended to take place. (It was also the hardest spot to get out of should the battle go against Rome, and you can bet that Marius had allowed for that also.)

Marius' Plan A – the one I had revealed in all its splendour to the Cimbri – envisioned the Cimbri advancing toward us across the Plain on a broad front, rather as they had done against the army of Manlius at Arausio. But at Arausio, the Romans had been overwhelmed before they could properly deploy, and that would not happen today. Our early start this morning was an indication of Marius' determination that rather than overwhelming Roman units struggling into position, the Cimbri would find Rome's veteran legionaries formed up, ready and waiting.

Or in the case of Marius' legions on the left, not waiting. Marius planned to launch a short, savage charge downhill as soon as the Cimbri came within range. Backed by most of the cavalry on the left flank, Marius' army would drive the Cimbri back until their centre, which would be attacking Catulus, would be forced to retreat also, since otherwise it risked being taken in the flank. Then Catulus could advance carefully and the Roman line would move forward until the Cimbri were swept from the plain. This was a typical Marian plan – solid, cautious and meticulous, intended to make modest gains at minimal risk.

However, it is a military truism that no plan survives contact with the enemy, and this would be especially true today, because the Cimbri had spent yesterday afternoon carefully studying that selfsame plan. The Marius plan was now completely obsolete, which made it all the more unfortunate that neither Catulus nor Sulla had bothered to inform Marius of the fact.

Thanks to Catulus' determination to place me in the middle of the action, I was nominally in charge of a mixed unit of some 800 cavalry. However it was made very clear to me that the real leader of the unit was a veteran military tribune called Saufienus. Saufienus had been in the cavalry since he was fifteen and had a damaged nose, scarred face and leathery skin to show for it. 'Look pretty, wave your sword and shout 'Chaaarge' when I tell you', Saufienus informed me, 'and the rest of the time keep out of my damn way.'

Keeping out of Saufienus' damn way left me largely in the company of my bodyguards. These consisted of a hulking junior centurion and his slightly smaller optio sidekick. After we left the main army to deploy into battle position, the centurion leaned over and murmured into my ear, 'Just so you know, Lucius Panderius, my family have been clients of the Domitii Ahenobarbi for generations. Our lands lie right next to theirs in Bovillae, and the Ahenobarbi have always been our friends and protectors. Also just so you know, you little turd, young Domitius Ahenobarbus rather likes and respects you, so he's ordered us to kill you quickly, rather than the slow death by disembowelment we have in mind - and which we might try anyway. Who's to know?'

It was hard to know if the centurion was serious, or simply trying a bit of the bullying intimidation that comes naturally to the centurion breed. Either way, he was an annoying complication. I looked at the *optio*.

'In your case it's pretty clear. Your mother screwed a Barbary ape. But what's with the other guy? Perhaps one of those gorilla creatures the Carthaginians reported finding deep in Africa, or maybe a troglodyte. He definitely takes after his father in any case.'

My escorts were prevented from replying by the clatter of hooves as a troop of riders emerged from the mist. Rather to my astonishment these men were led by Antonius and Porcellinus.

'Greetings Tribune!' said Antonius heartily. 'We asked and received permission from Catulus to fight on horseback today. As we were leaving Sulla decided to attach these newly-arrived Thracian mercenaries to your force. Where do you want them?'

'You'll have to ask Saufienus. He's the military tribune who's actually running things around here. Though to be honest, some three dozen riders are not going to make a big difference one way or another.'

'Oh, don't be so sure about that.' Antonius and Porcellinus pushed their horses to each side of me, forcing the centurion and sidekick grudgingly to take up position behind.

'Did you know that the Thracians fight with lariats as well as lances?' enquired Porcellinus enthusiastically. 'In battle they actually lasso enemy cavalrymen and pull them to the ground.'

From behind me came two startled shouts. Before I could turn in the saddle to see what was going on, Antonius took me by the arm and shook his head warningly. I winced slightly at the sound of armoured bodies hitting the ground and pretended instead to be paying attention to Porcellinus' exposition of Thracian cavalry techniques. When I finally did twist back to take a look, I saw two horses with empty saddles and a line of blond horsemen staring back at me with stony faces. Of the centurion and his sidekick there was no sign.

'Sulla says don't make him regret this', said Antonius, and I was reminded of my patron's oft-repeated maxim that no-one was a worse enemy or better friend than he. Well, thanks to Sulla's friendship I had one less thing to worry about today. I turned back to my cadets.

'You two, stay in the second rank and no heroics. I don't want to have to explain to your parents how I let you get killed. You are here to observe and learn, not win the grass crown for winning the battle through your personal efforts. Now report to Saufienus so that he can tell you the same thing.'

Because I missed the first part of the battle, the account which follows is taken partly from Sulla's memoirs (Particularly the chapter that should have been entitled 'How I won the Battle of Vercellae and Single-handedly Saved Italy'). The other, somewhat more balanced part, comes from a detailed description given to me by Madric. Yesterday, after watching me leave the Cimbric camp alive, Madric had slipped over to the Roman side along with several dozen other Gallic deserters who had seen a Roman army from the pointy end and had no wish to repeat the experience. Assigned to the rear ranks of the Marian force, Madric had an excellent view of events as they unfolded.

'Best battle I ever fought in my friend, a walk in the park I'd call it, if only it wasn't so accursed dusty. But then dust was what you might call the whole point of it all, wasn't it?'

But let's go back to the beginning, when the first Cimbric troops spilled out on to the plain. The sun was just rising and Cimbric prisoners later revealed that the massed ranks of the Roman army made an impressive sight. They were drawn up on a slope so that every rank was visible, and the morning sun sparkled off polished bronze helmets and shield bosses. Filtered through the mist, it seemed as though the Roman ranks were wreathed in fire.

Madric on his hill saw the Cimbric army come

together - not as did the Roman army, with columns deploying into neat ranks, but with clumps of individual family and tribal groupings turning up in their own time, and being directed to their place in the Cimbric battle line by organizers from the King's council. The scene was somewhat reminiscent of spectators arriving for a large outdoor event, especially as the Cimbri had brought their families along for the day. A distant line of wagons containing the Cimbric women and children filled the back of their end of the plain, and from these woman occasionally darted to give their menfolk forgotten pieces of armour or a last minute kiss.

Even with perfect organization it takes a while for tens of thousands of men to get lined up and pointed in the right direction and the Cimbri were far from perfectly organized. The watching Romans waited stoically. Most had grounded the bottom end of their shields and were watching the Cimbric deployment with arms folded over the rim at the top. Paradoxically, as the morning light grew stronger visibility actually decreased as dust from the plain was kicked into the air by tramping feet to gradually obscure the Cimbric ranks beneath a light haze.

Behind the Roman line was Marius with a crowd of attendants and Momina by his side. As Rome's war-leader for the day it was Marius' duty to sacrifice an ox and thus determine what the gods willed as the outcome of the day. When the Harsupex examined the liver of the sacrificial animal and pointed out the signs to his general, Marius' triumphant shout rolled down the hillside. 'Mine is the victory!'

As if in reply, the sound of Cimbric trumpets merged into a steady blare and drums started a deep booming behind the Cimbric army. (I later found that the Cimbric women covered their waggon beds with leather and used these as massive drums.) At the sound the barbarian mass began to march forward, carpeting the plain with warriors. There was a crude rhythm to the advance, step-step-stamp, step-step-stamp, with dust spiralling up from the earth as the plain shook from the synchronized pounding of tens of thousands of feet. With each step and stamp the Cimbric army bellowed their deafening battle cry of 'Wo-tan-DA!' and the sound hit the bluffs and washed back like a wave over the waiting Roman force.

Centurions moved busily along the ranks of the assembled Roman army, steadying the men, checking kit and muttering quick words of encouragement which were almost drowned out by the roar from the advancing enemy. Commanders on both sides checked their intelligence reports with the reality of the enemy deployments now manifest in front of them.

King Boiorix and his advisors would have noted that the Roman deployments matched those in the plans revealed to them yesterday, with the exception that Catulus' soldiers were deployed slightly further forward than they should have been. Catulus from his command post on his hillside would have been anxiously scanning the front rank of the Cimbri arrayed against him. The Cimbric council - helped by myself – had identified the army of Catulus as the weakest link in the Roman line. After all, the Cimbri had chased Catulus from the Alps, from his camp across the Adige, off the battlefield at Tridentum and across north Italy.

Now the army of Catulus was pinned against the bluffs at Vercellae with no escape. So the Cimbri intended to throw their entire force against the army of Catulus and crack it apart. With panicked legionaries fleeing left and right and disrupting the Roman lines, the Cimbri would wheel left and overwhelm the far smaller force of Sulla before turning to finish off Marius.

To hit the army of Catulus with massive force, the Cimbri intended to form their army into a huge blunt wedge, with their noblemen and best fighters at the crushing edge. To ensure that the wedge stayed solid and unbroken, those in the front rank had linked themselves together with chains locked around their waists. That had been a suggestion of Claodicus, and so ridiculously macho that I could not believe that the other Cimbric nobles had accepted it. But now Catulus, squinting through the dust at the front ranks of the advancing enemy, saw those chains and breathed a sigh of relief that they were in use.

There was a general shifting and preparing among the leading cohorts of the Marian line as legionaries loosened swords in their scabbards and hefted the pilums they would hurl before their downhill charge. Then came a cry from the legion tribune, which was taken up and echoed by centurions along the line.

'Stand! Stand! Hold the line!'

The Cimbric infantry tumbled aside, and cavalry came boiling through the ranks, huge mounted warriors with pigtails streaming beneath their elaborate helmets, dust rising in clouds behind them as, screaming with fury, they drove towards the Roman line. Had such a charge been directed against Catulus' green levies at Tridentum, the line would surely have broken as the legionaries fled from that terrifying wave of men and horses twice as tall as they.

But the Marian legionaries were veterans and they simply locked shields and stood their ground. The sight of charging cavalry is less terrifying to men who know that the charge won't be followed through. Horses are not stupid, and the prospect of throwing themselves at a spiky shield wall with more spikes behind does not appeal to even the most ferocious of steeds. So the legionaries stood and swore at the oncoming Cimbri who predictably swerved their horses at the last moment, unleashing their javelins as they did so.

Higher up the slope, Madric watched the Cimbric cavalry gallop off past the left of the Roman line where their mass broke into swirling knots of individual combats as the Roman cavalry engaged the attacking horsemen.

'Worth a try', he muttered. 'It might have broken greener troops.'

As it was, the Marian veterans paused to steady their line, remove javelins inconveniently stuck into shields and awaited the signal for their postponed charge. It was Marius himself who gave that order, riding level with the front ranks and leading his men into the almost opaque wall of dust thrown up by the cavalry.

It was a matter of guesswork where the front rank of

the Cimbric army was, so the centurions waited until the last possible moment before bellowing 'Throw!', and the front ranks paused, leaned back and sent shower after shower of pilums into the murk. Then with a hoarse roar, the legionaries drew their swords and charged. And charged. And charged some more until their sandals were clattering over the pilums they had launched twenty seconds before. Of the Cimbri there was no sign. Trotting along in the rear ranks, Madric and his fellow Gauls exchanged puzzled looks. By now their cohort should be slowing down as the front ranks crashed into the enemy lines. Instead the legionaries pushed forward with rather the same sensation felt by a man who body-charges a locked door, only to find it was open all along.

Finally Marius was forced to call a halt, and his cohorts came to an untidy stop while the troops shuffled back and forth to re-dress their battle-line into proper formation. Marius sent runners to probe into the dusty murk - made thicker by the Romans' own charge - and everyone waited with drawn swords for the answer to one pressing question – where in Jupiter's name was the enemy?

Catulus could have told them, and the sight before him was no less ominous for being expected. His part of the battle front being less active, there was much less dust to obscure the view (while between Catulus and Sulla's army the mist still lay in pools undisturbed by the advancing enemy, for the Cimbri were for the moment completely ignoring Sulla's contingent).

So Catulus got to see how, as their cavalry swirled by, the Cimbri had turned left and sprinted across the plain to join the mass of men advancing on the Roman centre. He watched sourly as the Marian cohorts threw their pilums and charged into a cloud that contained nothing but dust. For the moment the best half of the Roman army had been taken out of the battle for the cost of nothing more than a faked cavalry charge.

Even that charge had caused problems for Catulus' relatively inexperienced army. At the sight of the Cimbric cavalry heading away from them after the feint against the Marian troops, some of Catulus' men raised a shout that 'the enemy are retreating'. Several men broke ranks to pursue, only to be savagely beaten back into the ranks by furious centurions who wielded the flats of their swords in place of their vine-stick badges of office.

It didn't take long for the enormity of that mis-judgement to become apparent. Far from retreating, the Cimbri resumed their 'Wo-tan-DA' advance and battle cry and from their position on the slopes Catulus' 20,000 men could see that they now stood alone against an army five times larger than theirs.

This represented the crux of the debate in the Roman command tent, a debate which had raged for much of the previous night. Given their history of defeat and humiliation at Cimbric hands, how would Catulus' men react to being singled out for the undivided attention of the enemy? Petraeus, the *Primus Pilus* of Catulus' legions had been called to the council and anxiously questioned on that very point, over and over again.

The senior centurion had stubbornly insisted, 'I tell you that they're ready. We had raw levies when we took them to the Alps, and the army was barely half-baked by the time we took to the field at Tridentum. But we've been drilling the men every day and they've seen and skirmished often enough with the enemy that they no longer fear them as monsters from legend. Above all, since we got here the men have had to put up with the taunts and insults of Marius' veterans. They're not just ready to take on the Cimbri – just say the word and they'll storm the Marian camp as well. The men have their self-respect. Take a look at their pilums, Sirs – you'll find CAT for 'Catulus' engraved on the shaft of every one of them. The men want the Cimbri to know exactly whose men are going to shove their barbarian arrogance down their own throats.'

Now the truth of the senior centurion's words was made evident in the attitude of the legionaries who were to bear the brunt of the Cimbric assault. There was some shifting of feet and murmuring in the ranks, but it was the murmur of men eager to get into the fight and take out some of their pent-up feelings on the enemy. Centurions moved along the lines with the same message. 'Remember boys, one pilum volley, and a short, sharp counter charge. Just enough to take the edge off their momentum. Then they're going to push you back. Expect it, but give up ground one step at a time.'

Cimbric and Roman lines engaged with a crash that

was heard across the battlefield. Sulla's men in their splendid isolation on the right flank both saw and heard the violent collision and saw the Cimbric line shake as Catulus' legionaries hurled themselves across the short distance between themselves and the enemy. The clang of sword on shield echoed from the bluffs and across the plain penetrating the dust cloud where a frustrated Marius was still desperately re-organizing his troops.

Not knowing where the enemy or their cavalry had gone, Marius had been forced to form his men into a rough square that could fight off an attack from any quarter, and in this formation his legions began to edge forward once more. The clash of armies behind and to the right had men looking over their shoulders, but then Cimbric skirmishers engaged their front, and the Marian troops prepared for imminent action – which never came. Eventually Marius ordered his square to resume a cautious advance.

In the centre, the sheer fury of the charge of Catulus' legionaries seemed to stun the Cimbri for a moment, but the chains binding the men in the Cimbric front ranks ensured that while their line bent in places, it could not break. Nor could the legionaries sustain the momentum granted to them by their short downhill charge. Gradually the sheer weight of the tens of thousands of Cimbri pressing against them forced the Romans back, step by step up the hill towards the bluffs.

Both Catulus and Petraeus were right behind the front ranks, ducking javelins, shouting half-heard exhortations and frantically directing reserves to wherever the lines looked like buckling. This was the crux of the battle. Both sides knew it, and the Cimbri knew that they were winning. Their chant of 'Wo-tan-DA' swelled in volume, and at every 'DA', the Cimbric line pushed forward and the Romans gave back another step.

It was savage face-to-face fighting, with still relatively raw levies against the cream of the Cimbric nation. With this in mind Catulus had made sure that his instructions were drilled into every man – defend, defend, defend. The legionaries were fighting against men who knew every move and counter-move, every stab and slash. So the legionaries countered, blocked, and sheltered behind their shields and the shields of the comrades at their shoulders.

From the rear of the legionary line came a steady trickle of men, one clutching the side of his face whilst blood dribbled between his fingers, another staring blankly at the near severed forearm he cradled with his other hand and another, uninjured, who bore a shield chopped into mangled matchwood. This man hurriedly exchanged his shield for a fresh one before stepping back to the combat, pausing only to clap a comforting hand on to the shoulder of a comrade who staggered from the ranks, limping with a bloody thigh.

Every man who emerged from the line was whooping for breath, and on that fact was based Catulus' strategy. The Romans could at least rotate out of the melee, with every wounded or exhausted man replaced by a fresh legionary in the file behind. The Cimbri chained together in the front rank had no such respite but had to fight their way grimly uphill against a continuously replaced line of fresh opponents. Yet such was their ferocity and skill that the Cimbri still pushed the Romans back.

It seemed inevitable that the retreat would go on until the legionaries were pinned against the bluffs, and then the army would split apart like a ripe apple beneath the foot of an ox. Legionaries would break left and right looking for shelter, falling in an untidy wave on to Sulla's hastily re-deployed lines which would break into confusion as the Cimbri came piling in behind like wolves on to a wounded stag.

But well before that could happen, the Cimbri reached the posts. These were no flimsy makeshift defences, but solid logs buried in the dead of night down to almost half their depth in the sandy soil of the hillside. Some of these logs had formerly made up the gates of Catulus' camp, and others had been hastily pillaged from the village at Vercellae, but now they all stood like fence posts without a fence, ten paces apart and chest-high, absolutely no obstacle to an advancing enemy – unless that enemy had linked themselves together into a single line by the chains locked to their waists.

The men at the front of the Cimbric wedge were the finest fighters of their nation, but even they could do little with their chains caught against posts as thick as a man's thigh that stubbornly prevented any further advance. Nor could the linked line of Cimbri retreat, for the press of warriors behind them was still trying to shove forward, frustrated by the sudden delay and determined to push past it. Catulus' legionaries were able to back off just out of sword range and contemplate the sight of warriors slashing at the empty air in front of them, hacking at the posts and bellowing at the men behind them to back off before the chains cut them in half. Then two or three legionaries would pick a man at leisure and rush at their pinned victim to hack him down before retreating to select their next target. Trapped against the posts, the chained Cimbri could do nothing but stand and take it.

Behind the front line of legionaries a relieved Catulus was hastily organizing the mass of his men for another downhill charge. Behind him the trumpeters sounded a single long blast, their higher note cutting through the flat blare of the Cimbric instruments. That was my signal.

Liber XIV

Until that morning I would have said that waiting for a battle to start is one of the least pleasant ways of spending time that a human can imagine. Now I shall update that opinion to observe that it is even more unpleasant for the battle to have already started and to be waiting to join it – especially if you have no idea of how the battle has been going so far, or what you are about to charge into.

For the past three hours my nerves had been wearing away into frazzled little stubs as I waited along with eight hundred increasingly restive cavalrymen in the mist-covered lake-bed I had discovered in my previous trip to the Raudine Plain. You can cram an exceedingly large number of men and horses into a relatively narrow space provided that they are all amenable to the idea, and we had basically pushed that concept to the limit.

From the Cimbric point of view, we were a shallow puddle of mist a hundred paces wide by seventy long, sitting innocently between Sulla's men and the mass of the Cimbric army. That is, assuming that the mass of the Cimbric army had attacked Catulus according to plan. We had no idea if this was the case, because to maintain this deception, no-one could come or go from our foggy little depression. We had no idea of what was going on outside our mist-shrouded world.

Seldom have I cursed with more venom the barbarian tendency towards disorganization than I did as that morning wore on. The warmth of the day began slowly burning off our cover and still the Cimbri were shuffling around, picking their noses and generally deciding if they wanted the battle to start in the late morning, afternoon or – hey, why not? - perhaps they could make it an evening affair.

The mist around our heads was thinning and I was about to order everyone to dismount so that we might keep a lower profile when the same order was passed along, presumably from the highly competent Saufienus. Actually, most people, including myself, were dismounted anyway since just sitting on a stationary horse can tire the animal, it's a bad idea to ride into battle on a horse that already needs a break. The dismount took place with a certain amount of muffled cursing as hooves came down on unwary feet, or those on foot found themselves crushed between the flanks of the tightly-packed horses.

Maphronius received a particularly vehement complaint when he abruptly emptied his bowels and the cavalryman behind was unable escape in time. Overall, tensions in our little warband were rising toward fever pitch even before that first 'Wo-tan-Da' war cry rolled across the plain. The sound led to a general checking of sword belts, hitching of armour, muttering of prayers and all the little preparations that men make when they know that sudden death is approaching fast.

My personal nightmare was that the Cimbri had made a last-minute change of plans and had decided to begin the battle by taking out Sulla's half-legion.

If the barbarians had done that, then the first we would know of it was when a human wave of well-

The Battlefield at Vercellae

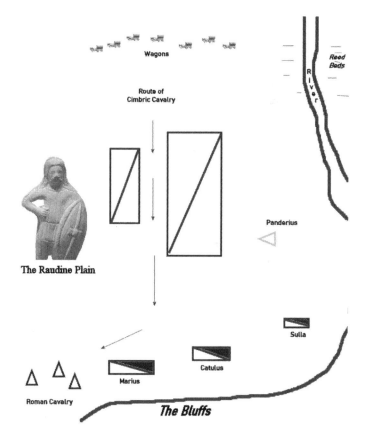

Wagons

Route of
Cimbric Cavalry

River

Reed
Beds

Panderius

The Raudine Plain

Sulla

Catulus

Marius

Roman Cavalry

The Bluffs

armed warriors crashed into the flanks of the unprepared cavalrymen in our misty depression. So it was with considerable relief that I heard the muffled chant move along and past my front. Even with the waggon drums pounding away in the background, everyone heard the clash of arms as the Cimbric line smashed into Catulus' legionaries on the slopes.

Thereafter, we were kept in touch with events through the yells, shouts and groans of the Cimbric rear ranks, who were observing the battle on the hillside with the enthusiasm of the crowd at a mass gladiator combat. Eventually the cheers lost their energy and gradually changed to groans and puzzled yells of frustration, a good indication that the Cimbric uphill advance had stalled at the posts. I was about to advise the man next to me to get ready when the same message was passed along to me in a tense murmur. Saufienus was ahead of the game once more.

It wasn't hard to imagine what was happening on the hillside above. With the Cimbric advance halted, Catulus' legionaries would be taking the opportunity to soften up their stationary opponents with volley after volley of heavy pilums. Thrown downhill and with a high trajectory the pilum is a lethal missile.

When five pounds of spear descend at speed, all that energy is focussed on the tiny pointed pyramidal tip of the weapon and that generally gives it more than enough force to punch through a shield and into the body of the person sheltering behind.

At least some of those pilums would have been equipped with additional lead weights which the legions use to give their traditional calling-card that extra bit of emphasis. Even if the warrior on the receiving end of one of these volleys has the extra protection of armour, a pilum-perforated shield is little more than an encumbrance in a melee, and the pilum's pyramidal tip makes the thing cursed hard to remove. And that's even if the shank has not been made of sub-standard iron – as it often is – causing the rest of the spear to droop away from questing hands trying to yank the thing out.

Catulus' trumpets signalled us just as we heard the savage shout of 'urrah!' which told us that the legion had launched itself at the disorganized and somewhat demoralized Cimbric line. Without waiting for the inevitable order from Saufienus, I straightened myself in the saddle and in deference to his earlier orders, tried to look pretty as I waved my sword over my head and yelled 'Chaaarge!'.

Two days ago on the plain, I had been somewhat shocked and surprised when a dozen deer had suddenly popped up apparently from nowhere. It was not hard therefore to imagine the effect on the average Cimbric rear-ranker when the ground of the empty plain beside him suddenly erupted with hundreds of cavalry, all charging with homicidal fury.

We burst out of the mist to find the enemy shockingly close – thousands and thousands of them spread from fifty paces distant all the way to where a huge pall of dust hid the further side of the battlefield. There was no time to glance uphill to see how Catulus' legions were doing – it was all I could do to brace for impact as we hurtled headlong into the disorganized crowd in front of us.

I may have mentioned earlier that if infantry form up properly, a cavalry charge has no chance at all. However, it would be an understatement to say that the enemy before us did not form up properly. These were not the front-rank hardened warriors. These were the farmers, the farriers, the untried teenagers and the occasional grey-haired veteran. They had less than twenty seconds to prepare and spent most of that in a state of shock and absolute panic. I had a brief, startled glimpse of men literally climbing over each other in their desperation to get away before Maphronius hit the first of them with his shoulder and I tried and failed to decapitate the man with a backhand slash as he spun away.

The plan was not for us to tear deep into the mass of the Cimbric army, because eventually we would become embedded and our momentum lost in the mass of armed humanity who could then cut us down at leisure. Instead we split, four hundred men rampaging down the side of the Cimbric mass, and four hundred of us charging up the slope towards Catulus' men, spreading chaos and panic as we went. The Cimbri had observed the ease with which cavalry could get trapped within the small pocket between the bluffs and Catulus' army and had decided to use their horse only on the open flank – especially as the original Roman plan that the Cimbri had seen did the same thing for the same reason. So we were an unexpected and nasty surprise -

and there was no opposing cavalry to mitigate our nastiness.

If all was going according to plan behind us, Sulla's force had already wheeled left and was moving at speed toward the open wound that our charge had left in the enemy's flank. My section of the cavalry had the task of moving uphill as the Catulan legions moved downhill, so that those Cimbri facing the legions could have the full demoralizing benefit of knowing from screams and shouts that something horrible was happening behind them.

From the fact that I was hoarse for days afterwards, I must assume that I was doing a good deal of shouting – or screaming – of my own, though I confess I was unaware of it at the time. My main thought was what a great job it was to fight with the cavalry, since so far I had been fighting men whose earnest ambition was simply to get out of my way. Maphronius quickly got the idea that he needed to get alongside a running man so that I could bring my long cavalry sword down on his skull or shoulders. If the man stood, shield raised, Maphronius would simply run him down – someone had trained the sorrel well.

Apart from registering an ever-increasing tiredness in my sword arm, only flashes of that wild uphill charge remain. Maphronius skittering aside as a completely severed head bounced downhill towards us. A Roman cavalryman pulled from his horse and falling unto a cluster of men who stabbed viciously downwards again and again, a man staggering from a cluster of warriors and desperately trying to contain the intestines spilling from his belly. Lifting my sword to swing and being briefly blinded as a mix of blood and brains from my previous victim splattered off the blade on to my face.

Then seeing a bald-headed warrior with a beard spilling down his naked chest step forward from nowhere and thrust a long-bladed spear right at my side. The killing thrust was aimed where my armour opened slightly to allow me to sit easily in the saddle, and with the sudden clarity of pure terror, I knew that the leaf-shaped blade was aimed to pierce my belly. Then it would take one twist of the shaft to slice open my intestines. I had just slashed downwards, and now I brought my sword up, already inside the stabbing tip, so that my forearm that caught the haft of the spear and sent the tip skittering up my armour where – I later discovered – it opened a deep cut in my jaw.

The violence of the manoeuvre was such that I felt myself tipping sideways and backwards off the saddle, and managed a wrenching twist in midair to break my fall with the palms of my hands before my face smashed into the sandy soil of the plain. Winded, with every bone and joint in my body protesting, I rolled just as a spearhead stabbed into the ground where I had landed. Instinctively I kicked out, and felt my boot connect with a leg as I scrambled backwards into a sitting position.

A snarling group of warriors faced me with spears levelled and I fumbled at my waist to produce my belt dagger. Still propped up on the other arm, I waved that pathetic little weapon at the enemy and was astounded to see the expressions of my attackers change from savagery to consternation and fear as they turned and fled.

Then a Roman maniple rushed past, jostling, bumping and swearing at me for cluttering their advance. A nail-soled Roman sandal stabbed into my thigh as someone stumbled over me, yet really, I did not mind at all. Then I was looking at the mail-coated backs and nodding plumes of the legionaries as they advanced downhill, and sympathetic arms were lifting me gently to my feet.

'Been through the mill a bit, have we, magistrate?'

It may not have been fair, but being recognized as a drinking buddy of the chief centurion of the legion guaranteed me quick service from the medical first response team following close behind the action. The *capsarius* stitched me up with swift precision and gently pushed me over to an assistant with the brusque instruction, 'Get his armour off, and strap his chest. He's probably fractured at least two ribs.'

Then even before I could thank the man, the *capsarius* turned away and gave his full attention to the next legionary in line. Trying to breathe as shallowly as possible, I walked gingerly from the first-aid group to collect my horse.

Ten minutes later, I was mounted and proceeding very gently down the slope. Maphronius seemed to understand that his rider was in delicate condition and picked his footing with exceptional care. Riding was so painful that I had debated whether to return to the camp, but in the end the urge to see things out to the bitter end overcame the acute discomfort of being on horseback.

Rome had won. Of that there was no doubt. From my position on the slope I could see over the heads of Catulus' legionaries who were still steadily chopping down their panicked opponents as methodically as the foragers whom I had recently seen stripping a field of barley. As the Roman killing machine moved steadily downhill it left a carpet of bodies in its wake, with auxiliary skirmishers following up to briskly spear or stab anyone who was still moving.

Still further down the hill, Sulla's army was a blunt spearhead embedded deep in the side of the Cimbric mass, while Saufienus' cavalry made short, lethal charges at any warriors who attempted to get behind the unit's back. Even then, most who did attempt this were less concerned with outflanking manoeuvrers than they were with reaching the relative safety of their waggons parked at the back of the plain. Just about the only Cimbri still fighting were those trapped between the mass of their own army and the swords of the advancing legionaries. At the rear of the Cimbric army an ever-increasing flow of men was breaking away and jostling to flee the battlefield.

Then from the rear of the dust cloud cloaking the side of the plain stepped rank after rank of Roman legionaries – Marius' men, whom their commander had kept in good formation. After a frustrating morning of stumbling about without meeting the enemy, Marius' veterans were abruptly confronted by the sight of half the warriors in the Cimbric army streaming by, paying the legionaries minimal attention as they headed at speed for the exits. A single trumpet call, a shower of pilums and the legionaries charged.

From my position on the hillside the remnants of the Cimbric army looked like a fat, tortured snake. The head was being remorselessly consumed by Catulus' men making their way downhill to where the upper body bulged away from me, pushed by Sulla's advancing troops. The tail was swaying back towards the Cimbric waggons as men fled from the advance of the Marians. From each front came hoarse shouts and screams as the Romans mercilessly butchered the disorganized and demoralized enemy.

'It is a terrible sight, no?'

The question came from another rider – a Macedonian officer, if I judged aright the insignia on his linothorax armour. The man had one arm in a bloodstained sling, and used the other to guide his horse as it gingerly picked its way over to me across a carpet of corpses.

'Oh, I don't know', I replied mildly. 'It seems rather pleasant to me.'

'Look there', suggested the Macedonian. 'The rout has reached the waggons. The women are none too happy about it.'

This was putting it mildly. The Cimbric women had climbed from their waggons and were roundly cursing their menfolk, grabbing them and physically turning them back to the fight, or belabouring the fleeing men with brooms, pans and other household implements. Some warriors, trapped between the waggons and the advancing Romans, turned to make a fight of it and many of the women snatched up spears and fought and died alongside their men. With the legions in complete killing mode and the best of the Cimbric fighters long slain, the remnants of the Cimbric horde stood little chance.

'Deus!' exclaimed the Macedonian and pointed to where a woman had cut the traces of the beasts pulling her ox-cart. As the cart tipped backwards the woman was pulled into the air by a noose she had rigged around her own neck. Yet what made the sight more appalling was that as the cart tipped further it revealed that the woman had noosed an infant to each of her ankles and these were strangled along with her as she hung.

'They may have lost, but these people are brave', exclaimed my companion. We were nearing the actual fighting now, so we stopped and I rested my hands on the saddle horn and watched the slaughter.

'It takes less bravery to kill yourself than it does to face an uncertain future', I replied. 'True bravery would involve giving your children a chance at life. They could always kill themselves later if they disagreed.'

'And what life would they have, as slaves of the Romans? Look, some of your legionaries are accepting surrenders now. What life awaits those people?'

'You are Macedonian, yes? Well I once met the grandson of your king Perseus. When he was captured, his young son was brought to Rome where he ended up working as a clerk in the courts. Married a girl from Chios, and made a pretty good life for himself. That -', we watched as a group of women with kirtled skirts made a suicidal rush at legionaries who cut them down without taking a scratch in return. 'That is cowardice, plain and simple. Suicide is hiding from the future.'

'You do not like these barbarians much, do you?' observed the Macedonian.

'I hate them.' I replied simply.

'But why? They are our enemies, yes, but they are noble warriors …'.

'Oh, don't give me that horseshit! They are a people who rejoice in blood and death. When they see a farm, they devastate it, when they see a work of art they deface it. They live for pillage and war. They build nothing and they create nothing. They destroy the work of those who do build something and then they praise the destroyers.'

'You Romans do a lot of killing and pillaging also. Remember that I'm Macedonian, and my people have seen your legions at work.'

'Oh yes, Rome pillages, and massacres and terrorizes, but as a means to an end, not as an end in itself. And we don't act as though doing it is somehow brave or noble, and we don't do it as random cruelty. It's messy and imperfect and whether you like it or not ...' (I briefly thought of the late Scipio Dextrianus at this point), '… Rome is building something. When we cause death and destruction, we bring something out of the ruins. For these people -', I stabbed a contemptuous finger at the corpses underfoot, '- death and destruction are the end objective. Leave civilization to them and in another thousand years all we'll have is a legacy of more suffering, more corpses, and flea-infested savages still shitting in middens. Oh, and a few more ballads celebrating blood-crazed killers.'

'So don't try persuading me to admire such people. I don't.'

The Macedonian was clearly taken aback by my vehemence. 'Well, Roman, you have nothing to worry about. All that is left of the day is for your victorious soldiers to round up prisoners, loot the Cimbric camp and start the oh-so-civilized rape of their female captives. You've saved Rome – now let's see what Rome makes of your victory.'

With that retort, the Macedonian turned his horse and rode off, leaving me alone on a field of corpses.

From a hundred paces away came cheers and shouts. With victory complete, the legions were losing their shape with men embracing, clasping each other's forearms and yelling praises to their patron gods. Others were already spreading out to go back over the battlefield and loot the more wealthy-looking of the bodies strewn on the ground.

I turned Maphronius and watched the shadows of clouds chasing each other across the bluffs. In an absent-minded way I noticed that it would have been a beautiful day for the tens of thousands of men who had not lived to see it. Rome had won an epic victory and the Cimbric threat was over - for once and for all. Yet somehow instead of elation I felt somehow disconnected and unaccountably depressed. Perhaps it was the constant nagging pain from my ribs.

Sighing, I turned Maphronius and left the battlefield to the rejoicing soldiers. I needed a drink.

Epilogue

Later that evening, the sky was golden overhead as I took my horse slowly up the hillside to where two riders sat in their saddles, silhouetted against the horizon. I always take a small private stash of opium with me on campaign, and this precaution had ensured that, though my ribs still hurt like fury, I didn't really care about it any more. Instead my sense of detachment had increased still further, so that the mass of pale bodies carpeting the plain below seemed somehow unreal.

The two riders were talking quietly, but the man furthest from me broke off what he was saying at my approach. 'Oh, it's you.'

This was Catulus, who sounded distinctly unenthusiastic about my arrival.

Sulla chuckled. 'Relax Quintus. I asked him to be here. Panderius is one of the few people who knows the true story of what happened here today, so he may as well see what he has wrought.'

'*He* wrought? I thought it was our plan that did this.' Catulus waved an arm to indicate the plain, where the darkening shadows of evening were starting to close over the stripped corpses and the scavengers, human and animal, which moved among them.

I pulled Maphronius up carefully, making sure that I stopped with Sulla between myself and Catulus. The Proconsul did not look as though he had forgiven or forgotten. Like me, Sulla seemed somewhat disquieted at the sheer enormity of the deaths spread out below us. 'It is a great victory', he muttered, almost as though trying to convince himself it was so.

'Oh, it definitely is', agreed Catulus. 'Petraeus was so right that the men were ready. They're cock-a-hoop right now and can't wait to rub it into the Marians. They won the battle single handed – excepting your contribution also, Sulla.'

'Lucius did his part', observed Sulla indicating me with a tilt of his head.

'You're wounded', observed Catulus, looking at me more closely. 'What happened to those bodyguards I assigned to keep you safe?'

The re-specification of my bodyguard's duties drew a wry smile from Sulla as I answered with complete truth and minimal honesty, 'We seem to have become separated. It was very confusing out there for a while and they must have gone their own way.'

'Ah.' This from Sulla. 'My scouts did report picking up two men making their way to us from the remnants of Vercellae. The men claim to have been abducted from their horses, blindfolded and stripped naked. This explains why, when they were captured they were wearing peasant women's dresses which were much too small for them. Apparently that was all they could find. We were not sure if the men were deserters or madmen, so I've held them in the cells in the camp. They will be released back to you, Quintus, of course.'

'Of course', said Catulus sourly. 'Your doing, I suppose, Panderius?'

'Absolutely not, Sir,' I said honestly. 'But some of the cavalry do have a rather robust sense of humour.'

'Which is more than can be said for our noble leader', observed Sulla, deftly changing the subject. 'They tell me he is spitting nails.'

Catulus replied loftily, 'I don't see why. As overall commander of the army, the victory belongs to him - however minimal his actual contribution to the fighting.'

'*Victor pulvis* they are calling him. 'Conqueror of the dust'. Somehow it's not the noble title that the man who has just saved Rome feels that he is entitled to.'

I chimed in, 'Actually, Marius is already putting it about that his men turned up somewhat earlier than they really did and it was his flank attack that saved the day.'

'What? How do you know that?'

I shrugged. 'From Antonius and Porcellinus. They were the only two of your trainees who saw action today, and they were bragging about it to some of Marius' cadets. They picked up that bit of information in return.'

'Well, Marius will have to account for the fact that it is my command tent, not his, which is bulging with captured standards and banners. Come to that, my men had their pilums marked with my name. We'll get independent witnesses – hmm … Parma is the nearest town – and they can examine the enemy corpses and verify whose men did the hard fighting. I won't be cheated out of my share of a triumph, nor my soldiers either.'

Catulus went on, but my attention had wandered. Among the prizes taken in Catulus' tent was that same golden calf that I had last seen being brought up for the soldiers of the fort at Sarni that they might swear to fight no longer for Rome. I wondered what had become of Metus. His father's body, they told me, had been recovered from the battlefield, but of the young spymaster there was no sign. The obnoxious Claodicus had been captured.

'… and tell no-one of this, ever. Panderius! Are you even listening?'

'Huh? Excuse me, Sir. The opiates …'.

Catulus repeated himself with forced patience. 'Marius loves you little enough as it is. If he ever discovers that you were partly responsible for causing him to spend the morning charging aimlessly around in a dust cloud during what should have been the greatest victory of his career, then I can't protect you. Sulla can't protect you. Marius will get you no matter what, if he finds out that you, not the Gods, did this to him.'

'Oh, that. Actually Proconsul, the events of the past few days are a total blur to me. I hit my head when falling off my horse - again – and I very much doubt that the memory will return. However, it's certain that I spent the missing time peacefully instructing your cadets in the theory of warfare so little of value has been lost.'

'Exactly so, indeed. And know that I am indebted to you for your … ah … service. It will be remembered, and you can call on me should you require recompense. And Panderius …'

'Sir?'

'Should you ever be called on to serve under my

command again, make sure you decline the offer very firmly. Because trust me – I'll make sure you spend the most miserable days of your life in the short time immediately before your untimely and rapid death. Are we clear?'

'Do not serve again in the army of Catulus. Got it.'

'I may however, patronize the dining rooms at your establishment in Rome. They tell me your cooks are among the best in the city.'

'The first dinner will be on me, Sir. To celebrate the return of peace.'

Sulla had been uncharacteristically silent during this exchange. Now he broke in, his voice sombre. 'I wouldn't be so sure about that.'

'About what?'

'Peace. We're going to see precious little peace over these coming decades. Rome has removed one threat to her existence, yet the removing of one threat has simply made the others more imminent and dangerous.'

'You foresee trouble ahead?' asked Catulus quietly.

'I see nothing but trouble. The inequalities in Roman society are tearing the city apart and we, the powerful, are too blind to see it. The Marians see it and use it for their own ends, not those of the masses. Eventually the people's frustration is going to boil over.'

'The Italians might get us first', I added gloomily.

In reply to Catulus' questioning look I nodded at Sulla,who said, 'We've spies all around the country. The Italians are not just restive under Roman rule. They are actively plotting rebellion and given how we've mis-managed our relationship with our allies, I can hardly blame them.'

'So peace? Peace is not going to happen – look there, over the piles of corpses to the horizon. That gentlemen, beautiful as it is, is an omen of what is to come.'

Each lost in our own thoughts we sat quietly, our victory forgotten as we studied the western sky which glowed with the dying light of the blood-red sunset.

Author's afterword

The challenge that I set myself with the Panderius novels was to write an accurate 'history'. That is, Panderius' adventures should align so well with the known facts that a historian presented with the text should be unable to demonstrate that any part of it is actually untrue. Fortunately with regard to the Vercellae campaign, this still leaves me considerable room for manoeuvre. The sources for events at this time are vague, scattered and contradictory. Therefore it has fallen to me to take incidents described by various ancient writers and decide when, where and how these fit into a timeline of events.

As a historian it behoves me to show my work so that the student of the period can be clear what is based on the ancient sources and what is my own invention.

Chapter one's Maphronius did not exist, but his unethical practices certainly did. Tacitus gives us a close description of very similar conduct by corrupt recruiters among the Batavi people in Histories 4.14. Note also that the Republic was considerably more prudish than the later empire with regard to pederasty, and even two centuries later northern Italy was famously conservative. Hence the potential for black-mailing those who had purchased boys for immoral purposes.

The Tridentum campaign unfolded as described, with my description based on reports by (the very unmilitary) Plutarch, Appian, Orosius, Florian and others. Lutatius Catulus was unable to hold the Alpine passes mostly because Marius had left him with too few troops who were largely raw and untrained. That the location of the unguarded passes was betrayed by a spy in Catulus' camp is my own invention.

From Plutarch's *Life of Marius* 23 we discover that Catulus did indeed set up camps on both sides of the river Adige, and the Cimbri destroyed the bridge between them as described. We hear from Pliny the Elder (NH 22.11) that the P*rimus Pilus* Petraeus was awarded the *corona graminea* (grass crown) for leading a breakout and so saving part of the army, and I have placed that breakout on the eastern camp, along with the shameful conduct of young Aemilius Scaurus,which was also as described. (Frontinus 1.13)

There is also a separate and totally incompatible description of events where the soldiers on the 'fort on the other bank of the Adige' fought hard and surrendered on terms. I have opted to use both descriptions, with the defence of the fort at Sarni fitting this second description. The siege ends in this book with the defenders swearing on a golden calf as our alternative sources say actually happened, and this calf was in fact later captured by Catulus' men. Metus, our young spymaster is an invention, though his father Boiorix is a real character as is Claodicus, who appears later.

Plutarch seems to assume that after the struggle at the bridge between the twin camps, the next phase of the battle happened immediately. It's hard to see how, since Plutarch's description left the Cimbri on the other side of the Adige, with the bridge destroyed. Thus it seemed reasonable for me to give the Cimbri a few days to get across to Catulus' side of the river. When the two sides eventually squared off on the battlefield at Tridentum, Plutarch tells us that Catulus' men did indeed start an impromptu retreat (the Cimbric out-flanking move is my invention) and Catulus did put himself at the head of the retreat to give it some dignity.

The Cimbri attempted to bottle up Catulus army as it was retreating, though our source (Frontinus *Strategems* 1.5.3) does not say when. The logical place to put this event is after the non-battle of Tridentum. The manner by which Catulus cleared the ridge is as described by Frontinus.

We have no record of any cadets serving with Catulus, though we know from Sallust's *Jugurtha* and Caesar's *Gallic War* that young aristocrats did join generals in this way. Domitius Ahenobarbus and Antonius are real characters, as is Lafranius who went on to become a leader of the later Italian revolt. Marcellus Porcellinus and Scipio Dextrianus are ima-ginary. (Though as a traitor to Rome, Scipio's family would have declared him *damnatio memoriae*, which would have resulted in the young man being scrubbed from the historical record in any case.)

Momina is based upon Martha, a Syrian priestess who prophesied for Marius and was as described by both myself and Plutarch, though I've gone into more detail about the lady's supernatural abilities. Madric, the spy who supplied the actual information, is fictional.

The 'haunting legionary love song' *Bona Barca Veneris* is my translation of a modern song popular with the British army in less progressive times. Translate back at your own risk.

The meetings with the Cimbric ambassadors and king went as described in the ancient sources (mainly Plutarch), though there is no record that Martha/ Momina suggested the actual venue for the battle at the Raudine Plain.

Our sources for the battle of the Raudine Plain are a mess, with no two writers agreeing on much. The battle-map in Chapter XIV is my own reconstruction, for in reality we do not even know where the battle took place. In the battle, according to our sources, we have mist, a dust cloud and the Cimbri simultaneously blinded by sunlight. Oddly enough, there seems general agreement on the two most bizarre aspects of the battle. Marius did indeed charge into an empty dust cloud and spend the rest of the battle groping about in the murk while trying to find the enemy. (cf Plutarch *Marius* 26), and though the opening Cimbric cavalry charge is as recorded (by Orosius), the suggestion that this was for the express purpose of raising dust is my idea.

Incredibly, the Cimbri were indeed stupidly macho enough to chain their best warriors together to attack Catulus' men. How in reality Catulus actually stopped the Cimbric advance is unknown but I decided that, if forewarned, the Romans could stop them with strategically placed 'fence-posts'. The idea is not original, for Sulla dug in sharpened logs behind the front rank of his legionaries at the battle of Orchomenus in 85 BC, causing havoc to an attacking wave of Pontic scythe chariots.

While I have invented Panderius' cavalry charge out of a mist-filled depression, there are reports that an unknown individual led a cavalry charge at the crucial moment. (Sulla later tried to hint that this person was himself). An academic reader of this text has pointed out that Panderius spends a lot of time falling off his horse, and several other characters likewise take a spill from horseback. I am assured by those re-enactors who have tried Roman cavalry manoeuvrers that despite the deep chair-like Roman saddle the unfortunate lack of stirrups means that Panderius' number of falls is actually somewhat below average.

It is to be expected that we would have absolutely no information on the espionage war that Cimbri and Romans doubtless waged. The Romans regarded intelligence gathering as a somewhat ungentlemanly business best left to unsavoury individuals such as the brothel-operator Panderius, and contemporary historians rather liked to pretend it did not happen at all. This has left our Lucius Panderius with a free hand to go about saving Rome in whatever manner he felt best.

Other Lucius Panderius books

The Gold of Tolosa
Philip Matyszak

Introducing Lucius Panderius, war hero, connoisseur of fine wines and Germanic prostitutes - and the perpetrator of the biggest gold theft in history. This first novel by well-known writer and historian Philip Matyszak takes us from the mean streets of Rome to the even meaner streets of Gallic Tolosa in a journey filled with ambush, intrigue, battle and double-cross.

In 105 BC Rome is faced with extinction, both from a huge army of invading barbarians and by a dark curse that has been festering for generations. It falls to Lucius Panderius to avert both threats, and incidentally to make himself richer than Croesus. Though fiction, the *Gold of Tolosa* is historically accurate and explains how enough loot to recapitalize a third-world economy was taken in a theft that really did happen.

Whether Lucius is crossing swords with barbarian warriors or Roman magistrates, the pace is never less than frantic, and ancient Rome has never been more fun ...

'Great atmosphere, a good story, and a strong sense of fun all combine to make this a wonderful excursion to the world of Republican Rome.'
Adrian Goldsworthy, author of *'Caesar: Life of a Colossus'*

'Fun jaunt through the bloody landscape of late Republican Rome.'
Ancient Warfare Magazine

Monashee Mountain Publishing

Other Lucius Panderius books

The Servant of Aphrodite
Philip Matyszak

After returning from the dead - or at least from the river Arausio - Lucius Panderius finds himself back in Rome, and an unwilling participant in the snake-pit of Roman politics. Whether dodging assassins in the back-alleys, or ducking missiles at political rallies, our hero finds that the streets of his home city can be just as dangerous as the battlefield. And on the battlefield, at least you know who your enemies are …

Rome, 104 BC is a city on edge; torn by social conflict and threatened with destruction by a massive barbarian invasion. To survive the turmoil, Lucius Panderius needs to be every bit as ruthless and duplicitous as his shadowy and powerful enemies.

'The Servant of Aphrodite' is the second of the Panderius Papers, and as with its predecessor, this novel combines detailed historical research with non stop action and adventure.

Monashee Mountain Publishing

Made in United States
Orlando, FL
15 March 2025

59490229R00166